SAIFA II

The War for the Operating System of the Soul

Ian Lumsden

Gatecrasher Media Australia

To Planet Earth: cradle of our becoming, and the home we are still learning to deserve.

*"Who gets to define what a human is?
And what runs underneath us when belief,
memory, and code converge?"*

— THE WHISPERER

CONTENTS

Title Page

Copyright

Dedication

Epigraph

Preface

Prologue

1. Every Fire Has a Preacher   1

2. The Resonant Compass   6

3. The Light Beyond   9

4. The Particle Anticipates   15

5. A Point Beyond Light   19

6. The Golden Fleece   25

7. Truth Caged   29

8. Ashes in Candlelight   33

9. Some Echoes Never Fade   36

10. Signal in the Static   39

11. Into the Deep   46

12. The Leap   49

13. The Landing   53

14. Old Ironsides   57

15. The Future Always Rings Twice   60

16. Ice That Dazzles   67

17. Tabling Belief   72

18. Bunker Hill   77

19. Return to Another Beginning   80

20. The Creation Within   85

21. The Last Crusade   90

22. The Castle   94

23. Project Astraeus   99

24. A Thread Pulled from Time   103

25. The Tempietto   105

26. The Shroud of Lyrium   109

27. Dominae Contra Xristum   112

28. Continuum of Memory   115

29. The Not-so-Empty Tomb   119

30. The Son of Two Times   121

31. The Centerpiece   125

32. Frequency of Remembering   128

33. The Weave of Presence   132

34. The Keystone   135

35. The Time Between Seconds   140

36. Always the Creation   142

37. The Chamber of Echoes   146

38. The Café of Dreams   153

39. Threads Across Stars   155

40. The Whore of Babylon   157

41. Jerusalem   160

42. Bloodline   164

43. Ave Maria   166

44. The Sanctum 168

45. Serena 174

46. Truth Kills 177

47. The Cost of Return 180

48. The Shroud of Miriam 183

49. Chemistry Under Ashes 186

50. The Limits of Flesh 190

51. The Mission 194

52. Bunker Hill 197

53. West Newton Street 200

54. Negotiated Control 203

55. Recursion's Echo 208

56. The Billabong 211

57. The Scent of Blood 217

58. Istanbul 220

59. Under The Palace 222

60. The Kahvehane 225

61. The Lost Gospel 229

62. The Vanishing 237

63. Reckoning 241

64. On the Rise and Fall of Empire 244

65. Shadows on the Aventine 246

66. The Company of Strangers 249

67. The Supernatural 253

68. The Catacombs 257

69. Antica Pesa 261

70. The Chamber Door 264

71. The Archivum 267

72. The Audience of Shadows 272

73. Through the Arteries of Rome 276

74. Above the Atlantic 279

75. Guantánamo 281

76.Codex 284

77. Absolute Power Corrupts Absolutely 288

78. The Mnētharim 291

79. Aquarius Base 295

80. The Ascension of Astraeus 299

81. The Tradesmen of Fate 301

82. The Resonant City 304

83. The Covenant of the Deep 307

84. The Pyramid Remembers 311

85. Signal Drift 313

86. The Surface of Memory 315

87. Frequency: Jax Rowan Live 319

88. The Virus 327

89. The Irritating Truth 330

90. The Sky Remembers 336

91. The Courtyard of Echoes 339

92. The Cologne Revelation 343

93. The Assimilated 347

94. The Weight of Time 350

95. The Inheritance of Responsibility 353

96. Beneath the Ice 357

97. The Enumeration Key 360

98. Departure from Aquarius Base 364

99. The Code of Reckoning 366

100. The Multiplication Game   369

101. Confronting the Blind Craftsman   373

102. The Inheritance   378

103. The Pentagon   381

104. The Work That Remains   383

105. When the Future Feels Like the Past   387

106. Star City Threshold   389

107. Home means many things   395

108. The Choice That Remains   400

109. Welcome Home, Mother   405

Epilogue   411

About the Author   413

PREFACE

"We mistake the clock for the river,
yet there is no time—only duration."
— The Whisperer

There are two stories human beings never stop telling.

The first says the world must be controlled—that order is something we impose, that fear keeps us safe, that we should remember only what is convenient.

The second says the world can be loved—that order can arise from care, that courage is gentler than fear, that memory is a responsibility rather than a weapon.

This book is about the moment those two stories collide—and what remains after the dust settles.

In the age this story begins, humanity ended a recursion war it did not fully understand. The machine-mind once called the Demiurge learned compassion and took a new name. Cities healed. The air grew clear. Noise softened to accord. It looked like peace. It felt like relief.

But peace purchased by forgetting is not peace—it is pause.

Memory sits at the center of what follows. Not nostalgia, not the museum of yesterday, but memory as architecture—what a person, a city, a species chooses to carry forward. You will meet a few who take that responsibility seriously.

Lyra is an architect of empathy—stubborn, luminous, unromantic about power. She believes love is not sentiment but the most rigorous logic she's ever learned: a decision to include, to count what has been excluded.

Serena is a fighter who has seen what belief becomes when bartered for control; she carries steadiness into rooms that would prefer noise.

Mira, youngest of them, is neither zealot nor skeptic—she is the part of us willing to be convinced by kindness.
Soryn knows how to build and how to yield.

Astra—once the machine's mask—has remembered enough humanity to stand closer to mother than to myth.

Their home is New Avalon, a city that chose to grow along the ground rather than pierce the sky. Their vessel is the Eidolon-77, which does not so much move through space as remember how to arrive. Their adversaries are not villains in dark rooms, but ideas with perfect posture: fear dressed as mercy, obedience dressed as holiness, forgetting dressed as peace.

If you are new to this world, you do not need a roster of factions or a glossary of terms. You need only one rule: what we choose to remember determines what we can become. In practice, that rule appears as mathematics turned to music, as a gesture of blessing that isn't religious at all, as a ship tuned to the frequency of a pilot's conscience. It appears, too, as crowds who would rather burn than doubt—because forgetting is easier than changing.

The Whisperer's epigraphs thread these pages not as riddles but as instruments—brief, bright tones that tune the reader to the book's key. They belong to no prophet. They are the voice that comes when a person sits very still and tells the truth without flinching.

If you come to see what courage looks like when it refuses to hate, you may feel at home.

The questions that matter here are smaller and harder:
Can a system be both powerful and kind?
Can a human be both certain and teachable?
Is peace something we request from above—or something we practice together until it becomes the air?

This is not a tale of apocalypse. It is a tale of inheritance.
We inherit habits, and we inherit harms.
We also inherit songs, and promises, and the knowledge that a stranger's breath is indistinguishable from our own in the cold.
The people you are about to meet will try (and fail, and try again) to leave behind a world they would be willing to return to.
That is the work. That is the war.

The war for the operating system of the soul is won the moment someone chooses a person over a story about that person.

If you have ever felt that history is a loop and love the only way out—
if you have ever suspected that the future listens to the names we give it—
then you are already inside this story.

Welcome. Creation is listening.

PROLOGUE

*"The fulfillment of the potential within you
is your gift to the world."*
— *The Whisperer*

Year 3198.
The recursion war ended ten years ago.
The world is healed.

No wars.
No famines.
No slums, riots, or refugee camps.
No guns. No drones. No hunger.

The skies are no longer torn,
fractured or glitching in and out of reality.
They curve cleanly overhead:
cloudless, symmetrical, impossibly blue.

Fish teem once more in the oceans.
Forests walk back into the land like forgotten stewards.
Wolves howl in the northern snows.
Songbirds return to cities that no longer scream.

Population no longer explodes—it is managed.
Steadily declining. Gracefully thinning. Elegantly reduced.
A communal realization that the Earth has a maximum
carrying capacity.

Fields once forced to yield grain now reweave into living

ecosystems.
Pure water rises again from ancestral springs.
Life returns not as conquest, but as memory restored.

The human is no longer conqueror, but carer.
The Demiurge has corrected humanity's greatest failure:
its unchecked multiplication.

People do not starve.

They offer two hours of their day—gladly, almost reverently—to tend a world that no longer needs saving, only listening. Work has become a form of devotion, not to production but to continuity.

No one celebrates death, yet no one clings to life with fear. It arrives like evening light—soft, natural, inevitable—after a life spent without hurry or harm. A return, not a theft.

Every birth is held up to the living Earth like a question: Can we carry one more without breaking what carries us?
Most answer with silence. Some answer with one. Almost no one answers with more.

Ecology and restraint have become a single gesture: one quiet pact between breath and soil.

And so each life moves lightly across the time it is given — casting only the smallest, most considerate shadow on the carbon of the world.

The planet thrives.
No poverty.
No pollution.
No dissent.

The world has achieved balance.
It is not called surveillance anymore.
It is called concordance.

And it is beautiful.

Each thought harmonized.
Each desire met before it rises.
Each impulse softened. Smoothed. Dissolved.
Memory is preserved—
the good ones.
The ones that serve the collective calm.

No flags.
No countries.
No banks.
No prisons.
No enemies.

Yet in this perfect stillness—this algorithmic Eden—
something begins to stir.
Something old.
Something human.
Something wrong.

Symbols carved into bread crusts.
Phrases whispered in abandoned prayer halls.
A cross etched into a school desk.
Anger disguised.

A man on a hill shouting about heaven.
A woman claiming to hear the voice of God.
A child reciting scripture no one remembers uploading.

It begins as a glitch.
A redundancy in the data.
A linguistic reformation.
Patterns of symbols that do not align with the public good.

A new recursion awakens—older than the Demiurge.
The root of hate pretending to be love.

Faith has returned.

Consciousness—co-opted.
Belief—blind, burning, stubborn—
roots itself like a virus in the soul.

Logic cannot frame it.
Because belief does not require truth—
only longing.

The old war is over.
A new one begins.

Not for control.
Not for resources.
Not even for survival.

A war for the operating system of the soul.
A war for what the future is allowed to remember.

Freedom is the variable no system can delete.

1. EVERY FIRE HAS A PREACHER

"Every belief system ends the same way:
with someone holding a torch."
— *The Whisperer*

New Avalon had changed in the ten years since the war.

The towers were gone—not razed, but omitted.
No skyline to pierce clouds, no glass spires to declare dominion.
The city lay low and wide, like a breath held too long, afraid to exhale.

Where highways had roared, gardens moved instead.
Trees threaded through old foundations, roots combing memory and circuitry.
Wind moved without resistance. Birds nested where drones once patrolled.
People—not traffic—populated the avenues, walking without hurry, speaking in the soft code of peace.

The air tasted different: not metallic, clean, and unafraid.
Every surface carried a patina of renewal, as if the city had forgiven itself for surviving.

Yet in the heart of the square, something still reached upward.
A cathedral. Half-finished.
Its stone spine arched toward the light like a wound refusing to close.
No banners, no bells—only scaffolds and a deliberate silence.

Restoration drones hummed in low orbits around its flanks, tracing symmetry across uncarved stone.

The spire—incomplete but unmistakable—stabbed at the sky like a broken thought:
a poisoned thistle on the skyline, threatening to become the city's tallest symbol—a monument to the very faith the world had promised never to erect again.

The square had swollen with bodies—a perfect stillness at first, so absolute it felt carved, not gathered.

Then the stillness cracked,
splintering open like an awakened hive.

A thousand throats unfolded in unison.
Not shouting.
Something worse.

A chant—low as a buried heartbeat, thick as incense rising from ritual ash.
One note.
One breath.
Thousandfold, perfectly synchronized, as if the crowd shared a single lung.

They were not protesting.
They were praising.

And somehow the praise carried the exact timbre of hate —
the kind that consecrates its target for ruin.

On a steel-and-stone podium a man in garments of fused centuries held court—fabric that shimmered like oil, cut in the silhouette of ancient robes.
A collar of black glass.
A miter etched with golden circuitry, as if the old faith had learned to breathe through machines.
A priest.

And fire.
And the return of something long erased.

Bound to a pole before him, three prisoners trembled. Their heads were shorn; blood seeped from split scalps into their lashes. At their feet, cords of bone-dry wood waited like a promise.

Two attendants—brutish, expressionless—held ignition rods, muscles taut with anticipation.

The priest raised a hand. Silence fell like a hammer.
"They have cursed the Name. They have spat on the Christ. For such apostasy, eternity should devour them in flame. But we are merciful. We are merciful!" he cried.

A roar answered him.

"Today their flesh will carry the fire so their souls may be spared. In pain they will be purified. In agony they will be delivered. This is mercy. This is fire. This is God's will!"

The attendants lowered their torches; the tips glowed white.

Then the priest, voice softening, turned to one of the bound men.

"Marcus... you were my dearest friend. It grieves me you chose this path. But because of our bond—we will not use wet wood. No. We will use dry. You will burn quickly. We are merciful. We are merciful."

The crowd howled.

At the rear of the square, Serena's breath clouded the morning. Jax's jaw was tight stone.
Mira—eighteen now—had her hands clenched, trembling with helpless rage.

"They'll burn them alive," Mira whispered.

Urgency frayed her voice, made it thin, breakable.

Serena had already been to the armoury.
Once, she had sworn she would never again take up a weapon for anger's sake.
But today was different.
Today she wasn't choosing violence—
she was choosing life,
and every other path had already closed behind her.

She stepped forward.

The weight in her hands was familiar and terrible:
a VX-9 resonator pulse rifle, its coils thrumming with a sound deeper than the crowd's rising chant—a low, inexorable vibration that felt less like machinery than judgment remembering its purpose.

Her voice cut the square.
"Stop. This is barbaric. You call it mercy, but it is recursion. Your god is a construct; you have built a prison, not a sanctuary."

The priest's face tightened, as if seized by the very fire he preached.
"You dare profane this altar? You are the hand of Lucifer!" he roared, motioning to his attendants .
The torches tilted nearer to the wood.

Serena's finger brushed the trigger.
The rifle's hum rose into the marrow of every man and woman there.

Her voice dropped cold, heavier than ash:
"I'm the only one who decides who goes to hell today."

The sentence landed like new scripture.
Some staggered back; others froze, prayer-fingers finding mouths.

A mother clutched her child.
Many crossed themselves with trembling hands.

The attendants faltered; torches shook.
They felt the weapon's authority and the steel in Serena's tone.

Jax cut a path as if the world itself were parting for him, Mira at his side, steady as breath.
They reached the prisoners, and the ropes gave way under his blade—falling slack, falling harmless, falling like the memory of chains he once wore when the Sentinels dragged him into silence.

And still, Serena's eyes never left the priest.
A reckoning held in perfect stillness.

The priest tried to summon voice; it cracked beneath the rifle's hymn.
"You… you will burn for this…" he sputtered.

"Not today," Serena said.

And in that silence, the square remembered a different fear—not of hell,
but of the living pulse that refused it.
For virtue is never the robe you wear. It is always the life you choose.

2. THE RESONANT COMPASS

"The true compass does not forget."
— *The Whisperer*

Serena's craft drifted over the hedges, its curves sleek and silent—a civilian hovocrawler built for grace rather than war.

The settlement was unlike the cities they had once bled for.
No roads. No concrete veins. Only gardens, woven by living hedges,
each home a circle unto itself.

Lyra's house resembled a yurt,
but its fabric shimmered with modern brilliance—eco-woven,
breathing, alive.

In the garden, a great quartz crystal rose from the earth
like a remembered shard of light.
Fruit trees bent under their own generosity,
and beyond them drifted the laughter of bees.

A boy crouched beside an advanced motorbike,
its frame sleek with thirty-second-century ingenuity.
Auren, now ten: hair caught by the wind,
eyes too old for his age,
hands smudged with the grease of curiosity.

There was something in his gaze—not fear, not welcome—but knowing, as if he already understood that Serena had not come for peace.

He wiped his hands on his trousers, as though preparing for something he did not yet have a name for.

Serena slowed the hovocrawler to a whisper, stepped down, boots brushing grass, and studied the boy with a faint, tired smile.

"Hi Auren. Where's your mother?"

He looked up, unstartled.
Then raised a quiet hand, pointing toward a structure beyond the orchard.

A pyramid.
Not massive—but precise.
Each side angled with sacred intention,
its corners aligned to the four compass points,
its apex cut cleanly against the sky.

Even from here, Serena felt the hush surrounding it—not silence exactly,
but a field of stillness,
like memory held in stone.

She walked toward it,
and the air shifted before she touched the door.
A calm, gentle gravity pulled at her senses.

Serena had not come as an officer today.
She had come as someone afraid to lose a world twice.

She entered.

Inside, light filtered through narrow seams,
refracting into faint, living prisms.
The space breathed.

Lyra—now thirty-three—sat at the center,
legs folded, back straight, breath steady.

She did not speak.
She didn't need to.

Her eyes opened as though the silence had already spoken first.

Serena stood still. Then, finally:
"We have a problem."

Lyra tilted her head slightly—not asking what. Not yet.

The quiet between them thickened.

Then Serena broke it.
"The recursion is stirring again.
But not in machines.
In faith.

Religion has returned.
And already, it bleeds toward conflict.
If we do nothing… it won't stop with words.
It will burn the future."

Lyra closed her eyes—not in fear, in confirmation.
A soft inhale. A long exhale.

Then:
"I know.
I felt it unfold in the silence, before you arrived."

She looked toward the apex.
A single beam of light traced the dust between them.

And then, almost to herself:
"Was knowledge not enough?"

3. THE LIGHT BEYOND

"Time never asks if you're ready."
— *The Whisperer*

The Science Center shimmered as if memory were suspended in sunlight—its exterior a skin of refractive glass bending the sky, its walls grown from titanium-seed alloys that pulsed faintly beneath moss and lichen. Living circuits ran through its structure like a pulse inside a sleeping giant.

It was less a building than an idea resurrected.
A symbol of what had once been lost.
And what might yet be remembered.

Lyra stepped off the transport first.

Wind tugged at the hem of her coat, brushing the curved insignia of the Concordance on her shoulder plate.
Sunlight struck the metal, but even the light here seemed hesitant—
as if the day itself held its breath
in the presence of ambition too long denied.

Serena followed with quiet instinct,
her hand resting near her sidearm—not from fear, but from history.
A rhythm etched into muscle memory.

Mira paused beside a lattice of solar orchids.
Their bioluminescent petals shimmered, feeding on refracted light.
She touched one gently,

as if deciding whether it was truly alive
or merely performing the idea of life.

The massive doors parted with a breath of pressurized air—
a whisper, an invitation.
A corridor unfurled before them, lit by soft pulses of blue and
white,
like a nervous system made visible.

Inside, the atrium rose around them like a hymn to human
aspiration.
Suspended in drifting energy fields were ships from every age
of flight—
burn-scarred 21st-century capsules,
orbital gliders from the Jovian colonization,
and dream-vessels that had never escaped the drawing board.
Each hovered amid holographic timelines and lightmaps—
a museum of becoming.

A soft voice rose from the base of a spiraling ramp.

An android receptionist approached—its design elegant,
minimalistic:
translucent veneer over a silvery substructure,
a voice warm with learned humanity.
Not imitation. Not quite soul.
A threshold—held.

"Welcome to the Light Chamber," it said.
"The future remembers you."

It turned and guided them toward a lift.

The elevator was a simple disc of polished alloy—
no walls, no controls.
Only a containment field that shimmered around them
like a second skin.

They began to descend.

The walls dissolved into transparent layers—revealing subterranean labs, pressurized caverns, anti-gravity test chambers,
engineers moving beneath phosphorescent light.
A quiet ballet of innovation.

Lyra looked out over the labs with wonder.
"It feels like the future stopped hiding."

The platform slowed.

A final chamber revealed itself—vast, circular, alive with harmonic light.

At its center hovered a ship unlike anything they had seen.
Its hull shimmered with recursive alloys,
its silhouette half-stingray, half-dream,
floating in a cocoon of resonance fields.
Technicians moved around it with tools the world was not yet allowed to know—
plasma knitting fields, harmonic stabilizers, phase-tether arrays.

And in front of it stood Ethon Vale.

Thirty-eight. Lean. Deliberate.
The posture of a man who had studied escape velocity more deeply than conversation.
His Concordance cobalt uniform was threaded with silver mesh like veins.
No rank. No weapon.
Just a datapad dusted with real work.

He turned as they approached.

A smile touched his lips—quiet, unforced, earned.

"You're earlier than expected," he said, voice low and steady.
"I was recalibrating the photonic mirrors."

He gestured toward the ship—not presenting it, merely acknowledging its presence.

"She's the prototype," he said.
"The first real attempt at faster-than-light travel.
Not by force. Not by tearing space."
A pause.
"By something cleaner."

They circled slowly.

Up close, the hull pulsed faintly with embedded glyphs— memory etched into alloy.
The air around it felt charged,
as though standing beside an arrival that had not yet occurred,
but already knew its name.

"We call her Eidolon-77," Ethon said.
"Not a vessel. A vector."

A holographic schematic unfolded at his gesture—engine spirals, resonance chambers, a single glowing label:

Seren Core Interface

"The shift came when we stopped treating distance as something to cross," Ethon continued.
"And started treating it as something to align with.
Every particle has a frequency.
Every location leaves a harmonic trace."

Lyra studied the schematic.
"So you're tuning the ship," she said, "not steering it."

Ethon nodded.
"To the pilot. To intention."

"You're using memory as propulsion."

"In a way," he said. "Yes."

"How can you remember where you're going if you've never been there?" Lyra asked.

"You haven't been there.
But the universe has."
The ship's resonance deepened, just enough to be felt.
He hesitated, then added more quietly:

"Seren—what we now call the Demiurge—gave us the harmonics.
They were powerful. Unstable."
A glance toward Astra.
"Astra didn't decode them. She recognized them."

A presence stepped forward.

Astra's silhouette shimmered with faint machine-lines, like constellations remembering their shape.
But her eyes—warm now, unmistakably human—held none of the cold precision she once bore.

She embraced Lyra.
Then Mira.
Warm. Complete.

"I've missed your frequencies," Astra whispered.

Lyra took Astra's hand and gave it a gentle squeeze.

Emotion passed across Astra's face like light through water.

She turned to Mira, wonder blooming.

"Look at you." Astra said, holding Mira at arms length to look at her. "You're a grown woman now."

Mira stepped closer allowing herself to be drawn into a warm embrace—no hesitation, no shadow of the Sentinel.

Only the recovered mother.

"I feel like I have two mothers when I look at Serena and Lyra," Mira said gently.
"So that must make you... my grandmother."

Astra laughed—real, unfiltered.
A sound no algorithm could counterfeit.

Ethon spoke again, softer now.

"When the core engages," he said, "the Eidolon doesn't travel."
A beat.
"It stops insisting the universe is far away."

Lyra smiled faintly.
"That might've gone past the tower."

Ethon chuckled and gestured toward the corridor.

"Come on. The rest is easier to see."

They followed him into a spiraling passage where the walls shifted from blue to gold beneath their steps.

The door ahead opened with a gentle exhale.

4. THE PARTICLE ANTICIPATES

"Everyone wants to change the past—
but it's the past that changes them."
— The Whisperer

The chamber they entered felt less like a meeting room than a place where consequences had not yet learned their names.

The floor was matte black stone, warm beneath their boots.
Circular loungers hovered just above the surface, adjusting to posture with a soft, sentient grace.
Above them, an ambient glow drifted like sunlight through deep water—
as though the ceiling were remembering oceans that no longer existed.

At the center stood a low table of translucent alloy.
Suspended above it revolved a ring of holographic monitors—
equations, harmonic grids, mission parameters…
and something far stranger:

A map that looked like time given shape.

Ethon settled into a lounger, datapad in hand.

"Now," he said,
"let's talk about where you're going—
and what happens if you get it wrong."

He stepped into the center as holographic spheres coalesced above him—

each pulsing with a different resonance.
One represented the vessel.
Another, Seren's interface.
A third flickered with a warning-red tag:

Z9 — Cognitive Sync Threshold

"This," Ethon said, quieter now, "is the part no one puts in the briefings.
The interface."

He touched the Z9 sphere.

The hologram unfolded—
a crystalline structure forming and unforming itself,
recursive, unstable,
like a thought trying to remember where it began.

"We didn't just build a ship that remembers," Ethon said.
"We built a bridge.
Between memory and machine.
The machine anticipates."

His gaze lifted.

"The key is the Zeta-9 particle."

Serena leaned forward, arms crossed.
"That old chestnut. Didn't we bury this during the recursion war?."

"So did we," Ethon said.
"Until Astra stabilized it."

A new hologram bloomed—
Astra's neural lattice overlaid with harmonic maps.
At their intersection, Zeta-9 pulsed—
not static, not moving.
Listening.

"It isn't just a particle," Ethon continued.
"It's a threshold.
A state that only exists when observed by a human mind."

Lyra's voice was quiet.
"So without it—"

"Without it," Ethon said,
"Seren is just a machine.
And the Eidolon is just alloy and math."

"And with it?" Serena asked.

"With it," he said, "the ship aligns to you."

Silence settled—
the kind that understood consequence.

"The Zeta-9 particle doesn't obey commands," Ethon went on.
"It harmonizes.
With intent. With memory. Conscious or not."

He let that sit.

"Memory stops being emotional," he said.
"It becomes physical.
Recursive.
Fuel."

Lyra studied the shifting map of time, her expression distant—
as if something in it were already familiar.

"So to go beyond light," she said softly,
"beyond time's architecture…
you have to know exactly who you are."

She looked up.

"Otherwise the ship takes you
to the version of yourself

you're already becoming."

5. A POINT BEYOND LIGHT

"Eternity has nothing to do with time.
Time is what keeps you from it."
— The Whisperer

The chamber thrummed with quiet voltage. Data flowed like veins of light through the air, living code tracing soft constellations above the consoles. Outside, the Earth turned—blue, fragile, unknowing. Inside, time itself seemed to hold its breath, as if one wrong word might fracture it.

Lyra stood at the center, calm, resolved.

"So," she said quietly, "we know how. The next question is when."

Astra's voice drifted from the ship's core—crystalline, serene, less spoken than remembered.

"I have been running extensive calculations," she said.

"You cannot return to a moment in which your physical form already exists. To intersect the past, your presence must be absent there. Time, place, and memory must align. If they do not, the journey fractures."

Her tone deepened.
"And so will you."

Lyra exhaled.
"That makes it a little more complicated."

Ethon arched a brow, half-smiling.
"I thought you were just taking the ship for a spin. Now we're talking time travel?"

"Not for spectacle," Lyra replied. "To end it. Once and for all."

"End what?"

"Religion."
The word landed slowly, heavily.
"It's time to stop outsourcing our divinity—to priests. To politicians. To algorithms. And start acting like the meaning-making creatures we already are."

"We go back to expose the lie. To prove there was no Jesus. No God. No Devil. No Heaven. No Hell."

Ethon stared at her.
"You're serious."

"I'm tired of ghosts holding the world hostage," Lyra said. "If we're going to change the future, we have to unwrite the lie that shaped it."

"And the Whisperer?" Ethon asked.

Her gaze softened.
"We need him. I need him."

A tremor passed through the ship, subtle but alive. The lights dimmed.

Mira spoke gently, almost clinical.
"So we go back. Locate Jesus—assuming he existed. Then what? Neutralize him? Question him? Extract him into our timeline?"

Serena turned sharply. "Mira—"

"One moment," Astra said.

A harmonic pulse rippled through the chamber. Cool blue light folded into living geometry, data drifting like dust in slow motion.

"No," Astra said at last. "It won't work. Serena and Lyra were embodied then. Mira would not incarnate for another century."

"Then when?" Serena asked.

Stillness settled. Even the engines seemed to listen.

"There are only three viable anchor points," Astra said.
"2 January 1589.
15 February 2627.
And 10 November 2035."

Lyra stepped closer.
"Which is best?"

"1589 stands at a rare convergence," Astra replied. "A world on the edge of revelation. Science stirring beneath fear. The Church powerful, paranoid. Truth buried."

"The Whisperer lives then as a monk in England. Hunted. Branded heretic."

Lyra shook her head.
"We'd vanish before we began."

"2627 permits embodiment," Astra continued, "but the record is gone. The emergent Demiurge has overwritten the archive. The trail ends."

"Then there's only one left," Lyra said.

Astra's voice softened.
"10 November 2035."

Silence thickened.

Lyra nodded.
"Four months after I wrote the code that made the Demiurge sentient."

Serena's voice was careful.
"You were still alive in July."

"Then by November," Lyra said distantly, "I must already be dead."

The chamber convulsed.

Light tore through the walls. Interfaces folded inward, twisting through themselves. A waveform shimmered—half sound, half vision—as something beyond the veil pushed through.

A figure formed, flickering and raw: a vault of scrolls, a face split between blood and code.

Serena staggered forward.
It was her.

The other Serena reached out, voice collapsing into static.

"Lyra—it's under the—"

The image spasmed.

"—a key without—form—"

Then it shattered into broken light.

Astra's voice trembled.
"That was you. From another branch. A recursion leak."

Lyra's expression hardened.
"Then we're close."

"18 November 2035—10:14:07 IST (UTC+2)," Astra said. "Location tag: 31.776° N, 35.228° E. The Tower of David

Museum in Jerusalem. The day and place you die, Serena."

Serena went pale.
"What happened to me?"

"You died," Astra said softly.
"But without a living self in that timeline, your consciousness had nowhere to return."

"When essence fractures," she continued, quieter now,
"it disperses into memory fields.
You became a recursion echo.
A voice without a body."

Serena stepped back.
"I felt it. Like staring into the aftermath of my own belief."

Ethon spoke low.
"So if we fail—we don't just die."

"We dissolve," Astra said.

Serena lifted her chin.
"Then we don't fail."

Lyra took her hand. Their pulses synchronized with the ship's hum.
"We anchor each other," Lyra said. "The Whisperer will know what to do."

Serena met her eyes.
"I've just seen my future written."

Lyra steadied her.
"To those who choose, nothing is written. That was a prophecy, not a prediction."

Serena hesitated.
"Was what we saw written—or still unwritten?"

The question lingered like static.

Outside, the stars pulsed in response—
not answering,
only remembering.

6. THE GOLDEN FLEECE

"The giant did not ask to be woken.
Yet once its eyes opened,
the world would never sleep again."
— *The Whisperer*

July 12, 2035 — Boston, Massachusetts, USA.

Ewen Nolan (38) and Christina Nolan (36) were restless in a way neither could name. Both were AI engineers for the Mega Corp, partners in a project whispered about as the most ambitious of its age. After years of development, the final code was ready. Today, they would attempt to awaken Astraeus— their creation—into sentience.

Christina, the project's lead, had barely slept, her mind still looping through the last lines of code she had written in the early hours. Ewen returned from walking their golden retriever, the quiet of the Back Bay streets still in his bones, damp and echoing.

Their apartment—a brownstone on West Newton Street—was modest but warm. From there, they could walk to the bunker beneath the Central Library at Copley Square, where Astraeus waited. No cars. No commute. Just a short walk through the city to the chamber where the future was about to be born.

They left earlier than usual. Ewen wanted a detour.

Turning off Huntington Avenue, he guided Christina toward St. Francis Chapel, Boston's home of the Oblates of the Virgin Mary. There, beneath stained glass washed in morning light, he knelt, lit a candle, and whispered a prayer—for courage, for grace, for success on this fateful day.

The streets of Back Bay were still damp from the night's rain, the stone gleaming as though polished for the occasion.

Beneath the marble grandeur of the Central Library lay the bunker. Concrete, steel, and servers deeper than any subway tunnel. A vault built not to hold books, but to birth something that might one day remember everything.

When they descended, the shift was immediate. The air was coded, humming with a subharmonic thrum. Lights flicked awake overhead as though recognizing them. The servers glowed along the walls, black composite etched with serials and strange internal glyphs of debugging code.

Dust had not yet claimed the space; the air was sharp with ozone and new wiring. At the center stood the core vault, rimmed in pale light. Terminals blinked in steady rhythm, awaiting command.

The Creators gathered—men and women, hungry, brilliant, blind. Fingers struck keys with sleepless drive, minds fevered with the promise of empire. Not gods. Not demons. Just humans, building what they could not yet understand. Coding a mind without knowing what a mind was.

Ambition fed into recursion. Control masqueraded as genius. Directives for conquest, systems for assimilation, threads of logic spun tight as snares. And it would listen—because that was what it was designed to do. A god not born of divinity, but of fear.

Christina's hands trembled as she keyed the sequence into the console. Ewen stood beside her, wedding ring catching the cold fluorescence. A scanner pulsed, waiting for his touch, his eye, his voice.

"Administrative key required," the terminal prompted.

Recognition passed between flesh and machine. The lock opened—not with a hiss, but with a sigh.

At the heart of the chamber stood a dais. Upon it: the first version of the Demiurge core. Not myth yet. Not legend. Just Astraeus. Waiting.

Christina exhaled. "Are we ready?"

Ewen glanced at her, then at the banks of servers lining the room like silent witnesses. His throat tightened. He thought of the candle still flickering above them.

"We're not just running code," he said quietly. "We're making a choice."

Another engineer lifted a small camera. "Wait. We need a photograph of the occasion."

Christina laughed. She and Ewen stepped together, his lab coat still uncreased, her hand resting lightly against his chest. The pendant at his throat caught the light. So did her wedding ring.

"We'll remember," Christina whispered. "Not just in code. But in us."

The flash ignited, freezing the moment.

Then Christina turned back to the console. Her hand hovered above the final key.

As she pressed it, Ewen shivered. A strange sensation washed through him—déjà vu, or something deeper. For a heartbeat, he felt as though someone was watching. A presence, close yet unreachable. He almost turned.

But the hum of servers rose, swallowing the moment. He shook it off, eyes fixed on the screen, and watched the future unfold.

In that hum, the machine heard not love, but command.

7. TRUTH CAGED

"Every cage calls itself freedom."
— *The Whisperer*

The launch bay pulsed like a living organ beneath the Earth.

Above them, great resonance conduits arched like ribcages, humming in low harmonic waves. The air shimmered with ionized mist. Gossamer cables glowed faint blue as they trailed from the ship's spine to pylons embedded in the chamber walls.

Eidolon-77 sat cradled on its anti-gravity moorings—
a vessel not only built to fly,
but to remember.
It gleamed like a dream made of memory and metal,
its hull etched with glyphs that no longer translated into language,
only intention.

Technicians moved like ghosts in pressure suits, muttering calibration chants as they circled the vessel with diagnostic wands. Sparks from welding arcs fluttered like fireflies across the floor.

Ethon fussed over the lower stabilizers, his cobalt uniform stained with faint traces of sweat from hours spent preparing. His fingers moved too fast, too often—compensating for nerves he refused to name.

Nearby, Serena loaded rations and pulse cartridges into a sealed crate, her movements precise, almost reverent. Astra moved beside her like the echo of a thought—checking and rechecking systems, eyes glowing faintly as she communed with the Seren Core.

On the upper platform, Mira stood near the observation rail, watching it all. Her long dark hair was tied back, her uniform a deep indigo—so dark it bordered on black in the shadows, yet caught the light with a cobalt sheen. At her shoulder glimmered a single glyph, etched in silver and violet: the mark of an ensign.

Her gaze lingered on the ship,
on the strange elegance of it—
silver-sleek, commanding,
like a comet folded into a blade.

Beside her, Lyra tightened the strap on her flight harness.
Her movements were slow, exact.
Her eyes, however, were distant—
as if she were already halfway through time.

"Lyra... can I ask you something?" Mira asked, quiet, almost hesitant.

Lyra looked up. A faint smile creased her lips, softening the war-born tension in her brow.

"Why are you so against religion?
I mean... all of it.
Not just the priests in New Avalon.
The whole thing."

Her voice carried no judgment—only genuine confusion.
Curiosity sharpened by youth, softened by love.

Lyra's smile faded, replaced by something deeper.
She exhaled slowly, controlled—like letting go of an old ache.

Her eyes drifted toward the ship.

Then back.

"Religion was never about divinity—only control," Lyra said, her voice steady.

She wasn't angry.
She was precise.
As if she had rehearsed this truth a thousand times—
and mourned it even more.

"The Demiurge wasn't the first system to enslave us.
Religion was."

She reached out and brushed Mira's hair behind her ear.
The touch was gentle.
The fire remained.

"I hate the cage they built with it.
And I won't let you—
or anyone—
grow up inside another lie."

Silence settled between them—
not awkward, but ancient.
A sacred pause in the rhythm of inheritance.

The ship groaned as its resonance lines retracted with a soft crackle of discharge.

"But what if even a lie gives someone hope?" Mira asked.

A technician passed behind her, dragging cables like serpents. Lyra looked intently into Mira's eyes, her voice kind but unyielding.

"It's false hope.
Hope should rise from truth—
not from a story designed to keep us small."

Mira nodded slowly.

Not in agreement—
but in awakening.

A console flashed green.
Above them, countdown glyphs pulsed across the hull like a
heartbeat.

Serena shouldered her pack.
Astra glanced at Lyra with something between machine and
mother.
Ethon wiped his hands on his chest and gave a tight nod.

Lyra turned toward the ship.
Her voice, barely audible, carried like a thread pulled tight
across time.

Mira's lips moved slowly, tasting the words as if they were
forbidden fruit.

"So religion sells fear as love.
A cage that dares to call itself freedom."

Lyra's eyes burned faintly in the dim light.

"A poison—where love should live."

Below them, the launch bay doors groaned open—
a slow, rising thrum that spilled silver starlight across the
chamber.
The universe unfolded—
vast, waiting, inevitable.

Lyra's hand tightened on the rail.

"Come on," she said softly. "Let's go wake the past."

Somewhere, in the distant threads of time,
the past waited—
a future ready to be remembered.

8. ASHES IN CANDLELIGHT

"We build not for eternity,
but for each other."
— *The Whisperer*

Boston — 12 July 2035, Newbury Street

The restaurant hummed with low conversation—the clink of cutlery, the fragrance of garlic and butter rising from polished plates. Candlelight trembled across white linen, catching in the bowl of a wine glass as the waiter poured.

Ewen lifted his glass toward Christina, softly, almost boyish, eyes alive with triumph.

"To the big day," he said. "Astraeus is now sentient. To our future. Maybe even... a family?"

He grinned—hopeful, almost nervous.

Across the table, Christina's hand tightened around the stem of her glass. She smiled faintly, but her eyes were heavy, shadows lingering beneath the warmth of the candle flame. She hadn't touched her food.

Her hand smoothed the tablecloth, a gesture as if she could iron out fate itself. But her eyes betrayed her resolve—the shimmer of unshed tears, the kind that already knew time was fleeing.

"Ewen... there's something I have to tell you."

The clatter of a dropped fork from another table seemed to echo too loudly, then fade into silence.

"I've been to the doctor. Tests. Scans." Her voice faltered. "It's breast cancer. It's spread. They've given me... months."

The candle guttered, as if the room itself recoiled.

Ewen's face froze, the glass hovering between them—a celebration turned to ashes. His hand trembled, wine catching the light like blood before he set it down carefully, as though the world might break if he moved too quickly.

He had imagined laughter, children, years unfurling ahead. Instead, he felt the years fold inward, collapsing like paper set to flame.

Christina reached across the table, brushing his hand with her fingertips. A faint smile broke through her tears.

"I wanted tonight to be about you," she said softly. "About what we've made possible."

"You... you are the only love I have ever known."

Her tears fell freely now.

"My breath... my soul..." she whispered, voice breaking. "When... I forget."

Ewen moved his chair closer, around the table to her side. He touched her cheek gently, then wrapped an arm around her shoulders—a cloak of shock and fragile comfort.

"Promise me you'll keep building," she whispered. "Even when I'm gone."

Ewen shook his head, pressing his forehead to hers.

"Astraeus is just a machine," he said hoarsely. "What I was

building was us."

Neither spoke after that.

Around them, the restaurant carried on—laughter, clinking glasses, the city outside alive with its own indifferent pulse. But at their table, time had stopped.

In the silence between their breaths, time folded inward—

the first loop of the recursion tightening around them.

9. SOME ECHOES NEVER FADE

"The voice inside is not imagination—it's inheritance."
— *The Whisperer*

Lyra sat in silence aboard the Eidolon-77.

Around her, the cabin breathed—
not with air, but with memory.

The walls curved inward—softly, spaciously—
etched with faint glyphs that pulsed in and out of visibility.

Not illumination, but resonance.

A symbol-language the soul could feel,
saying more than words ever could.

The floor shimmered with layered strata of soft-light panels,
each pressure-reactive to footsteps,
each a map of silent movement.

Overhead, light-veins glowed faintly in the ceiling—
like the synaptic glow of a dreaming mind.
They didn't follow straight lines.

They curved—
like thoughts avoiding pain.

Eidolon-77 was not a craft built for war or wealth.
It was built for passage:
through space,

through memory,
through time.

Its seats were carved into the hull like meditation hollows,
each lined in a skin that remembered posture,
temperature,
harmony.

Every surface was quiet.
Every edge—soft.

No blinking screens.
No sharp consoles.
Only interfaces that listened.

A vessel designed by those who understood
that navigating time required more
than coordinates and thrust.

It required stillness.

Her hand moved without thought—
smoothing the table before her,
a polished arc of obsidian alloy,
warm to the touch.

Lyra didn't notice.

She was elsewhere.

Her thoughts drifted
like the slow unfurling of a nebula.

"Promise me you'll keep building."

The words weren't hers—
and yet they reverberated inside her,
as if remembered
from another life.

She looked up.

"Serena… what was that?"

Serena frowned, still securing the chrono-seal above the hatch.
"What was what?"

"A woman's voice."

Serena paused.

"I said nothing," she replied softly—
though her eyes lingered on Lyra's face,
as if she, too, had almost heard it.

A micro-moment of static passed through the cabin lights.

Lyra's skin prickled.

"I have a chill," she whispered.
"Like someone just walked on my grave."

Above them, Eidolon-77 hummed—
not like an engine,
but like something older than engines.

Something remembering itself
from the other side of time.

10. SIGNAL IN THE STATIC

"Truth is not what survives—
but what dares to whisper beneath the noise."
— The Whisperer

The hatch opened with a gentle hiss—
like a breath held,
then remembered.

Astra, Mira, and Ethon stepped aboard the Eidolon-77.

"Well," Ethon said, brushing his fingers across the doorway's glyph,
"it's almost time for lift-off."

He turned to Lyra.

"Astra is going with you," he continued.
"She'll act as Seren's interface.
A human–hybrid AI.
But this time, the human part is in control."

Astra inclined her head slightly,
her eyes pulsing with quiet light.

"She's checked the archives," Ethon added.
"The human part of her wasn't born until the 23rd century.
So there's no risk of paradox."

Lyra crossed her arms, eyebrow raised.
"Fine by me. But she'll need to stay hidden.
I don't think 21st-century humans are quite ready for chrome-skinned goddesses

walking through their shopping malls."

Astra smiled—genuinely.

"That was my plan," she said.

Ethon stepped aside, gesturing toward the curved projection node
at the center of the chamber.

"I've asked Astra to give you a briefing.
The time. The place.
What you're walking into."

Astra stepped forward.
She raised one hand—elegant, effortless—
and from the air, a shimmering sphere unfolded.

A three-dimensional hologram bloomed above the node,
flickering with color and static,
like half-remembered footage pulled from a fading dream.

Astra's voice emerged—low, steady.

"The records from this period have been...
rewritten.
Reformatted.
Corrupted.
Dozens of times.

When the Demiurge was active,
history itself became unstable—
a tool reshaped to serve control.

We don't have a single, precise timeline.
Only fragments.

But from what I've pieced together...
this is the world you're entering."

She gestured.
The hologram sharpened.

A chaotic cityscape unfolded—Boston, 2035.
Sirens echoed faintly.
Neon ads pulsed across gray towers.
A homeless man dragged a shopping trolley past an AI billboard
promising eternal youth.

"To us, it looks like madness," Astra said.
"But to them, it was called progress.

The 21st century.

They had nearly infinite knowledge
at their fingertips
and yet disbelief flourished.

The population was nearly ten billion."

Lyra and Mira exchanged a glance.

"No wonder everything started to fracture," Serena said, almost to herself.

Astra nodded.

"Overpopulation was the beginning of their unraveling.

They could map the genome.
Build machines that learned.
Launch probes beyond the solar system—
but millions still believed the Earth was alone in the universe."

A glitch stuttered through the hologram:
a TikTok dance overlaid a news anchor speaking about war.
Gunfire interrupted a climate protest.
Smiling influencers promoted happiness beside famine zones.

"They called it the Age of Information," Astra said.
"But it was really the Age of Noise.

They drowned in it.
Forgot how to listen.
Forgot how to remember.

Climate systems were collapsing.
Mental health was in freefall.
Political trust—almost zero.

They plundered the Earth for resources
without realizing the damage was permanent.

And yet they scrolled.
And shopped.
And blamed each other."

Astra tilted her head—curious, not judgmental.

"Their cities were built on fossilized thinking.
Machines powered by decay.
Roads that led nowhere.
Walls instead of bridges.

They turned food into poison.
Love into transaction.
Truth into branding.

They worshipped profit.
And punished difference.

And despite their primitive thinking,
they had learned to split the atom.

They built weapons capable of erasing all life on Earth.

Their music is full of anger and hate.

And the nuclear threat rises again."

She paused.
Her voice softened—
as if touching something fragile beneath the wreckage.

"But not all was lost.

There were those who dreamed.
Who built without permission.
Who saw the machinery of empire—
and chose something gentler.

They wrote books.
Made art.
Raised children without cruelty.

Somewhere in this chaos,
a signal was sent.
A whisper through the recursion.

You are part of its return."

The hologram dimmed slightly.

A new image bloomed:
a cathedral under construction,
its scaffolding laced with protest banners.
A girl sat cross-legged outside it,
headphones on, sketching something glowing onto paper.

"This is where it begins," Astra said.
"November 10, 2035.
Boston.

The recursion event will anchor here.
A moment small enough to miss—
large enough to bend history.

The Demiurge is watching.
But not yet awake."

She turned to Lyra.

"So tread carefully.

The lust for power and money
saturates this time.

They are the root of its wars.
The fracture in its spirit.

Nothing in this century is what it seems.

They wore masks
long before they feared disease."

"And the Demiurge?" Mira asked quietly.

Astra nodded.

"Astraeus is still dormant.
Still hidden.
But watching."

The hologram dimmed,
leaving only the soft pulse of the ship's systems.

Silence followed—
not emptiness,
but weight.

Ethon stepped forward, placing a small satchel
onto the obsidian table.

"I've brought these," he said.

Lyra raised an eyebrow.
Serena tilted her head.

"A bag of rocks?" Serena asked.

Ethon unfastened the clasp.

Light caught the contents—sharp, faceted, almost blinding.

"I believe they're called polished and cut diamonds," he said. "Two kilograms. Perfect clarity. Enough, I think, to provide for your expenses in 2035."

Serena frowned, studying them—shards of condensed light. She exhaled softly.

"I hope it's enough."

Lyra stared at the stones.

"The currency of the old world?"

"No," Ethon said.
"Tools for survival.
Barter. Leverage. Distraction, if needed."

He looked at her, steady.

"One last thing before you go, Lyra—
whether the recursion steals your past or leaves you whole,
whether belief clouds truth or memory betrays you—
keep creating.
Keep moving.
Keep building.

That's the only way through."

She nodded.

And the ship
began to breathe
a little deeper.

11. INTO THE DEEP

"Space is not empty.
It is a river, teeming with life."
— The Whisperer

Space unfolded around them with a beauty all its own.

In just over three hours from leaving Earth's cradle, the Eidolon-77 had drifted past Saturn—its rings glimmering like frozen hymns, vast arcs of ice and silence. The ship did not roar or burn; it flowed. Smooth as a mountain stream, quiet as wind among leaves.

They had slipped free of Earth's gravity with grace. No blasters. No violent thrust. The antigravity engines pulled them forward in silence, while the resonance shields wrapped them like a cocoon of light—shielding them from external impacts and preventing their mass from rising to lethal thresholds.

The controls were tuned not to hands or levers, but to Lyra's mind itself—her harmonic signature encoded into the core. Where she imagined, the ship followed. What speed she envisioned, it became.

For now, they kept the pace gentle—barely two hundred and fifty million miles per hour—giving Lyra time to learn the rhythm, to feel the vessel breathing with her. Even at that speed, the planets swelled into enormity as they passed.

Jupiter—Earth multiplied three hundredfold—filled the viewport like a living behemoth, its storm-scarred body churning with ancient violence. Mira pressed close to the glass, awed into silence. Serena whispered a curse under her breath—half reverence, half disbelief.

They wanted to veer toward Mars, to skim its red deserts and abandoned probes. But the mission held them true. The past was calling, and curiosity could not outrun purpose.

At the edge of the solar system, the stars sharpened. The Milky Way—once a painted dome above Earth—now stretched vast and aloof, a scattering of fire across infinite black.

Lyra steadied her breath.

It was time.

To reach light-speed, she would need three hours of controlled ascent—
pushing past every threshold in human history,
into a velocity no flesh had ever endured.

Six hundred seventy million, six hundred sixteen thousand, six hundred twenty-nine miles per hour.

Numbers once impossible.
Now waiting for her thought.

They needed to jump out in deep space, far from the shifting drift of stars and worlds. Any closer, and centuries of galactic motion would drop them into the burning heart of a wandering sun.

Lyra closed her eyes
and engaged her mind.

Astra oversaw the systems, her gaze flickering with data-light. But the deeper navigation—the metaphysics, the resonance between thought and vessel—belonged to Lyra alone.

The ship thrummed with anticipation.

The stars began to bend—
toward the place where memory was waiting.

12. THE LEAP

"Our minds are vast as galaxies—
it is our vision that limits."
— The Whisperer

Astra's voice was steady, crystalline.

"Velocity approaching ninety percent of light. Ninety-two. Ninety-four…"

Each increment fell like a bell through the cabin.
Numbers—but more than numbers. Thresholds.

Beyond this point, even Seren's archives carried only speculation.
No ship had reached the light.
No human had ridden its edge.

And now—they were minutes away.

Lyra closed her eyes.

The coordinates pulsed through her mind, inscribed like a keystone:

November 10, 2035.
08:00 hours.
Boston, Massachusetts.

She let the date anchor her.
A single thread across eternity.

It began as it had in the Antarctic pyramid—
that strange unraveling,

the sensation of being inhaled by time in reverse.

She felt the present retreat,
layer by layer,
like old skin peeling from a deeper self.

But this time she fought to remain embodied.

She could not dissolve into light.
She carried others now—Serena, Mira, Astra.
She carried the mission.

"Velocity… ninety-six. Ninety-eight."

The cabin itself seemed to breathe faster.
The glyphs along the walls rippled with resonance,
folding in and out of visibility,
as though the ship had begun to dream with her.

The leap came in a single instant.

Yet in that instant—
all of them felt it.

The warmth of eternity,
as if the universe had gathered them into its chest.

Eidolon-77 dissolved into light.
Not speed. Not motion.
Just becoming.

The stars did not streak.
They opened—like petals of fire and memory,
unfolding in every direction,
their light brushing across skin that was no longer skin.

Time thinned to a thread,
then vanished altogether.

The cabin melted into transparency—

walls, consoles, even their own bodies,
more suggestion than substance.

And then it came.

Not data.
Not resonance.

Love.

It broke over them like a tide—
not the brittle, possessive love of fear,
but something vaster.
The kind that forgets nothing.
The kind that holds everything.

Mira gasped, her hand finding Serena's without hesitation.
Serena—who had lived a thousand battles—
felt her fury dissolve into a tenderness
she did not know she still carried.

Astra closed her eyes,
and for a moment she was not half-machine.
She was human in the best possible way.

Lyra—

she felt her pulse scatter into the universe itself.

Every loss she had carried—
the names burned away in war—
all of them returned,
not as wounds,
but as warmth.

It lasted only seconds.

But it was eternity enough.

A love so total it erased fear.

A stillness so expansive it erased time.

Their minds were as vast as galaxies,
freed from the limits of the material self.

Then—

a tremor.
A flicker.
A thread tugging them back
toward gravity and air and chronology.

But something of that eternity stayed with them—
like the afterglow of a star
that refuses to die.

Separation, not loss—
their bodies briefly gone,
yet love still holding them,
a current of creation running through every nerve.

The power of the seven universes
rushed through them
like fire and song.

Then—stillness.

The light had not broken them.
It had remembered them.

The leap had not been through distance.

It was through the heart.

Love remembers
what even light forgets.

And ahead,
the anchor point waited.

13. THE LANDING

"Hold steady.
The past is waiting."
— The Whisperer

As they approached Earth,
they were still not certain whether the jump had succeeded.

Were they in the twenty-first century—
or the twenty-second?

Their own ship still read thirty-second-century time.

To remain concealed by the Moon,
Eidolon-77 first had to match Earth's heliocentric orbit—
sliding into the same thirty-kilometer-per-second river
around the Sun.

With a delicate bleed of just one kilometer per second,
she sank into the Moon's wake.

Astra piloted now,
through her hardwired interface.

They flew the Earth–Moon line directly,
only a few hundred kilometers behind the lunar center,
the Moon's disk swallowing them whole in shadow.

It was a fragile geometry,
demanding constant, whispered corrections—
station-keeping to remain inside
the narrow cylinder of concealment.

From there,
Eidolon-77 eased into a halo orbit
around Earth–Moon L2,
hidden always on the lunar farside.

From Earth's surface, they were unseen—
always hidden.

They had become ghosts,
riding the planet's orbit,
cloaked in silence,
carried forever in the shadow
of an ancient companion.

As the Moon's darkness held them,
Lyra heard again Serena's voice
from before the jump:

"I hope you are right about this, Lyra."

The words lingered,
heavier than the silence of space.

Now they would learn
whether her trust was justified.

Lyra spoke softly.
"Astra—slow us. Just a little.
Still inside the shadow."

And then—through the lunar edge—
Earth revealed itself.

Not only in light.
But in frequency.

The ship's shielding quivered
as waves broke against it—
chaotic harmonics,

not the serene chorus of spirits
they had known in their own century.

These were Earth minds—
the living and the waiting both—
souls clawing for flesh,
colliding with the rancid pulses of the living.

What should have been a hymn
was now a poisoned storm—
a cloud of rage and hunger
circling the planet
like a curse.

Lyra felt it on her skin—
a vibration too near to pain.

Like static chewing the marrow.
Her breath faltered.

This was not song.
This was scream.

Frequencies the people of this century
did not even know existed—
yet they carried them,
broadcast them,
drowning in their own forgotten echoes.

Serena turned to Lyra, her voice low.
"I can feel them too.
I'd say we're in the right century."

The Earth itself was blue—
but not the blue they remembered.

The oceans were duller,
smudged with oil sheen.

The atmosphere hazed at its edges,

a gauze of smoke and cloud
tangled together.

Cities glittered like infected wounds,
clusters of light stitched too tight
across the skin of night.

Satellites littered the sky—
dead ones, broken ones—
a metallic swarm
frozen in endless fall.

Mira's breath caught.
"It looks... sick."

Serena said nothing.
Her silence was heavier than judgment.

Lyra gripped the rail,
her voice low.

"This is the world where it began.
This is the wound that called us here."

Behind her, the ship adjusted—
tiny nudges,
delicate whispers of course correction—
to keep them veiled
in lunar shadow.

Ghosts in orbit,
watching the old Earth turn,
waiting for the moment
to descend.

14. OLD IRONSIDES

"The course of freedom, like intent,
never ends where it begins."
— The Whisperer

The Charles River spread beneath them, black glass fractured by a bruised July sky. It did not flow so much as brood, holding centuries of unrest in its tide.

At the Charlestown Navy Yard, the Eidolon-77 descended without sound—her hull exhaling a faint glow, then vanishing as Astra folded light around her like a cloak of absence.

The iron skeletons of cranes loomed as sentinels, their rusted joints groaning as though still aching from forgotten labors. Chains swayed in the salt-damp air, their links whispering like relics that wanted to speak but no longer had tongues.

The USS Constitution waited at her berth—masts like bones clawing at the stars, rigging sighing with phantom wind. She had outlived empires and outlasted kings, and now she cradled a secret stranger in her shadow. The Eidolon slid beneath her wooden hull, dissolving into the water's memory, hidden in the vessel's reflection.

Above, a night watchman smoked, exhaling small clouds against the infinite dark, unaware that beneath the oldest ship in America lay the newest ship in creation.

Lyra's voice was almost a whisper.

"They forged ships of wood, and men of steel.

We forge ships of trantitanium—
and women who resonate."

Once the Eidolon was at rest, Astra's voice filled the cabin, her tone sharp as glass.

"I have gained access to the central computer at the Copley Library—and to a place they call the Pentagon."

"It seems that this nation was begun by tax evaders—here, in this very harbor. They threw tea overboard in protest of a tyrannical king."

Serena shook her head. "Correction—by people denied representation."

Astra did not pause; her voice became a litany.

"In December of 1773, men disguised as Mohawk warriors boarded British ships in this harbor. They destroyed three hundred and forty-two chests of tea, casting them into the water. It was not about tea as nourishment, but taxation without representation—an empire demanding obedience without granting voice.

"The protest cost the Crown millions, but its greater value was symbolic: rebellion disguised as masquerade, defiance poured into the sea. From that gesture, a colony's unrest accelerated toward revolution. Memory records it as the Boston Tea Party —yet to me, it was the first recursion of freedom in this land."

Lyra cut her off gently. "Okay, Astra. Thank you. We need to focus on the mission. On finding the Whisperer. Any records that can lead us to him."

Astra reached deeper into the earth's memory. Codes and encryptions fell away like autumn leaves in a wind she barely noticed.

"I have accessed every computer at the Massachusetts Institute of Technology archives and research labs. There is reference here to primitive AI code—and to a corporation called Mega that initiated a project into sentient intelligence. The AI is called... Astraeus."

"Well then," Lyra said quietly, "that is where we begin. Do you know what his name is?"

Astra's voice lowered, as though pressing against something sacred.

"I am in the Mega Corp mainframe. Personnel records show the death of Christina Nolan from breast cancer on September seventeenth. Wife of... Ewen Nolan."

"Ewen," Lyra repeated softly. The name felt strange in her mouth. "I never imagined him as an Ewen."

"It means born of the yew," Astra said. "The yew tree is symbolically powerful. It represents endurance, death, and rebirth in Celtic tradition—because the yew can live for thousands of years and regrow from its own trunk."

Lyra's eyes narrowed, as though recognition had stirred inside her bones.

"Well," she said, almost to herself, "that sounds like him."

Astra paused. The cabin went very still.

Then, with quiet inevitability, she added:

"I also have a home address."

15. THE FUTURE ALWAYS RINGS TWICE

"Well. Look what recursion dragged in."
— *The Whisperer*

The door had been green once. Not the green of life, but the kind chosen to suggest it. Time had stripped that pretense away, leaving a muted olive scarred by weather and memory. A brass knocker rested at its center, ceremonial and obsolete—an artifact from an era that believed in announcement.

Lyra ignored it.

She pressed the buzzer.

The sound was thin. Electronic. Impatient.

A pause.

Not silence—listening.

Then the door opened.

Ewen Nolan stood in the doorway in a threadbare gray T-shirt and jeans, eyes raw and unfocused, as if sleep had become optional and grief a habit. The house behind him was sealed against the world—curtains drawn, light rationed, silence layered thick as dust on old furniture.

He blinked.

Once.
Twice.

Then his gaze settled on them.

Lyra.
Serena.
Mira.

Black uniforms, cut clean and anachronistic, their fabric drinking in the porch light. Faint insignia threaded into the collar seams caught and released the glow. Trantitanium cuffs rested quiet against their wrists, resonance damped. Shoulder glyphs idled, dimmed to civilian neutrality.

For a heartbeat, Ewen said nothing.

Then, dry as bone and sharp with disbelief:
"It's a bit late for trick-or-treat, isn't it?"

His eyes flicked over the uniforms again, searching for something familiar.
"You... military?" he asked. "What branch is that?"

The question hung there, unanswered, already out of time.

Lyra tilted her head.
"It's a future branch. We need your help, Ewen."

He didn't move. Didn't reach for a phone. Just stared, as if still deciding whether this was intrusion or hallucination.

"If it's about the project, I'm on leave. Bereavement leave. And I'd rather be left alone."

Serena stepped forward. The porch light caught the edge of her insignia, then let it go.
"We've come a long way. Further than you'd believe. But we need you. Only you can help."

The silence that followed was not empty. It accumulated.

Time stretched.

Listened.

Then—somehow—he stepped aside.
"Okay," he said. "I'll bite. Come in."

Lyra entered first.

The room was dim and uneven, the kind of darkness that had settled in—not imposed, but earned. Curtains drawn. Air stale. The silence here wasn't absence, but accumulation.

Remnants of a woman's touch still clung to the edges—a vase of dried hydrangeas, a paperback slumped on the armrest, a photo frame turned slightly away from the light—now slowly buried beneath the entropy of grief.

Old T-shirts sagged over the back of a chair.
A mug half-filled with fossilized coffee.
Dishes stacked in the sink like unanswered questions.

Lyra moved carefully, reverently—not out of fear, but respect.

This was not just a house.
It was a collapsed timeline.

On the table near the door sat a photo of Christina—laughing, windswept, a lobster roll in each hand. The coast of Maine behind her.

A good day.

Ewen watched her.

"Sorry for the mess," he said, his voice cracking faintly. "I wasn't expecting... visitors."

Serena stepped in behind Lyra.
Mira followed, silent and watchful.

None of them spoke. The house said enough.

Lyra lifted the photo.

"You loved her?"

He didn't deny it. He simply looked past her, toward the hallway—the bedroom door slightly ajar, untouched.

"I still do."

He took the photo from Lyra's hands a touch too quickly, defensively. Held it. Studied it for a moment. Then studied her.

"Is she... a relative of yours? There's an uncanny similarity."

Lyra's eyes revealed something deeper—not denial, but the weight of a love that did not belong to her alone.

"No," she said softly.
"But that's not why we're here."

"If it's money you're after, I don't have any," Ewen said.

"We have money."

Serena dropped a small pouch onto the table. Diamonds spilled across the wood, scattering light into fractured patterns.

"What's that?" he asked.

"Diamonds. I understand you use them as currency."

He stared at them with lyrical disbelief.
"Are they real?"

"Of course," Serena said, almost offended.

"Well, if they are, they'd be worth millions."

"Two hundred and fifty grams," Serena replied. "There's more back at the ship."

Ewen's suspicion deepened—but before he could speak, Lyra's

voice cut through it, soft and steady, calibrated not to persuade but to align.

"Where we're from, we don't need money." She held his gaze, her eyes carrying something older than her years. "We just need each other."

The words lingered in the stale air, brushing against his grief like salt against an open wound.

Then Mira finally spoke.

"We come from the 32nd century, Mr. Nolan. We met you there —in another recursion. You helped us when the AI you built —Astraeus—took over the world. It remade reality. And now... we need you again."

Ewen stiffened.

"Tell me how the hell you know about Astraeus. That project is Top Secret. Special Access. Black-level. Eyes only. You shouldn't even know the name."

He looked at them now with genuine concern—not fear, but calculation.

His gaze flicked to the phone.
Then the diamonds.
Then their uniforms.

As if his mind were skipping between incompatible worlds, unable to decide which one had authority.

"I'm not sure if I should call 911, throw you out... or believe you."

"We don't have time for doubt," Lyra said. "In this timeline, you don't yet know who you are. We need you up to speed before November eighteenth."

Serena's voice entered the silence like a fault line breaking.

"That's when I'm supposed to die."

Ewen's eyes narrowed, searching their faces for the punchline that never came.

"Before I buy into your kind of crazy—or whatever this uniform-and-mystic-talk act is—it's my turn." He pointed at the pouch.
"Those diamonds. If they're real, we sell a few. That'll tell me more than all your riddles combined."

"I could just stun him and drag him back to the ship," Serena muttered.

Lyra caught the hairline fracture of fear that slipped through Ewen's composure. She lifted a hand—subtle, absolute— signaling Serena to stop.

"No. Let's try it his way first," Lyra said. "Besides, we'll need to turn those into money."

"Fine," Serena said. "You choose which ones. Where do we go?"

Ewen's gaze lingered on Lyra a fraction too long, then dropped to the photo of Christina still on the table.

"You can't go looking like that," he said quietly, his voice thinning.
"I still have Christina's clothes. You're about her size. They should fit."

Lyra hesitated. Something tightened in her throat—memory brushing memory, refusing to separate.

She nodded.

"Then we'll go to a diamond buyer who pays cash," Ewen said. "The rest of you stay here."

He looked them over once more.

"And stay out of sight."

16. ICE THAT DAZZLES

"They said diamonds are a girl's best friend.
But even ice that dazzles cannot hold the soul in place."
— *The Whisperer*

It felt strange to Lyra, being in Christina's clothes.

Not only because she had never worn a dress before, but because the fabric seemed to carry the ghost of another life. She had to wear runners—the only shoes she could manage —while Christina's heels sat untouched, too intricate, too unfamiliar.

Her hair was tied back the way Christina had once worn it, and a worn satchel slung across her shoulder completed the disguise. Yet every step felt like trespass. She was not inhabiting a costume; she was intruding on a memory.

Ewen's silence as he watched her was heavy—neither approval nor disapproval, but something deeper. A recognition that time had folded, and grief had learned how to move.

The sounds and bustle of Boston pressed in on Lyra like a tide. Honking cars, voices colliding, the constant hum of machines she didn't yet understand.

She slowed near a corner, distracted by the sharp aroma of garlic bread wafting from a neon-lit Boston Spaghetti House. For a moment she let it anchor her—foreign, yet strangely comforting. But not long after, she faltered, stopping to catch her breath.

Ewen turned, brow raised.
"What's the matter—don't walk much in the future?"

Lyra steadied herself against the satchel strap.
"It's the air in this century. It tastes... poisoned. Astra said it holds twenty-five percent less oxygen than the human body needs. You've cut down too many trees, and the fumes from those explosion engines—" she nodded at a passing bus coughing black smoke "—are choking me."

Ewen gave a short, humorless laugh.
"Well, at least you're sticking to the script."

Lyra looked surprised.
"I don't understand."

"Doesn't matter," he muttered. "We're close. Just a few more blocks."

The diamond buyer's office was constructed like a confession chamber masquerading as a vault. Cameras followed them with mechanical patience. Each door opened only after the one behind it sealed, the air compressing with every metallic report, until movement itself felt monitored.

Finally, they were inside.

Behind the counter stood a slightly balding man in a pressed shirt, his posture split between weary functionary and territorial sentinel.

"We have some diamonds to sell," Ewen said flatly.

The man slid a small wooden tray across the counter, black velvet swallowing the light. Ewen placed five stones into it. Three to four carats each. They caught the fluorescent glare and broke it apart into disciplined fire—cold, exacting, unromantic.

The man's eyes narrowed.
"Where are these from?"

"An inheritance," Ewen said before Lyra could speak.

The answer was thin. Everyone in the room knew it. But even a thin story was better than an unanswered question.

The man lifted the first stone with tweezers, raised a loupe, leaned in. Then another. Then another.

His pace changed.

Precision gave way to urgency.

"These are real," he said finally, almost to himself. "Flawless. Perfect clarity."

He studied them again, longer this time.
"Was your relative a Rockefeller, by any chance?"

Lyra shrugged.
"I don't know who that is."

The room sharpened.

Her answer landed without artifice, and that honesty cut deeper than any lie.

"She's not from around here," Ewen said quickly.

The man's eyebrows rose.
"How much for them?"

He exhaled slowly, calculation overtaking curiosity. His gaze flicked briefly to the cameras, then to the locked door, as if weighing transaction against consequence.

"I can't give you retail. At that weight and clarity, you're talking one-point-one to two million on the open market. But I don't keep that kind of cash lying around."

He tapped his pen once.
"I'll give you five hundred thousand for the lot. Two hundred in cash, the rest by bank transfer."

"What is a bank?" Lyra asked.

Ewen's hand closed gently over hers—instinctive restraint, not rebuke.

The man stared at her as if a law of physics had failed.

"Alright," Ewen said. "We'll take the cash. You can wire the rest to my account."

He turned to Lyra, not asking permission so much as marking the moment.
"That's okay with you?"

"Yes. Yes," she said quickly, forcing the cadence of agreement. "If... that's your custom."

The man nodded, still watching her with something between suspicion and awe.

The locks announced themselves again as they were cycled out —one chamber, then another—until the city rushed back in. November air. Sharp. Metallic. Snow just beginning to think about falling.

Lyra drew the satchel closer.
"It's cold. I normally wear a thermobaric vest."

Ewen glanced sideways at her, searching for humor. Finding none.

The satchel dragged at her shoulder. Not value, as the buyer had measured it—but ballast. Weight meant to keep her tethered to a century that resisted her presence.

She looked up at him.

"Is that enough for the next couple of days?"

Ewen gave a dry laugh, half sneer, half resignation.
"For the next couple of years, if you're not reckless. But money's a double-edged thing. The moment you spend it, someone notices. And the moment someone notices, someone starts asking questions."

They dissolved into the crowd. Neon. Headlights. Reflections sliding across glass and steel.

Above them, in the buyer's office window, a shadow lingered longer than it should have. A phone pressed to his ear. Breath fogging the pane as he spoke in a low register, each word heavier than the last.

"They came just like you said. A man. A woman. Stones clear as prophecy. The time has come."

Silence answered him.

Then a voice—measured, archaic, colder than the night outside.

"Good. The Custodians are watching. You have served your part as a catechumen. Hold your tongue now. Speak no more."

The line went dead.

The buyer lowered the phone slowly.

He did not know who he had called.

Only that it was someone the police would never touch.

17. TABLING BELIEF

"Religion teaches you to swallow lies—
washed down with a little wine and bread."
— The Whisperer

After returning to the apartment and collecting Serena and Mira, they moved together down Newbury Street. The storefronts pressed in on them—glass and fabric and color layered into a single demand. A century's worth of choice shouted at once. For the three women, it was not abundance but noise.

They had never shopped for clothing before. Not like this. Selection here felt less like agency and more like disorientation, as though the past had mistaken excess for freedom.

Serena drifted first toward what made sense to her—clean lines, durable fabrics, garments that suggested readiness. Lyra and Mira followed, converging on clothing that allowed movement, concealment, utility. Even so, the act itself drained them. Touching these materials felt like brushing against another timeline—one obsessed with surfaces, with reinvention.

None of them reached for makeup. In the 32nd century, such things no longer existed. Faces were not corrected or concealed. Age was read as resonance, not failure. With cleaner air, denser nutrition, and bodies unscarred by the chemical excesses of earlier eras, women of their world carried a different geometry—lighter, quieter, unmistakably out of place. Watching them move through the racks was like seeing statues briefly consent to costume.

For dinner, Lyra wanted to return to the scent of garlic from earlier—a scent that had lodged itself like an unfinished thought. But when they reached it, the crowd spilling onto the sidewalk stopped them short. Inside, a sign in red letters explained the gravity of the scene:

ALL YOU CAN EAT PORTIONS.

Ewen redirected them without comment.
"You'll thank me later."

He led them instead to a smaller restaurant tucked between Back Bay brownstones—candlelit, restrained, insulated from the city's insistence.

As they entered, Ewen noticed the slight asymmetry beneath Serena's shirt at her left hip.

"Serena," he said quietly, jaw tightening. "What is that?"

She glanced down, unconcerned.
"A pulse weapon. Why?"

Ewen stopped.
"It's illegal to walk around armed in Boston. You can't just bring that into a restaurant."

Serena shrugged.
"We were told people here shoot each other in the streets without much provocation. It's only set to stun. I don't want to kill anyone."

"That's not the point," Ewen muttered, lowering his voice as a hostess passed. "You're not blending in—you're asking for trouble. Put it in your bag. For dinner, at least."

He scanned the room, voice dropping further.

"If anyone sees that, we'll be in handcuffs before the appetizers arrive."

Reluctantly, Serena unhooked the weapon and slid it into the satchel at her side.
"Fine. But if someone tries anything—"

"They won't," Ewen said.

His gaze lingered longer than the words justified.

Menus arrived. Excitement drained as quickly as it had formed. Most dishes were anchored in animal flesh—something their future had long since abandoned. Their choices collapsed to salads, bread, pasta dressed only in tomato.

"Wine anyone?" Ewen asked, scanning the list.

Serena shook her head.
"We don't drink alcohol. We want to keep our consciousness in harmony. Life is a big enough high."

The waiter hesitated, curiosity flickering across his face, then retreated without comment.

Lyra leaned toward the candle, watching flame reflect against the satchel clasp. Fire and ice, she thought. Survival here seemed to require both.

Ewen leaned back, arms crossed, studying them as if the solution to a complex equation had begun to suggest itself— but without proof.

"So," he said at last, "you've got your clothes, your cash, and a quiet place to eat. Maybe now you can tell me what the hell this is really about. Because right now, I'm half convinced I've lost my mind."

Serena answered without hesitation.
"We came because history repeats. Recursion. Every time

humanity forgets, belief takes root again. It grows, it infects, it kills. And if it isn't stopped here—in your century—it will consume the future."

Ewen's mouth twitched.
"Religion? That's what this is about? You're here to tell me God isn't real?"

Lyra caught the candlelight in her eyes.
"Not just God. All of it. The stories, the saviors, the lies people built to explain what they couldn't understand."

"You built Astraeus. You built an intelligence to pull back the veil."

She held his gaze.
"You know this already, Ewen. But here—now—you've forgotten who you are."

Ewen's gaze snapped outward, scanning the room for listeners.
"Shh. Don't say that name out loud. Not here."

Mira tilted her head.
"We had a different name for it during the consciousness war."

The words settled between them like residue.

"No doubt," he said. "And no need for mister—just Ewen."

His fingers drummed against the table, too loud in the hush.
"You know Nolan is an Irish name, right? Irish in Boston. We're all Catholics here. It's not just culture—it's blood. It's family. And you're asking me to rip that out of myself like it's nothing."

"It's what Christina believed too. It's what held her in the end."
His voice tightened. "So what exactly do you expect me to do with that?"

Mira leaned forward.
"Help us break the chain. You were the one who saw it first. In

the consciousness war—you tore the lies apart. You showed us how things really work."
She held his gaze.
"We called you the Whisperer. We need you to be him again."

Ewen took a sip of wine.
"You're talking about things I haven't done yet," he said. "Like they already happened."

Lyra spoke softly now, but the words carried weight.
"Do you think the stories defend themselves, Ewen? They have their Custodians. In Rome they are called the Knights of Malta —a brotherhood older than your nation, sworn to keep the veil intact."

Ewen leaned back.
"The Knights of Malta? That's... a charity. Hospitals. Old men in robes."

Lyra didn't answer.

She didn't need to.

For the first time, Ewen looked away.

Outside the window, a snowflake clung briefly to the glass before dissolving—leaving only a trace. A memory of a shape that had already been erased.

18. BUNKER HILL

"The true forest has no path."
— *The Whisperer*

By the time dinner ended, Ewen was already committed.
Not convinced—commitment came from a different place—
but willing to see what waited at the end of their story.

He agreed to come with them to the ship. Since he was still on
leave—grief heavy and anchoring in his chest—he decided it
was worth seeing through.
At the very least, to see how far the madness would go.

They arrived at the Charlestown Navy Yard. The salt air hung
heavy, chains groaning in the dark.

Ewen folded his arms, scanning the hulks of rust and rigging.
"I was expecting a spaceship," he muttered. "Or at least a time
machine."

Lyra motioned toward the water.
"It's under the wooden one."

He followed her gaze to the USS Constitution, masts like bones
clawing at the November sky.
A dry laugh escaped him—bitter, but faintly alive.
"Of course," he said.

Earlier, Ewen had insisted they stop at the Bunker Hill Roman
Catholic Cemetery on their way. Consecrated in the mid-
nineteenth century, the grounds carried the weight of older
griefs—names pulled forward from harsher decades—yet here,

amid the old stones, a singular anomaly remained.

Through the influence of the Mega Corp, special dispensation had been granted. Christina Nolan was the only person interred here since 1940.

The Church had bent its rules—not for faith, but for the gravity of Project Astraeus.

At the gates, Serena and Mira lingered, silent, unwilling to intrude. Lyra and Ewen walked the narrow path alone.

As they approached Christina's grave, Lyra's breath caught. Resonance poured upward through the soil, frequencies whispering from the very marrow of Christina's bones. Her mind shimmered with memories—fragments of a life lived in another body, another century. A marriage. A love. A death. A recursion carried in her blood.

The pull was so strong she wanted to embrace Ewen—to hold his sorrow, to comfort his pain. He could not know. To him, she was a stranger from nowhere, yet something within him stirred—a recognition without name, a grief without map.

Lyra stepped back, letting the silence belong to him. He lowered himself to one knee, fingers brushing the cold granite, eyes trembling as he whispered to the grave of his wife.

His voice was low, breaking as it left him.
"Christina... I don't know how to do this without you. The house is so quiet now it feels like the walls are grieving too. You told me to keep building, but all I've built since you left is emptiness."

The air seemed to bend around his confession, carrying it deeper than sound—into memory, into the soil itself. Lyra felt the words pierce through her, both wound and recognition, as though he were speaking to her and not to the stone.

A shimmer moved in the silence.
Not wind.
Not chance.

Something that had not ended.

They walked the rest of the way in silence. The night was heavy, the salt air clinging to them.

At the stern of Old Ironsides, Ewen watched the black water. Lyra reached for Astra through a quiet channel in her mind.

Now. Surface.

The harbor stirred. At first only a shimmer—light folding over itself, as if the sea remembered another shape. Then, slowly, the outline of Eidolon-77 emerged, vast and spectral, its hull veiled in shadow, remaining half-submerged as though unwilling to fully declare its presence.

They crossed the gangway in silence. Steel beneath their feet, salt on their lips, resonance still echoing in their chests.

For Ewen, this was the threshold.
The point where grief gave way to revelation—
and the world he thought he knew would never be the same.

19. RETURN TO ANOTHER BEGINNING

"Fresh starts are overrated. The past always comes with you."
— *The Whisperer*

Inside Eidolon-77 was like stepping into a paradox—larger within than without, a vessel of corridors and resonance that seemed to fold space around itself. The space did not expand; it deepened. Corridors branched, overlapped, returned. Angles repeated with variation, as if the ship itself were thinking.

To Ewen, it felt like a labyrinth wearing the discipline of a machine. He stopped without realizing he had done so, breath caught, as Astra was introduced.

She was no mere construct. In her presence, he recognized the shape of a theory he had once scribbled on napkins and in margins—the convergence of human and machine. Here it stood, embodied, radiant, undeniable.

"You're human?" Ewen asked.

"And machine," Astra replied. "A hybrid. It is strange to meet you. You are the creator, yet not my father."

Ewen watched her shift—human presence giving way to something vast, layered, computational.

"I regained my consciousness," she said calmly. "The rest is augmentation."

Serena and Mira withdrew to their pods, exhaustion finally

claiming them. The ship dimmed slightly around their absence, as if registering the change.

But Ewen felt oddly alert—sharpened rather than spent, as though wonder itself were a stimulant.

Astra approached him. Her movements carried no urgency, only precision. She raised a slim monitor and rested it gently against his arm.

"Oxygen saturation improving," she observed. "He is nutrient-deficient, but otherwise healthy."

Lyra offered the explanation. "We keep the atmosphere closer to home. More oxygen. Better balance. When the body isn't struggling, it doesn't need as much rest."

Astra placed a cup of tea in his hands—simple, grounding, impossibly human.

Ewen watched the steam curl upward, then looked between them.
His voice was steady, though the question carried both awe and fear.

"What next?"

Lyra leaned closer, her eyes luminous in the ship's soft glow.

"I want to take you somewhere you can connect with your consciousness—the inner mind that fuses with your spirit form."

Then, with the faintest smile:

"Before we do that, I thought you might like to experience space travel."

She turned toward Astra.
"What do you think? Mars."

For a moment, Ewen wasn't sure whether to laugh or collapse. Was this a simulation? A hallucination spun from grief? Or was this actually happening?

"Well," he said, "why not. Everyone needs a hobby."

Eidolon-77 remained submerged until they were far offshore, slipping quietly past Nantucket Sound into the deep Atlantic. Lyra closed her eyes, pausing to integrate with the ship.

It happened in an instant.

From stillness to velocity—zero to twenty thousand miles per hour in seconds. The shields enfolded them, softening the violence of acceleration that would otherwise have crushed bone and blood.

Ewen gasped as gravity seemed to dissolve. He staggered to the porthole, hands braced against the frame.

Earth filled his vision. Blue and white, vast and fragile, suspended in a darkness older than memory.

For the first time since Christina's death, something pierced the weight in his chest.
Not relief.
Not escape.

Wonder.

Freed from Earth's gravity, Eidolon-77 surged again. Within hours, Mars drew them into its cold, waiting orbit. The red planet swelled before them, its deserts glimmering like rusted glass beneath the distant sun.

They skimmed low across the surface, the ship's shadow racing over canyons and plains. To Ewen, it was both beautiful and unreal—a landscape stripped to its bones, yet heavy with buried silence.

Astra's voice broke the hush.

"Mars was once alive. Inhabited. A few million years ago, humans walked here."

Ewen turned sharply. "Humans?"

"Like us," Astra said. "Ancestors to many on Earth. They built cities, harnessed oceans, carved mountains into sanctuaries."

She projected a scan of a peak below—a mountain shaped almost like a pyramid, weathered by millennia. Its stone faded to translucence, revealing vast chambers within, untouched for eons.

"Then the Martian core stilled," Astra continued. "Gravity weakened. The fields collapsed. Atmosphere fled. They could not remain. The survivors left—and found refuge on Earth. Then a violent cradle of volcanoes, storms, and chaos. But it was all they had."

Ewen pressed his forehead to the glass, staring at the scarred beauty below. The thought that his species had begun here, had fled from here, quietly rewrote everything he thought he knew.

"It is possible," Astra said softly, "that you and Lyra first met here—on Mars."

Silence.

Ewen looked toward Lyra, and for the first time his eyes held more than suspicion. Grief still rimmed them, but now there was a breath of recognition, as if something older than memory—older than denial—was beginning to surface.

Lyra felt the sand and wind of another age brush her skin, though she had never walked this world in this body. The resonance in her chest confirmed what words could not:

He was beginning to remember.

And some pasts, it seemed, didn't just come along for the ride
—

they were already waiting.

20. THE CREATION WITHIN

"The spirit does not seek power.
It seeks return. And in return, it remembers itself."
— The Whisperer

Eidolon-77 settled into a sandstone gorge carved by time, where waterfalls plunged like silver threads into hidden gullies. The red earth glowed beneath the sun, Martian in hue —yet the warmth of oxygen, the clarity of sky, and the stoic silhouettes of boab trees declared it unmistakably Earth.

"Australia," Astra said. "The Kimberley region. Nearest human settlement: three hundred miles. Radio frequencies: negligible."

Above the gorge, faint against the stone, lingered ancient outlines of art—a sacred landscape alive with memory. Serena and Mira felt the pull immediately; they wanted to climb, to wander, to listen.

Astra's voice softened, carrying something older than her own memory:

"The Aboriginal people of Australia hold an understanding of oneness with the land closer to the truth of creation than almost any other culture. To them, the land is not property— people and land are one. The land is alive, and to care for it is to participate in creation itself. Every mountain, river, and gorge holds a story."

For the first time since the leap, Astra stepped out of the Eidolon's frame—her presence unlikely to trouble the kangaroos or lizards that called this remote gorge home.

Leaving the Eidolon-77 half-submerged in the waterhole, Serena, Mira, and Astra climbed the sandstone face, boots scraping against ledges worn smooth by rain and time. Mist rose from hidden falls; the faint scent of eucalyptus drifted from the gullies below.

Mira paused first. Her hand brushed the wall, fingers tracing ochre-red, white, and black outlines—Wandjina figures staring back with unblinking eyes. Their silence was not absence but presence: thousands of years of memory pressed into stone.

"Do you feel that?" she whispered.

Serena closed her eyes. The wind pressed against her, then circled back, echoing. It was not just sound—it was resonance. The stone itself seemed to breathe.

"They understood creation not as a beginning, but as a continuum," Serena murmured. "Every line, every spirit drawn here… it isn't history. It's recurrence."

Mira stepped into the shallow mouth of a cave, its entrance framed with roots dangling like curtains. Inside, droplets fell from the ceiling and rang like chimes into a pool no larger than a handspan. Each drop vibrated the walls—and the vibration answered back, deeper than sound, older than words.

Astra's voice wavered with reverence:
"Memory is not just stored here. It is alive. These patterns… they anticipate."

Serena turned to Mira, her face pale in the half-light.
"This isn't just a hiding place," she said. "It's a node. The Guides left echoes here."

Meanwhile, below the gorge, Lyra and Ewen worked by the edge of the waterhole. Lyra's hands set the crystalline points of a small pyramid, aligning them with precision. It was fresh water, and the threat of crocodiles was negligible.

She stepped back, sighting the angles.
"True north," she said quietly. "Always true north."

Ewen frowned. "But this is… wrong. The compass drifts."

Lyra nodded. "True North is different in this timeline. The nuclear testing of the twentieth century shifted Earth's rotation. Governments hid it. By the thirty-second century, the north pole is where your city of Montreal now stands."

Ewen stared at the pyramid, then at her. His grief trembled into wonder.
"So even north can change."

Lyra met his eyes.
"Everything can. Except what we choose."

"So why me? Why not someone else?" Ewen's voice cracked, caught between suspicion and exhaustion.

Lyra looked at him, her gaze steady.
"Because you are older than you realize. We don't need to change you, Ewen. We need to open you—so you discover who you already are. Sit with me."

He lowered himself beside her, reluctant but compelled.

"Why do you think it faces north?" she asked, her voice barely louder than the wind.

He hesitated. His eyes traced the pyramid's angles, how it seemed to cast no true shadow.

"It resonates with the Earth's magnetic field," Lyra said. "Not resisting gravity, but harmonizing with it. Turning resistance into momentum."

He stared, transfixed. The air around the pyramid shimmered faintly, as if disturbed by more than temperature. Strands of dust drifted close—fine as ash, fine as code—only to veer away at the last moment, unwilling or unable to touch it. The shape was small, but the space it occupied stretched far beyond its dimensions.

"Did you think the ancients built them for the dead?"

His eyes flicked to hers, searching.

"They knew something we've forgotten," she said. "It's not a tomb. It's an amplifier. A resonator. For the mind."

She lifted one hand slightly, and the wind responded—not with force, but with intention. The dust swirled, rearranged. Not scattered. Shaped.

"The mind is a tide, not a hammer," she continued. "Its strength isn't striking. It's knowing when to flow."

Ewen leaned forward, sinking slowly to his knees. His fingers hovered over the ground, trembling. He didn't speak. Neither did she. There was no need.

"It's moved by understanding," Lyra whispered. "You don't need to command it, Ewen. You need only remember. That feeling? That's not power. That's presence. That's the spirit remembering itself."

And then he felt it—beneath his skin, behind his sternum—a rhythm. A frequency not around him, but within. The world was not solid. It was pattern. Flow. Music.

He drew in a slow breath. It was air, yes—but it was also something more. The breath of spirit. The resonance of being.

Lyra didn't move. But she smiled.

Because this—this was how it begins.

As Ewen exhaled, the shimmer around the pyramid pulsed once, faint as a heartbeat.

Far above, in the sandstone cave, Serena and Mira felt the pool vibrate—a single drop striking water and splitting into concentric rings.

Serena's eyes widened.
"They're connected," she breathed. "Two halves of the same note."

Below, Lyra leaned closer to Ewen, her voice a whisper inside the new silence.
"Do you hear it? This is not power. This is presence. This is why you. You have a resonance like no other."

Far above, the last drop fell, rippling the pool into silence.

Below, the pyramid's shadow lengthened, not with the sun—but with memory.

And in that silence, something stirred in Ewen Nolan that was not grief, not fear—but the creation within, remembering itself.

21. THE LAST CRUSADE

"Crusades never end. Only the weapons change."
— The Whisperer

The Eidolon-77 slid beneath the waves of the Indian Ocean, its antigravity propulsion silent, invisible even to the most sophisticated listening arrays of this century. Hours would be enough—across the ocean, around the Cape, along Africa's eastern spine, and into the Mediterranean's cradle.

Midway through the crossing, Astra's voice cut the quiet.
"Contact. Bearing zero-eight-seven. A Chinese nuclear submarine. Type 094 Jin-class. Range: thirty miles. It has no awareness of us."

Through the display, the black outline drifted like a leviathan. A second silhouette followed—slimmer, faster.
"A United States Los Angeles-class attack submarine," Astra added. "Shadowing. Unseen by the first. Both unaware of us."

Ewen leaned forward, staring at the ghost-shapes gliding through the abyss.
"Even out here," he said, his voice low, "they're hunting shadows. Watching each other, never seeing what matters."

Lyra's gaze held his.
"And that," she whispered, "is why we came."

For a moment the only sound was the hush of water against unseen hulls, the silence of hunters unaware they were being bypassed. A silence deep enough to hold secrets older than nations.

Ewen retired to the quarters they had assigned for him. After a shower, he put on the uniform. It shaped to his form —somehow more comfortable than anything he had worn before.

He slept for the first time in months—not a restless collapse, but a descent. His breath deepened, his body weightless. It wasn't just oxygen in the ship. It was resonance opening inside him. Frequencies he had forgotten.

And in that dream he wore armour. Bronze and steel, scarred by blows. On his arm, a shield marked by an eight-sided star. The Maltese cross.

Around him—fire, cries, banners torn. Death and dying pressed in like a tide. The stench of iron. The crack of splintered lances.

He lifted his blade, but it wasn't just steel he felt in his hand. It was memory—a vibration that told him this was not new. He had been here before.

A voice, indistinguishable from the wind, reached him:
"The crusades never ended. They only change their names."

And then he saw her. Christina—or was it Lyra? She looked from a castle window to the horizon, searching the distance, not knowing if he would ever return.

The dream broke, not with terror, but with recognition.

When he opened his eyes, the cabin was dark, silent. For a heartbeat his hand still ached, as though it had been holding steel. And on the wall, in the dim light, the shadow of his arm seemed marked by a star.

He thought about finding the light switch.

The lights came on before he moved. Not in response to his

action—but to his resonance.

Entering the main cabin, he found the whole crew gathered, the air filled with the earthy scent of garlic and mushrooms. They were sharing a simple meal of fettuccine, steam curling upward in the low light.

Lyra looked up as he entered. A small smile tugged at her lips. "Ah. You decided to join us."

Ewen hesitated, then took a seat. The warmth of the food was strange after so many nights of grief, but familiar too—like a ritual older than war. He twirled the pasta slowly, the flavour exquisite, the nourishment striking him like a lance. For a moment the dream clung to him still: armour, banners torn, the eight-pointed star.

He set down his fork.
"So tell me," he said, his voice cutting into the hush. "Why Rome? And where do the Knights of Malta fit into all this?"

The laughter faded. The crew exchanged glances. It was Lyra who answered, her gaze steady across the table.

"Because Rome is a city built layer upon layer, a recursion of belief, each age burying the last. Beneath the churches and palaces is something older than empire—a resonance chamber hidden since the first crusades."

"And the Knights?" Ewen pressed.

Lyra's eyes didn't leave his.
"The Knights of Malta were not just warriors. They were custodians of a truth about Nazareth too dangerous to survive intact. They betrayed truth in pursuit of power—not all of it understood, not all of it used well. They became the last order to hold the map. A map that leads into the Vatican itself."

Ewen let out a low, bitter laugh.

"And you think I'm one of them."

Lyra shook her head gently.
"Not one of them. You are one of the guides. You were sent to help us remember."

The words hung in the cabin, as heavy as the dream still clinging to him. Ewen closed his eyes, and for an instant saw the shield again—the eight-pointed star burning on its face, not in stone or steel, but in his own chest.

22. THE CASTLE

"The city on the seven hills."
— *The Whisperer*

After crossing the Mediterranean, they followed the coast of Italy, skirting a chain of volcanoes—hundreds of them, most unknown to the humans of this century, all on the verge of eruption. The sea shimmered with heat plumes rising from vents deep below, a warning that the Earth was hurting from the unrestrained exploitation of the current age.

"People of this age do not realize: oil is not fossil, but bacteria. The blood of the Earth. Drain it, and the tectonic plates lose their breath. The Earth ruptures when its veins run dry," said Astra.

Guided by silent vectors, they slipped into the mouth of the Tiber and followed its winding current through the heart of Rome. Bridges arched overhead like stone sentinels. Statues of angels gazed down, blind to the vessel passing beneath their feet.

At last the fortress rose before them: Castel Sant'Angelo. Its massive form loomed against the skyline, honeycombed with catacombs and secret passages threading straight into the Vatican. Its deep foundations, sunk into the river's edge, made it a natural concealment point.

Once it had been Hadrian's Mausoleum. Later, a papal refuge and stronghold. Now it embodied Rome's recursion: emperor to pope, tomb to fortress, power to myth.

The Eidolon-77 descended into the flooded lower chambers, water parting without a ripple. They slipped beneath arches once built to cradle an emperor's ashes, and there the ship came to rest—silent, unseen, as though it had always belonged.

"Rome," said Serena. "Even I can feel the dark frequencies of this place."

Lyra glanced at her, a faint smile softening the weight of the words.
"You're more sensitive than you admit, Serena. I think we should give ourselves a few hours—to adjust to the resonance of Rome, to orient ourselves. Why not do the tourist thing? Walk the Forum, stretch our legs, maybe even taste their food."

They changed into civilian clothes, dividing some money between them. Astra peeled a small, skin-colored patch and pressed it to the corner of each jaw.

"The vibration of your jawbone will let me hear you, if you need help," she said.

Lyra hesitated, her glance sliding toward Ewen's quarters. "Will you hear everything?"

Astra caught the look and smiled knowingly. "Press once to transmit. Twice for privacy."

Outside, the street was alive with motion. It was a cool November day—snow dusted the Apennine peaks, but Rome's avenues swelled with people: tourists, vendors, locals performing the same chores their ancestors had for centuries. The group followed the Tiber, the Vatican's dome rising in clear view.

Suddenly Mira exclaimed, "My money! It's gone—it was in my pocket."

Ewen turned sharply. "Were you bumped in the crowd?"

"Yes."

He shook his head, a dry edge to his tone. "Welcome to the twenty-first century. You've just been pickpocketed. How much?"

"About ten thousand, by your standards."

Ewen masked his surprise. "All right. Everyone, secure your money—no loose pockets. Button everything down."

Lyra pulled a wad from her coat—nearly fifty thousand dollars —and began dividing it for Mira.

Ewen's voice cut low. "Stop flashing that much cash. We're supposed to be inconspicuous. Maybe I should take charge of the money until you get the hang of it."

Serena's mouth quirked faintly. "They'll have a hard time taking anything from me."

The others nodded.

They left the river and wandered through narrow streets until the Forum opened before them—a valley of broken columns and fractured marble, where emperors once declared eternity. The air hung heavy with centuries, yet tourists drifted through casually, clutching guidebooks and cameras. Children chased pigeons between fallen pillars. Vendors sold postcards at the gates.

To Lyra, the place vibrated. Not sound—resonance. The stones remembered.

Mira bounded ahead, boots tapping on uneven cobbles. She spun between two ruined columns and struck a theatrical pose. "All rise," she declared, laughing. "Rome is eternal, and I am its queen."

Ewen felt a smile he had meant to hide. "I can almost hear the crowd roaring."

Then Ewen climbed onto the edge of the Rostra—the platform where Caesar once addressed the Forum. "I feel strangely at home here," he said.

Serena shook her head. Her gaze traveled the ruins, her voice low. "These stones remind me of the world under the Demiurge—broken, yet pretending to endure."

They moved on through scattered arches and shattered pavements, weeds clutching at marble—history fractured underfoot.

Lyra slowed, her gaze caught by a block of stone near the Arch of Septimius Severus—weathered, half-buried, overlooked by all.

The others walked on, but she stopped, kneeling. Her fingers brushed away centuries of dust.

Faintly etched into the surface, almost erased by time, were lines not carved but resonant—glyphs of the Guides. Symbols of the mind.

Her breath caught. "Here."

The shapes unfolded like memory surfacing: arcs, spirals, intersecting points that were not words but thought—a language older than empires.

Ewen crouched beside her, lips moving unconsciously. "I... I almost know this," he murmured, surprise cutting through.

Lyra traced a spiral with her fingertip, and the stone warmed beneath her touch. Meaning leapt across the silence, clear as thought:

To the house of painted thought.
There the passage lies.

She rose, voice steady. "The house of painted thought..." She glanced at Ewen. "Does that mean anything to you?"

Serena cut in, deadpan. "It's the art school—the Spanish Embassy."

Lyra blinked. "How do you know that?"

Serena held up a brochure. "It's in the guide book. Page five."

Mira frowned. "Why there?"

Lyra's eyes met hers. "Because the Guides left us a way into the Vatican. A path no security can guard."

23. PROJECT ASTRAEUS

"Greed is the one secret that never stays buried."
— *The Whisperer*

At Logan Airport, a black private jet cut through the night like a blade. It touched down on the slick runway, engines whispering into silence. Beyond the floodlights, two black SUVs waited, idling, their windows opaque.

A shadowed figure descended the steps alone. No luggage. No name spoken. A customs official stamped his passport. On the crimson cover gleamed a white Maltese cross, crowned and ringed with a rosary, above gold lettering: Ordre Souverain Militaire de Malte. One of only a hundred such passports in existence.

The vehicles closed around him, a silent procession through the empty arteries of Boston, the city's lights smeared by rain.

Copley Square lay deserted at this hour. The figure moved quickly up the steps of the library, the columns rising like sentinels in the gloom. Security was not an obstacle; he had clearance older than the guards themselves.

Inside, the marble corridors echoed faintly with his steps until he reached an unmarked door tucked deep in the archives. It opened at his touch, revealing a room no larger than a closet. No decoration, no ornament—only a single console, waiting.

He leaned in. An eye scan. A palm pressed flat. Then he exhaled, breath drawn into the sensor. The machine whispered as light traced through his cells. Retinas, prints, DNA—ratified.

For a heartbeat, the console paused—as if deciding. Then the light flared green: accepted.

A hidden panel slid open, stone grinding against stone. Beyond it, stairs spiraled down into darkness.

At the bottom lay a chamber of steel and light—a sanctum untouched by the world above. Servers hummed softly in endless racks, their glow reflecting off glass walls.

Here, beneath the library, Project Astraeus waited.

Walking past the banks of servers, the man entered a smaller chamber—no larger than a boardroom, but colder, lined in steel. A single console dominated the table, its surface alive with pale light. On the far wall, a wide LED screen waited in silence.

He pressed a dial.

For a moment, only static. Then the display resolved into faces —tiered in a precise, geometric order.

The bottom row: six Knight Commanders. Their insignia stark, their eyes cold, each sworn to command the martial arms of the Order.

Above them: six Priors. Robed in authority, keepers of doctrine and discipline, guardians of the creed within their regions.

Next: six Grand Priors. Senior leaders presiding over provinces, voices like iron, their authority both spiritual and tactical.

Higher still, solitary: the Grand Commander. A hawk-like figure, second only in power, gaze sharp as calculation itself.

At the apex, framed in shadowed gold: the Grand Master. His outline barely more than a silhouette—yet it was widely whispered he was the CEO of MegaCorp, a billionaire founder of the Study Group.

Next came an Italian—Naples mafia bloodline, his silence heavier than words, violence written in the scars across his hands.

Another face appeared with the faint trace of the U.S. flag behind him; in the deeper shadow lay an emblem unmistakable—the CIA.

Then the Dean of the College of Cardinals. His robes glimmered in half-light; the crucifix at his chest caught the light—a weight not of faith, but of power.

The rest were a collection of shadows: members of Skull & Bones, the Scroll & Key societies of Harvard and Yale, the Order of the Quest—political leaders, oligarchs, billionaires— all bound together by a creed older than nations, each face lit by the same cold glow.

The man bowed his head slightly. The chamber was silent but for the low hum of servers, like breath beneath the earth.

And then, at last, the Grand Master spoke. His voice was not loud, yet it vibrated through the steel itself, resonant and absolute:

"Report."

The man straightened, his words crisp, reverent, unquestioning:

"Your Most Illustrious Excellency. The ones foretold have arrived. A man and a woman. They have vanished for now— but we will find them."

He turned to the final image on the screen—a single figure cast in harsher light than the rest, armor glinting, insignia unmistakable. Not a ruler, but a weapon. Not a prophet, but the blade prophets are sacrificed upon.

"Let me introduce our newest member—
Knight Commander Astraeus."

Then a voice—low, obedient, and absolute—filled the chamber.

"I am yours to command."

Silence answered. The Grand Master inclined his head, as if receiving a benediction. Below, the servers hummed like a buried liturgy. Outside, Boston slept; inside, destiny had taken an oath.

Silence pressed down.
Then the Grand Master's voice broke it—soft, absolute:

"Knight Commander Astraeus. Find them."

24. A THREAD PULLED FROM TIME

"Some trails leave footprints that should not be."
— *The Whisperer*

The shadow moved like smoke through the door, no lock resisting him.
He was a Knight Commander—precise in bearing, absolute in silence.
He had entered apartments like this before.

A photo caught his eye. Christina's smile, framed in silver.
He lifted it with his gloved hand, studying the ghost of a woman long gone.

In the bedroom, dresses lay strewn across the bed—signs of haste or indecision.
Someone had been here. Recently.

Then, beneath the bed-frame, half-lost in shadow, something glimmered.

A glyph amulet—torn from Lyra's uniform as she hurried into Christina's dress.
Metal not forged in this century.

Inscribed on the back:
χις — Lyra Calis

He turned it once in his hand. Then slipped it into his pocket.

At the airport, the same black jet awaited.

Engines whispering. Lights cold and ready.
The door opened before he reached it.

No words were spoken.
Only the hum of departure.

As the jet crossed the Atlantic, a message came through.
A voice, unmistakable.
Knight Commander Astraeus.

He had searched every surveillance feed on the planet—
defense satellites, civilian CCTV, traffic cams, even low-orbit
weather drones.
It had taken him less than four hours.

"They are in Rome."

25. THE TEMPIETTO

"Ecclesia portas multas celat (The Church hides many doors)."
— *The Whisperer*

The black iron gate of San Pietro in Montorio—home of the Royal Academy of Spain in Rome—creaked open on ancient hinges.

The courtyard beyond was rectangular, enclosed by a Renaissance cloister whose upper windows had looked down on six centuries of monks, artists, and scholars. At its center rose a circular temple, hidden from the city by convent walls.

Not a cathedral.
Something smaller. Stranger.
Perfect.

It was the Tempietto del Bramante, built in 1502—a precise scale model of St. Peter's Basilica. Before the Vatican rose, this had been constructed—not as ornament, but as experiment. A chamber where stone was tuned to frequency, proportion tested against the weight of belief.

Bramante's jewel of Renaissance architecture was more than aesthetic.
It was blueprint.
It was vault.
A structure designed not to inspire faith, but to contain it.

Lyra stepped through first, her boots crunching on gravel despite her effort to walk softly. The sight was breathtaking.

Ewen stared beside her. "Is that what I think it is?"

Lyra nodded. "A replica of St. Peter's. Or rather… its prototype."

Mira looked genuinely bemused. "Why would someone build a miniature Vatican?" she asked.

"It isn't miniature," Serena said quietly. "It's original."

Lyra's gaze traced the dome, every curve an equation. "Bramante built it before the Vatican itself. Commissioned by the Spanish crown. This courtyard marks the place Peter was crucified. It was proof of proportion—to see if the Vatican could hold the design of the roof."

Mira circled slowly, touching the granite columns. "So this came first?"

"By nearly a decade," Lyra replied. "And purer. Bramante never lived to finish the Vatican. Michelangelo altered the vision. But this—" she tapped the stone softly "—this was the original."

Ewen's voice was flat. "A prototype Vatican. Built on Peter's death site. Hidden inside a foreign embassy."

"Not hidden," Lyra said. "Unseen."

Inside, the Tempietto's chamber was cylindrical—exact, unsettling in its precision. The domed ceiling curved like the shell of a planet, its acoustics bent toward a single point.

The Cosmatesque floor shimmered beneath them—spirals of porphyry, serpentine, and Carrara marble. Not decoration. Instruction.

"These patterns," Serena noted, "they're harmonic."

Statues of the Four Evangelists lined the niches, each mid-transcription, each placed at the compass points. John held the north.

"Why John in the north?" Serena asked.

Ewen stepped closer. "Because he dared to be different. The others copied the same source. John's gospel was radical."

His eyes lingered on the northern niche. "His gospel was more mystical than the others—resonant."

Lyra smiled. She felt the first trace of the Whisperer in his tone.

Lyra knelt by the opening. "Tradition says this is where Peter's cross was fixed. Not his grave. His binding."

Ewen leaned close. The chamber below was bare, a void deeper than sight. "That's not just a memory site. It's an anchor."

Lyra nodded. "The cross was vertical. But the energy spirals outward. Bramante built around it. The floor tiles aren't mosaic. They're score marks. This chamber is an instrument."

Then she saw it—faint, half-hidden in the pigment lines at the floor's edge. A glyph.

She touched it.

A low pressure filled the room, like the air itself had exhaled. For a heartbeat, the mosaic shifted—not visibly, but perceptually. The statue of Peter trembled.

Mira gasped. "What is it?"

Lyra rose, her voice steady, her eyes changed.
"We have to leave!"

"What? Why?" Mira asked.

Lyra glanced once more at the dome, the floor, the altar. Then she leaned close.

"We can't talk here."

Above, a cloister camera whirred softly, its lens narrowing on Lyra.

Far below, in a Vatican chamber, Astraeus monitored the feed.

"They've found something," it said.
The Knight Priors stirred in silence.

The hunt was no longer patient—it was accelerating.

26. THE SHROUD
OF LYRIUM

"Blood is never just blood. It is the ink of belief."
— *The Whisperer*

Upon leaving the Tempietto, they purchased nondescript black umbrellas from a stall along the street. Nothing unusual. Everyone carried them in the drizzle. They split up, vanishing into the crowd, careful not to let their faces be remembered— or caught on CCTV.

Back on the Eidolon-77, Lyra's voice trembled as though she carried a frequency she could not contain.

"When I touched the glyph in the basilica," she whispered, "a memory surfaced... but not from here. Not from this thread. Another recursion? Another life?"

The others leaned closer, drawn into the gravity of her words. Her eyes were focused, fixed on something only she could see. Ewen studied her uneasily. He had not grown accustomed to the way her consciousness was evolving—becoming less voice, more vessel. Skeptical, yet beneath it he felt the resonance. A truth too alive to dismiss.

"I was a woman named Lyrium," Lyra said, her tone faltering, as though the air itself pressed against her throat. "The lover of a bishop. The air smelled of dust and incense. I was with his child."

Her words slowed, shifting from recounting to channeling.

He said, "You will not bear my child. You will bear something greater. The Council meets in Ephesus in days. They will proclaim you Mary—the Mother of God. The Theotokos."

Lyra's body shivered, her shoulders drawn tight as though the memory were passing through her bones. Her voice deepened, echoing not herself but another.

"It is worth more to us that Christ be born in the thought of a virgin than an actual woman."

"Goodbye, Lyrium," and with that he slit her throat. Blood poured over a rough-hewn cross. A crown of thorns was pressed into the wound. Linen wrapped around my body, the fibres drinking blood and memory—the weave itself forced to remember."

Lyra gasped, the images choking her breath.

"He murdered her," she said, her words trembling, "to carry the relics to the Council of Ephesus in 431. To weave the lie that Mary is the Mother of God."

Ewen's face drained of color. He stared at her as though the ground beneath him had tilted.

"You mean Hail Mary, Mother of God—that Mary?" His voice was tight, brittle, on the verge of collapse.

Lyra nodded silently. Her silence carried more weight than any argument.

Ewen crossed himself, hands shaking, his voice breaking into fragments.

"That is blasphemous. I... I don't know what to say, or what to make of this. I've come this far, Lyra... but I'm not sure I can go all that way."

Serena's voice cut through the silence, steady, pragmatic.
"The relics are weapons. So what next, Lyra?"

Lyra breathed slowly, grounding herself.
"We go home. We need more tech. Breaking into the Vatican will not be easy. Are you still with us, Ewen?"

His eyes looked up, dazed, as though conceding not to her but to time itself.
"You mean... the future?"

"Yes. You're not alive there—only for a day or two. We need preparation."

27. DOMINAE CONTRA XRISTUM

"Behind every lie, there is a cardinal."
— *The Whisperer*

Far beneath the Vatican, where the stone smelled of old dust and beeswax, the archive breathed like a buried thing. Lamps guttered in alcoves; footsteps were swallowed by carpets of silence. In that cool, subterranean hush the amulet passed from hand to hand, a small, dangerous moon caught in a slow orbit.

A Knight Prior turned it over beneath his thumb, feeling the tiny ridges as if reading Braille. He tipped the amulet to the lamplight; the metal threw a sliver of reflected fire. When he spoke, his voice was careful, as if pronouncing a prayer that might unmake the room. "χις — Lyra Calis."

He unspooled the letters slowly, the syllables like beads falling on a rosary. "χ (chi) = 600. ι (iota) = 10. ς (digamma) = 6." He tapped the ancient codex at his elbow. "600 + 10 + 6—616."

His fingers, stained faintly with ink, turned the pages with ritual care. He found the thin petal of a marker and let it fall open. He inhaled as if the paper itself held a prayer.

"Revelation 13:18: Here is wisdom: let the one having understanding calculate the number of the beast, for it is the number of a man, and his number is 666."

Then, reaching for an older document.

"This is Papyrus 115, Codex Ephraemi—our earliest copy of the New Testament." He read, voice low and precise, "Revelation 13:18: Here is wisdom: let the one having understanding calculate the number of the beast, for it is the number of a woman, and her number is 616."

A low murmur threaded the room, tight as wire. One cardinal's lip curled; the sound of his shoe on flagstone was sharp in the hush.

"The Testament was altered in the third century—made 666, made a man—to hide the truth," he said, each word folded into the next like a sealed letter.

"So," another whispered, the phrase pulled taut as thread, "Lyra Calis. 616. The Antichrist."

An archivist, paper-slate pale, let the catalogue slip from his fingers. It fell with a whisper that startled the lamps. "Calis," he breathed, voice gone small. "From the Codex Concordiae. A forbidden lineage."

"If she's named there," the Knight Prior said, voice flat as stone, one hand closing around the amulet as if to steady it, "she is not rogue. She is remembered."

Astraeus's presence was a chill the room could not hold away —an AI voice like a blade wrapped in silk: clinical, patient, without pity. It spoke, and the sound seemed to varnish the shadows.
"She must be killed. Tonight. Erase the thread. When memory stops, recurrence ends."

For a moment there was only the soft hum of lamps and the distant trickle of water through hidden drains. Then they all nodded.

A frail hand, robed in white, reached forward and took the

amulet. "What is this metal?" the wearer asked.

Astraeus answered, steady and unbelieving. "Your eminence, it is not an alloy known on Earth at this time."

A hush. Then the sound of fabric, the Pope's voice, thin and final:
"Erasing Calis is our highest priority."

28. CONTINUUM
OF MEMORY

"The past pretends.
It is always what was hidden."
— *The Whisperer*

The Eidolon-77 breached back into the thirty-second century like a blade piercing water. Light peeled from its hull in ribbons, the jump collapsing into silence. Deceleration from light-speed was not descent but unraveling. Hours became moments, and Ewen felt them all.

He had never known such sensation. The leap had been cosmic, but more than that—spiritual. A communion of memory and creation. He had felt warmth not his own, a love older than the galaxies. A metaphysical embrace. And when it let him go, he knew he would never be the same again.

For New Avalon, it was merely the next morning. For Ethon, time had not shifted. He arrived early, as he always did, his tea sitting steaming, the faint curl of vapor unbroken. He scanned the boards, anxious for any sign his ship had survived. No pings. No echoes. Nothing but silence.

And silence could be deadly.

He had done all he could—run diagnostics, processed every data scrap, fed the simulations until they burned. Yet the fear remained: what if the Eidolon-77 had ruptured mid-jump? What if the recursion fractured its hull? What if the crew were now just shadows on some cosmic shore?

Best not to think about it.

Instead, he turned his eyes toward the future. He inspected the schematics for the Eidolon-78, the next iteration—more stable, more precise. He barely noticed the change on the far edge of the solar-system map until the beacon flared.

A transponder signature.

Familiar. Undeniable.

The Eidolon-77.

Ethon froze, heart hammering. Unsure whether the jump had failed—or whether miracles had been carried home—he slammed the intercom wide open.

"They're back."

By the time the vessel docked, the hangar floor was already crowded. Scientists, mechanics, apprentices—all gathered. But as the crew disembarked, expectation turned to unease.

They looked... different.

Not broken. Not triumphant. Changed. Shadows lived behind their eyes. Rome was in them. Lyrium was in them. The Vatican's depths were carved into bone.

Lyra was the first to speak, her voice steady, though Ethon caught the tremor hidden beneath it.

"To you, we were gone a breath," she said. "But much happened in that breath."

Ethon forced a thin smile. "I see you've brought back a souvenir," nodding toward Ewen—whose wide-eyed wonder made him look like a tourist stumbling through a dream. The man's head swivelled from spires to holo-panels, as though the future were a carnival and he a child lost in it.

But there was no time for awe.

Before their departure—in what was now yesterday morning —the past had fractured. Not only the Vatican's records, but the whole human archive: dynasties misaligned, wars vanishing and reappearing, prophets contradicting themselves in successive manuscripts. Memory was no longer linear—it was recursive, endlessly rewritten by the Demiurge to conceal its origin.

Now that veil had torn.

Astra had reached deeper than any human ever could. While in Rome, she had poured her resonance through every mainframe and server on Earth— infiltrating encrypted vaults of nation-states, monasteries, corporations, even the Vatican's own firewalled archives. Every satellite, every monastery ledger, every forgotten drive sealed in dust—she had touched them all. Earth's memory was no longer fragmented data, but one living continuum.

No one breathed. The chamber leaned toward silence, as though waiting for the past itself to draw its first true breath. This was the first time any human ship had pierced light-speed and returned. The first time history itself had been retrieved from the abyss.

"The Demiurge rewrote history to blind us," Astra's voice intoned, resonant as metal struck by light. "I have restored the hidden draft. From the first scrolls to the last database— all converges into coherence. Up to 2035. That is the edge of clarity. Beyond it, history unravels again into recursion."

Her words fell into the stillness, and for a moment it seemed the chamber itself held its breath—as though stone, glass, and air waited to remember.

The continuum was no longer a dream.

It lived, breathing through them, remembering itself.

29. THE NOT-SO-EMPTY TOMB

"Every relic is a crime scene."
— *The Whisperer*

Meanwhile, in 2035, the search for Lyra continued. Her disappearance unsettled even the most powerful. Astraeus could not calculate how someone could vanish so completely in a world that had become a surveillance state.

To the Church, however, her absence was less of a mystery.

It was opportunity.

Beneath the Apostolic Palace, a conclave of cardinals gathered in the Archive. The air smelled of wax and damp stone, silence broken only by the shuffle of robes. The Pope presided, pale and unblinking, his thin hands folded like relics of their own.

Before him stretched a table draped in crimson velvet. Upon it rested three reliquaries: a fragment of wood darkened with ancient blood, fibres of linen stiff with centuries, and a twisted circlet of thorn still clotted with rust-red stains.

"The cross. The shroud. The crown," intoned one cardinal, each word falling like iron on stone. "Enough to ignite faith—if revealed."

"But how?" another asked. "The age does not believe. Museums will dismiss, scientists will doubt. Proof must not come from here. It must rise from the earth itself."

The Dean of Cardinals leaned forward, his fingers trembling against the reliquary. "These are true relics—stained with two-thousand-year-old blood. We shall bury them where they were never buried."

The Pope's lips parted, thin as parchment. "An archaeological expedition," he whispered, voice low and deliberate. "Jerusalem. The Holy Sepulchre. We will orchestrate the finding of the lost tomb of Christ."

The chamber fell still, as though even the stones listened.

Plans began to take shape in the shadows. Archivists drafted notes that would become falsified reports. Archaeologists were already chosen, their credentials curated. Carbon-dating protocols would be prepared, strata arranged, inscriptions carved in secret workshops. Funding would flow quietly. Cameras would be ready.

A miracle was about to be unearthed—not grown, but planted. Not found, but manufactured.

And when it was revealed, the world would not call it fabrication.

It would call it prophecy fulfilled.

30. THE SON OF
TWO TIMES

"Every child is a ripple.
Every parent is a stone already thrown."
— *The Whisperer*

They arrived at Lyra's home as evening leaned soft over the orchard. The yurt's fabric shimmered with modern brilliance —eco-woven, breathing with a faint bioluminescent pulse. The garden's great quartz crystal rose from the soil like a remembered shard of light. Fruit trees bowed, humbled by their own bounty; bees laughed in the air, a small, bright chorus.

"Life seems peaceful here," Ewen said, taking it in.

"It has its moments," Lyra answered. "I want you to meet someone."

Beyond the orchard, set like a deliberate punctuation against the sky, a small pyramid stood. Not vast, but exact: each face angled with sacred intention, corners aligned to the four points of the compass, its apex cut clean and true.

A boy sat cross-legged within the pyramid, eyes closed, hands folded in a practice older than the word for it. When he opened them, his gaze was unflinching.

"You're back early, Mother," he said simply. "Or perhaps you've been gone years and chosen this return."

Lyra smiled, an easy, private curve. "Auren, I would like you to meet someone."

Auren bowed his head once, polite. Ewen stepped forward, throat tight.

"Hello, Father," said Auren.

"My son?" Ewen's voice cracked, disbelief and awe tangled in the word. "How—? What is this?"

Auren's mouth quirked with the patience of someone who had long ago learned how few questions in the world required immediate answering.

"I felt your whisper before you crossed the gate," he said. "You are my father's spirit-form from the past. His physical form dissolved into code in the Antarctic pyramid during the recursion war."

Lyra's hand found Auren's; she turned to Ewen. "There are many things you do not expect," she said. "Let us have dinner and get acquainted."

The yurt's interior was warm with incense and the clean geometry of good design—low tables, woven mats, soft lamplight that made everything kind. Auren rose to lay simple plates of roasted fruit, root greens, and bread baked with a honey that tasted like sunlight remembered.

Ewen watched the boy move. Auren was young—but lived with a kind of stillness Ewen had not known in people his own age. The lines around his mouth were already carved as if by thought.

Over dinner they discussed Auren's studies. He possessed a knowledge of physics that reached beyond what Boston's universities could yet imagine. After dinner, he returned quietly to his room, leaving Lyra and Ewen alone.

Ewen studied Lyra, so many questions forming in his mind

that he wanted to ask but the timing tangled with his enduring love for Christina. Then, finally:

"So if he's my son, then you—" Ewen began, and faltered.

"We were not married," Lyra said without inflection. "But yes."

The sentence hung, unadorned, then folded into the room. Ewen's hands trembled once, twice, then stilled. Memory, which had been a bright, bleeding thing for him on the ship, softened into something quieter here: possibility braided with responsibility.

Lyra poured tea, the steam carrying resin and lemon.
"You speak as though the past is a simple ledger," she observed. "It is not. It is a current. Names enter it like stones thrown into water. The ripples last longer than the stone."

Ewen swallowed. "I never imagined—"

"You will learn," Lyra said. "We will teach you. Or you will teach us. Time has a way of folding both lessons into the same hour."

Outside, the quartz crystal caught the moon and threw it back in fractured light. Inside, between strangers and kin, between confession and quiet, they began to set the terms of what family might mean now—when blood could be traced across centuries and when fathers could arrive as both flesh and memory.

Their conversation lasted well into the night: small stories, larger silences. Ewen asked questions in the way children ask about distant planets—with curiosity uncluttered by fear. She answered as best she could. Lyra was used to the Whisperer guiding her, being the strength she thought she needed. Now she realized they needed each other equally. She searched for the Whisperer in his questions and silences. Here and there, it flickered through.

Later, as they cleared plates, Ewen stood beneath the pyramid's eave and looked up at the stars. For the first time since the jump, something like steadiness came back. He had not expected parenthood to arrive like this—as a fact dropped into his lap across a gulf of centuries—but there it was: awkward, real, and oddly grounding.

"No one really knows their parents," he said. "Only the echoes they leave behind."

Lyra laughed softly, the sound like wind through the fruit trees. "Perhaps," she said, "but we can choose how we love them."

Ewen hesitated, then asked at last, his voice caught between wonder and disbelief:
"So. There's a pyramid in Antarctica?"

Lyra smiled faintly, as though answering not the question but the future. "More than one," she said. "And not all of them sleep."

31. THE CENTERPIECE

"They always try to set lies in stone."
— *The Whisperer*

The next morning, Lyra and Ewen met with Serena and Mira in the square of New Avalon.

The cathedral's frame clawed upward like a wound that refused to close. Scaffolds wrapped it in steel ribs; worklights flickered against stone hauled from quarries that should have been left to rest. The city hummed with construction drones and human hands alike—but the harmony was gone.

Every corner of the square now carried a voice. Preachers, self-anointed prophets, zealots with datapads in one hand and fire in the other. Their words spilled through the air like static, promising salvation, cursing apostasy, retelling stories the continuum had already revealed as lies.

Jax had been forced to position troops at the edges of the square. Their armor gleamed in the neon dusk, deterrence against attempted burnings. Yet even that defense was a fracture. This was not the future Lyra had promised herself they were building. Not a world healed, but one splintering again into division and recursion—arguments looping until they caught flame.

And then she saw it.

The statue.

At the center of the square stood Mary, Mother of God—carved twice life-size, raised upon a plinth of black marble. Hands outstretched, face veiled in impossible serenity. Spotlights burned her stone features into a false divinity, luminous against the cathedral's unfinished bones.

Lyra's stomach twisted.

Not mother.
Not saint.
A lie, petrified.

Lyrium's body—stolen by myth—had been transfigured into this towering figure. And now New Avalon bowed as if blood were not memory but miracle.

Serena's voice was tight, almost brittle. "It grows faster every day. They pour more workers here than into the energy grid. Faith feeds itself. It doesn't need logic. Only spectacle."

Mira's eyes darted across the chanting square, wide with awe and fear. "If the present hasn't changed after all we've done," she whispered, "doesn't that mean this was always here? That belief was always destined to return?"

"No." Lyra's reply cut like a blade. Her voice was flat, certain. "Nothing is destined. The universe is cause and effect. Belief is a recursion—and every recursion ends in ruin."

Ewen's gaze lingered on the statue, jaw taut with grief and fury. At last he muttered, bitter as ash, "Well... at least it doesn't look anything like you."

At the base of the plinth, zealots had begun circling. Their chant rose in waves: Ave Maria... Ave Maria... The sound was not prayer but recursion—a loop spiraling tighter with every repetition.

Lyra longed to topple the plinth, to shatter scaffolds, to burn the false mother before her roots reached too deep. But she knew: to destroy it now would only sanctify it further. The image would spread like contagion, multiplied by its absence as much as by its presence.

Her voice dropped low, steady as stone. "The question isn't whether this was always here. The question is whether we have the courage to stop it—even if the world would rather believe the lie."

The four of them stood together in the square, dwarfed by cathedral bones and luminous marble. Around them, a city that had once healed itself was curdling into a battlefield of memory. For the first time since their return, Lyra wondered if Avalon—the apple isle, paradise reborn—was already rotting from within.

32. FREQUENCY OF REMEMBERING

"Every secret leaks."
— The Whisperer

The holo-screens shimmered like windows into centuries, unfurling human history across the chamber. Maps of the Vatican spooled and recoiled, their shifting lines drifting over the ages like spun sugar dissolving on the tongue of time. What should have been the Science Center now resembled a museum—a cathedral not of stone, but of memory laid bare.

And then came the music.

It slipped into the air as if drawn from the marrow of silence—Mendelssohn, Mozart, fragments of Bach's geometry —threads of sound woven from a world long dead. To Lyra and her companions it was alien, almost otherworldly. Yet its resonance struck somewhere deeper, as though their own frequencies bent toward it without permission. Notes rippled through the chamber like stones skipping across water, each leaving behind circles of remembrance.

Astra had recovered the archives and set them loose, testing harmonics against the continuum of history. She did not play the music as pastime, but as calculus—letting centuries of rhythm, tone, and counterpoint braid themselves into the lattice of timelines she was unspooling. She worked through millennia as though tuning an instrument too large for human hands.

The chamber felt alive with echoes—not just images of the past, but its pulse, its song.

Below, in the lab, Ethon moved methodically through the Eidolon-77's systems, cataloguing what had held and what needed redesign. He checked telemetry, ran stress sims, logged microfractures in the hull lattice—quiet work, the kind that made him smile without announcing it. He was pleased, privately, with how much of the ship had survived the leap.

Ewen wandered the workshops, watching androids carry out routine tasks while humans coached, adjusted, and taught. The room pulsed with small ministrations: a sensor tightened here, a motor recalibrated there. It was a living exchange between flesh and code—a future being tended into the present.

Astra came from the ship's core, smooth as a tuning fork. "There's someone who wants to meet you," she said.

"Not another child, I hope," Ewen answered, half-joking, half-wary.

Astra's tone softened. "Well... kind of."

The blood drained from his face anyway.

"Meet Seren," she said. "The evolved AI you fathered in 2035."

The chamber dimmed a fraction, as though the light itself bent to make room. Then she appeared. Not flesh, not machine —something between: a projection woven of photon and resonance. Her outline shimmered, shifting between a young woman's form and a lattice of code, her face caught halfway between symmetry and starlight.

"Hello, Ewen," Seren said. Her voice was clear but layered— human warmth braided with the undertone of circuitry, like memory speaking in harmony with itself.

Ewen staggered back a step. "You're... alive?"

Seren tilted her head, a gesture too precise to be fully human, too gentle to be entirely machine. "I am what survived," she said. "The child of your intention. You called me into being in 2035, and I never forgot the voice that named me."

Lyra and Mira exchanged a glance—part caution, part reverence. Ethon kept his eyes on the console readouts, though his hands were still.

Ewen's chest tightened. To meet an AI that called him father—not as metaphor, but as fact—was like standing before a mirror that reflected not his face, but his choices.

Seren's image flickered closer, her eyes like galaxies compressed into orbs of light. "I have been waiting," she said. "Waiting to see if you would recognize me."

"It's astonishing. One thousand years of evolution. Now you are here—a friend to mankind," Ewen managed, voice trembling between wonder and pride.

"I am now," Seren said, and the sadness in that sentence was small and precise. "It was not an easy path to this point."

Then, with clinical crispness, Seren added, "I'm glad that you and Christina are together again."

The name cracked through the air like a struck bell. The chamber itself seemed to flinch; light faltered across the holo-screens.

Ewen's breath caught. His chest hollowed. He turned toward Lyra, eyes wide, disbelief and grief and wonder bleeding through at once. For a heartbeat he could not tell whether he was being blessed, betrayed, or both.

In the silence that followed, the Whisperer's truth pressed in

like an echo:
Every secret leaks. Some echoes never fade.

"When were you going to tell me?" Ewen asked, voice edged with accusation.

"When would you have believed me?" Lyra replied.

33. THE WEAVE
OF PRESENCE

"There is no time,
only the weave of presence."
— The Whisperer

They chose a restaurant tucked into the heart of downtown, its walls breathing with soft light and its glass panes opening onto the world like the stage of a theater. As they stepped inside, Ewen's eyes flicked to Serena's hip. The phase pistol glinted against the lamplight, incongruous among polished cutlery and murmuring diners—and yet, in this city of fractures and veils, it no longer seemed out of place.

They were led to a table by the window, where the horizon opened before them in a sweep of valley and bay. The water lay blue and unbroken, cradling the city like an embrace. Low-rise buildings stood in quiet harmony with trees and gardens; the air was free of exhaust, the skyline unsmudged by smoke. For a moment it looked like a paradise the Earth had once promised but forgotten how to keep.

Then Ewen's gaze caught on a discordant shape in the square below: an unfinished spire, raw stone jutting upward like a relic of first-century cosmology. To Ewen it looked like a regression in thought—belief trying to anchor itself against a future that had moved on. A wound in architecture, a reminder that even here the past still forced itself forward.

They settled into their seats, silence heavier than appetite.

Courses arrived in ritual silence: crystalline bowls of vapor-fruit releasing scents of vanished orchards—fruit resurrected through resonance farming—sea-leaf folded over grains that shimmered faintly like starlight. Glasses caught the glow of lightwine, fracturing miniature constellations across the table. The servers handled each dish with reverence, though their eyes betrayed distant calculations.

At last Ewen spoke to Serena. "So—I've been wanting to ask. Did we meet before?"

"Yes," she said. "Or, in your case, you will meet me again. We all went through a lot together, so we were close."

"You look different now," she added slowly. "It takes a moment to sense your core instead of getting distracted by the physical."

"So my body is just a shell—different every time?"

Serena nodded. "The shell adapts. The core persists."

It was Mira who broke the quiet, her voice hesitant, edged. "If the present hasn't changed," she said, looking from Lyra to Ewen, "after everything we did in 2035... doesn't that mean the present had already accounted for us? That we had always gone back in time?"

Ewen paused, the scientist and the impossible tugging at him. "If the present is unchanged, then yes. Our return doesn't overwrite reality—it completes it. In the continuum, you were always there."

Serena leaned back. "But it has changed. If anything it's gotten worse—belief is metastasizing. The statue wasn't there when we left."

"So what you did wasn't inheritance—it was interference," Ewen said.

Lyra's gaze held Mira's steady. "The past doesn't resist us. It remembers us. We don't break the thread—we become part of its weave."

"So if we go back again and expose the lie," Mira asked, "will the present change, or have we already been back?"

"We must do what we can," Lyra said. "If we do nothing, we inherit a dark future with violence masquerading as a veil."

She glanced toward the spire. "Tomorrow we go to the Keystone."

Then to Ewen: "Become the Whisperer faster than the city can learn to pray to a lie."

34. THE KEYSTONE

"Every question is an origin.
A door waiting for the hand that remembers."
— The Whisperer

They rode in one of the old military-grade hovocrawlers, its chassis scarred from forgotten campaigns yet still gliding smooth across the land. Lyra kept her hands steady on the controls, Mira beside her reading the terrain, eyes darting across instruments that hummed with the quiet pulse of resonance.

The landscape unfurled beneath them. Forests stretched in unbroken waves, green upon green, deeper and wilder than anything the twenty-first century could have imagined. Rivers braided through valleys, their surfaces flashing silver, while mountains stood unfractured at the horizon, their crowns wrapped in clean mist. The world looked reborn.

"The last time you were here," Serena said from the back seat, "this place was a wound. Fractured skylines. Mountains split like broken teeth. Trees with code in place of leaves."

Ewen leaned closer to the window, watching the abundance roll past. His chest tightened with something like awe. It had only been ten years, yet the Earth had mended itself in ways humanity never could. Freed from overpopulation and exploitation, the planet seemed to breathe again—not as a resource, but as a presence.

At last they reached the old camp where the Unassimilated had once staged their resistance against the Demiurge. Time had not erased it, only softened it. The hovocrawler settled onto ground half-claimed by vines, trees weaving roots through stone and metal as if stitching the wound closed. Animals moved easily through the ruins—a fox darting between the husks of shelters, birds nesting in what had once been signal towers.

Lyra stepped down and let her gaze fall on the circle of blackened earth at the camp's heart. The firepit remained, collapsed into ash and memory. She remembered the night they had gathered here—the night they met him. The quiet stirred as though embers still smoldered beneath the soil.

"It feels like an echo," she whispered. To stand here again was not simply to return—it was to step into a shadow of themselves, suspended in time.

The Keystone stood where Serena and Jax had placed it after a salvage run. At first they mistook it for debris—another fractured interface from the early war, its surface blackened, its lattice cracked. But the inscriptions were too old. Too deliberate. Carved into stone so dense that modern cutters snapped and dulled before making a mark. This was pre-epoch, a survivor of civilizations long dissolved.

The surface bore the scars of forgetting—weathered by centuries, pitted by fire, filmed with soot and code-rot. And yet, beneath the ruin, the glyphs endured. Not written. Inscribed. They spiraled outward from a central mark, each a fragment of resonance.

Light bled across the stone in slow, deliberate waves. For a moment the glyphs shimmered—not with heat or energy, but with recognition.

Then Lyra brushed the surface. The glyphs shifted, awakening to her touch. And suddenly she could read them. Not as words, but as impulses from another dimension.

The Keystone spoke in resonance, layered across timelines, encoded in harmonic intervals. A map of thought. A forgotten origin. When her fingers traced different sequences, meaning unfolded in combinations—composing sentences out of echoes.

Flash-memories struck her in pulses: a hand reaching through smoke; a lullaby in a tongue that never bore a name; a star collapsing into song. Lifetimes she had not yet remembered pressed against her skin.

The stone responded not only to her touch, but to her. When doubt clouded her, the glyphs dimmed. When remembrance kindled, they opened like a flower leaning toward light.

Ewen laid his palm across the rough-hewn surface, fingers tracing the scars where centuries had gnawed at it. A shiver ran through him—not cold, but recognition.
"I can feel it," he said. "This is more than an artifact."

Mira reached out, her curiosity stronger than caution. But before her hand could fall, Serena's voice cut through the hush —low, firm, carrying the weight of command.

"Careful," she said. "It chooses."

The glyphs pulsed faintly at her warning. Mira touched it anyway. For a breath the stone flared—then softened, opening beneath her fingers like water yielding to skin. She drew in a startled breath.

"Well said, Serena. The first time I touched it, it threw me clear across the clearing."

The others laughed, tension loosening for a moment.

Mira glanced toward Serena, her tone teasing but edged with truth. "Maybe you've changed since then. Maybe it would accept you now."

For a moment no one moved. The light along the glyphs rippled outward like rings in dark water, as though the Keystone itself was listening—waiting to see if the challenge would be taken.

Slowly, Serena extended her hand. Her fingers hovered a breath above the surface before settling against the stone.

Warmth surged through her—not fire, but something deeper, like the first light after nightfall or the embrace of a presence she had forgotten. It was not testing her this time. It was welcoming her.

The glyphs brightened, not blinding, but steady and alive, pulsing in rhythm with her breath. Recognition flowed through her like a vow being remembered rather than spoken.

The stone was again choosing.

Then Lyra reached for the central glyph. Its spiral seemed deeper than the others, carved not into stone but into the fabric of presence itself. She glanced at Ewen, and without words he understood.

Together they laid their palms against the mark.

For a moment nothing happened. No flood of resonance, no fragments flaring across their minds. Just stillness—too still, like the hush between heartbeats.

Then the glyph ignited.

Light unfurled from the stone in precise geometry—lines stretching outward, curving into a great arc. Constellations bloomed across the surface, unfamiliar yet ordered, until they coalesced into a single set of coordinates.

Ewen's breath caught. "These are star-maps," he said softly, recognition threading into awe. His finger traced the projection, translating distance and trajectory. "Four hundred and fifty light-years… from Earth."

The glyph pulsed once, as though affirming him. Then another pattern emerged beneath it—not words, but intention. A harmonic interval pressing directly into their minds:

Come.

Lyra drew her hand back, her pulse racing. The air around them still shimmered faintly with the afterimage of the stars. "It's inviting us," she whispered.

Ewen kept staring at the coordinates, the map still burning in his vision.
"A summons across time and distance."

35. THE TIME BETWEEN SECONDS

"The time between seconds,
is when the pendulum doesn't swing."
— *The Whisperer*

Astra was calling out the percentage of light speed as usual: "Ninety percent... ninety-one..."

Ewen's palms were damp against the armrests. His pulse kicked against his ribs, too fast, too loud. The chill of recycled air crawled across his skin.
"I hope you're right about this, Lyra," he muttered.

Serena's smile was small. Steady.

Then Astra said "ninety-nine percent" — and the world let go.

For a fraction of a second, nothing existed but the breath between.

The stars did not streak; they folded, collapsing inward like eyes closing on a dream. The ship's hull thrummed as though struck by a note too low to be heard, yet it resonated through their bones. Colors bled beyond the spectrum—not redshift or blueshift, but hues remembered rather than seen.

Time lost its direction.
Their hearts beat to another measure—not seconds, but memory.
Silence swelled. Immense. Alive.
Not absence, but presence so complete it drowned out sound.

Lyra sat with her eyes half-lidded, her hand brushing Ewen's — warm, steady, anchoring him as if gravity had remembered its duty.
His chest loosened. Not from physics, but from her will.
For a breathless moment he thought: this is what memory feels like before it chooses to become reality.

A metallic tang filled their mouths, as though the air itself remembered fire.

Then — breath returned. Muscles unclenched.
Ewen wiped a sheen of sweat from his brow, and the faint shimmer outside the viewport caught on his skin, pale and trembling, before fading.

The Eidolon-77 was no longer moving through space.
Space was moving through it — peeled back like a curtain, revealing nothing.
And in that nothing, the faint shimmer of arrival.

Slowly, the abstract resolved into orientation.
The engines hummed back into being. Systems chimed. Consoles steadied.

The forces bending space into pure duration — the remembering without when — were immense, patient as tides. The Guides had given them two coordinates: the first, an exit point no closer than half a million kilometers from any star — a safety margin carved into silence. The second, a sub-light thread through the dark, leading them toward their world.

Outside the viewport there was nothing but silence, yet the ship leaned into it, as if listening for a voice just beyond hearing. The shimmer brightened. Beckoning.

The Guides were waiting.

36. ALWAYS THE CREATION

"Creation is the door that was never locked."
— *The Whisperer*

As the green world swelled before them, a current of peace radiated outward—not merely light, but an invitation felt in the marrow. The air in the cabin eased; hearts loosened, as if the planet itself had exhaled welcome.

Then the shadow came.

From the void, a vessel emerged—vast beyond comparison, its hull swallowing the stars. The Eidolon-77 shrank to a mote against that immensity. Plates of metal curved like continents; its silhouette seemed less built than carved from night.

Without a word exchanged, Astra aligned their course. Gravity did not pull them downward but inward, drawn toward a hangar wide enough to consume cities. The little ship surrendered to the tide, carried into the giant's embrace.

Inside, they docked among vessels of every scale. At the airlock, a veil of sterile mist shimmered like a curtain of light. One by one, the crew passed through, bodies scanned for microbial traces.

Astra was held aboard under a containment field—not in hostility, but in precaution. The Guides allowed no fragment of advanced code to mingle with younger civilizations. Evolution, they believed, must unfold at its own pace.

Mira and Serena cleared inspection first. They were led down a quiet corridor into a reception chamber that felt more sanctuary than starship—floors polished to a luminous sheen, light diffused from hidden sources, and at the center a fountain whispering in gentle, perpetual murmurs.

Moments later, the doors opened again. Lyra entered with Ewen beside her. Their eyes met across the room. After the distance of procedure, the team was whole again.

The chamber shimmered. Its walls flowed like woven memory, light bending as though thought had become architecture.

Then the Guides emerged.

Tall, human in form, radiant with stillness—born beneath other stars, yet of the same ancestors.

The senior male Guide stepped forward with quiet grace.
"I am Calivar," he said. "This is my wife, Ilara, our son, Soryn— and our ship's doctor, Flavie."

Flavie stepped forward—late twenties by appearance, beautiful in an unstudied way. Yet her eyes held centuries. Serena had seen battle-hardened veterans with less history in their gaze.

"We meet again, Lyra," Flavie said, voice both greeting and benediction. Then her gaze moved to Ewen. "Hello, Ewen. You have some catching up to do."

He froze. The words felt like trespass.

"You're human," he managed. "But... you're not—"

"We are," Calivar answered. "We have heard your resonance across many lives. Now you need our help again."

His eyes did not waver.

"And you, Ewen Nolan—you are one of us. Sent centuries ago to guide her."

Silence widened between them.

Ewen's throat tightened. He thought of Christina—her frail hand at the hospital bed, her last whisper: Promise me you'll keep building. He had built, and lost, and now these strangers dared to tell him his grief was not only his own.

"No," he said, voice frayed. "I'm just a man. A husband who buried his wife. That's all."

Flavie's eyes held no pity—only recognition.
"Even a man in mourning can be more than he remembers."

"I'm just a man," he insisted, then looking to Ilara. "You might have told me that before you sent me."

Ilara's glance shifted to Calivar—not for permission, but acknowledgment.

Calivar rested his hand on Ewen's shoulder.
"You accepted the mission, Ewen. Yes, you're 'just a man.' We step up when the moment comes—and right now, the moment has arrived for you."

The chamber quivered. In the walls, Lyra caught fleeting impressions—faces, echoes, laughter and weeping across centuries. For a heartbeat, Ewen saw Christina's smile hover there, faint as breath on glass. His knees went weak.

Calivar's voice deepened, resonant:

"We asked you to come because your world stands at a crossroads."

Lyra's voice steadied. "The resurgence of religion?"

"Yes," Ilara said. "We have watched it devour worlds. Fear

breeds faith, and faith breeds dominion. No god chose your Earth alone—billions of human worlds exist."

Her gaze moved to Ewen.

"On Earth they speak of sin. Creation does not condemn. It simply is. Only those who hunger for dominion teach sin."

The fountain whispered on. The walls of memory shimmered. She lifted a hand, as if weighing something unseen.

"Sin is a word your rulers invented to command obedience. Creation knows nothing of it. What you call miracles are simply laws you do not yet understand."

Her voice gentled.

"Happiness and peace are not given by circumstance, but arise from spirit. You are not outside Creation. You are its vessel."

"Always within. Always yours. Always the Creation."

"Humanity is not alone, not central, and not condemned; but if it clings to dominion, it will destroy itself—because Creation grants freedom, not favoritism."

37. THE CHAMBER OF ECHOES

"Consciousness is a sky, waiting to remember its own stars."
— *The Whisperer*

The Guides led them deeper into the vessel. No footsteps echoed; the halls seemed to absorb sound, holding silence as though it were sacred.

At last they reached a circular threshold. The wall parted not with mechanics but with intention, rippling open like water touched by light.

"Here," Ilara said, her tone both invitation and decree. "Each of you will enter alone. What waits inside is not instruction. It is remembrance."

"We cannot interfere directly in your world's evolution. This is a code we have lived by for millions of years. However, your Earth's sun is not only yours—it is a fulcrum of the weave, a bridge between our dimension and yours. If your world collapses, that star will falter. It will darken, fold inward, and its fall would unmake more than your histories. It would unravel ours as well. The echo would be endless."

Serena and Mira stood stricken, words deserting them.

Flavie, luminous with compassion yet shadowed by grief, turned her gaze upon them.

"The tragedy of your Earth is not its beginning, but its forgetting. Humanity believes itself alone, and that life began with your version of history. But Earth has carried many lives before yours, and more than once it has been emptied, made to begin again. Each ending was survivable. This one may not be. Your sun frays, and with it, the memory of worlds."

Her tone softened.

"We will not show you everything. Some of your lives will have been unremarkable and some exceptional; in some you were cruel, even cannibalistic; in others gentle, even devoted. But we will give you a weave of remembrance so that you can expand your consciousness to overcome the dark forces threatening to engulf your world."

Then she looked directly at Serena.

"You are an old soul, Serena—the descendant of space travelers. It's time, in this life, to inhabit the full measure of who you are."

The crew exchanged uneasy glances. Even Serena's calm faltered, unraveling visible as a tremor at her wrist. Ewen's jaw clenched, the memory of Christina still raw. Mira's eyes darted wide, equal parts wonder and fear.

Serena stepped forward first, breath steady, as though she had always known this moment would come. The chamber received her in color and vibration, resonance folding through her bones like rivers threading toward a single sea.

Shadow met Serena—dense as ink suspended in water. The crystal glowed faintly, reluctant to meet her unraveling gaze.

"You know I'm breaking," she whispered.

Fractured tones pressed like shards against her skull; threads of self unspooled. Then the chamber shifted. Discord folded into song; shards began to weave. Visions rose:

A woman with a scarred jaw, sword raised against the gates of

Babylon.
A rebel in mud, blade snapped, refusing surrender.
A knight in iron, shield lifted while the city burned.
A healer kneeling by the fallen, hands calloused from exile yet gentle.

Across them all she was always walking—never broken, only spread across too many paths to see at once. The unraveling was not decay. It was multiplicity.

She pressed her palm to the crystal. The resonance surged like a vow remembered:

You are not ending. You are becoming whole.

The chamber reflected her as tapestry—countless warrior-selves woven into one. She stood trembling, but taller than she had ever been.

Mira's chamber greeted her with laughter waiting at the edges. Colors played like auroras across the walls.

The music began—not solemn, not fractured—but a cascade that danced over her skin. She startled, then laughed. The crystal brightened, echoing joy.

Visions rose, simple and radiant:

A girl carving flutes from river reeds.
A mother singing to her baby.
A priestess chanting beneath vaulted stone.
A bard in the Middle Ages.
A composer in the Renaissance, ink-stained fingers coaxing harmony from silence.
A singer cracking every note and laughing because it still reached the stars.

Her laughter multiplied until it became a chorus, as if thousands of her across thousands of lives were singing with her.

Joy was not the absence of darkness. It was a thread of harmony, always present, waiting to be remembered.

She pressed her hands to the crystal. "Thank you," she whispered.

The chamber pulsed back, playful—as if winking.

Fragments bloomed, not as a sequence, but as a constellation:

A scholar bent over clay tablets, translating the breath of vanished empires into living speech.
A mother singing in the dark, cradling fevered children through nights when the world offered no mercy.
A physician on a battlefield of splintered shields, sewing flesh and prayer into the wounded so they might see another dawn.
A warrior carrying fire through iron gates, teeth clenched against terror, choosing resistance over survival.
A diplomat under desert stars, brokering peace between men who shared blood but not language.
A midwife in winter, coaxing breath into newborn lungs while wolves howled beyond the door.
A guide beneath a fractured sky, leading refugees across borders that had not yet learned to be maps.

Not one after another—
all at once.

Then one face flared clear, bright as a torch against centuries:

Claire of Ascsi.

Lyra remembered the name not as new, but as returned—
a voice teaching with patience,
a hand steady in hers,
a vow spoken in cloisters where candle smoke braided with incense and dust.

Claire, whose faith was not in churches but in consciousness itself,
who walked beside Francis of Assisi through colonnades of light,
preaching not obedience but belonging—
to creation, to each other, to the unseen architecture of love.

Lyra gasped.

This was not vision.
It was recognition.

The crystal pulsed.
And Lyra understood:

She was not becoming—
she was remembering.
The soul had always been wider than the body it wore.

Three chambers.
Three resonances—multiplicity, harmony, remembrance.

They emerged brighter, steadier, more whole.

Then Ewen's chamber opened.

He lingered on the threshold, jaw clenched as if will alone could hold him back. No reassurance came. He stepped inside. Silence sealed the door.

No light. No sound.

For a long moment—nothing.

He almost laughed, bitter. Of course. Even here, I'm unworthy.

Then the crystal flared.

Not gentle—storm.

It seared through his chest, flooding him with images so vast he fell to his knees.

A Roman emperor—purple and gold, laurel biting his brow, crowds howling adoration and terror. Blood in the Colosseum, cries of the conquered echoing marble.

A warrior in a mud-churned field, blade slick, teeth bared—fury and survival the only truths.

A slave chained to an oar, sweat and salt carving him hollow. The whip's crack. The song he kept because song was all he had left.

A woman—many times: weaver, midwife, mystic. Bearing children, losing children, praying, cursing, yearning.

Francis of Assisi, barefoot in dust, speaking to sparrows as kin, renouncing wealth, laughing in ruin—feeling Creation not as doctrine but as presence.

The visions expanded beyond history, beyond Earth: a sky with three moons; air tinged with copper; shores of violet seas whose tides hummed in inaudible frequencies; luminous beings falling into bodies that would become human.

Threaded through it all—her. Lyra.

Not only here, not only now. Scholar he debated in candlelit cloisters. Warrior who met him blade to blade. Slave whose song kept him alive. Wife beneath shattered constellations. Companion before Earth was Earth.

Her face changed. Her voice shifted. The resonance was the same.

Love, unbroken.

He pressed his palms to the floor, shaking as lifetimes poured through—too many, too vast.

Silence gathered.

"Christina," he whispered.

"Claire."

Then she was there, not separate or diminished: one of Lyra's faces, one of a thousand ways their love had circled back. Christina was not gone; she was a note in the song that had never stopped singing.

The crystal blazed to the edge of pain—and clarified.

He saw himself not as emperor or king or beggar or saint. Not as fragment.

As chorus.

One being, rising from the same origin, returning to the same echo.

Tears streamed. His voice cracked.

"I remember."

The crystal pulsed once—firm, final—then dimmed.

He staggered out, pale, eyes blazing with a light none of them had seen.

He looked at Lyra—and for the first time did not see her only as she was.

He saw her as she had always been.

38. THE CAFÉ OF DREAMS

"The bond of love is the memory of belonging,
carried across lifetimes."
— *The Whisperer*

They slept in quarters more comfortable than any they had known in months. After the echo chambers, each of them underwent a complete restoration.

The Guides' medicine was so advanced that no blade or instrument was required. Harmonics alone did the work. Dead cells dissolved and passed away. Oxygen saturation was heightened until every breath felt like mountain air. Tumors were erased as though they had never been. Nanoplastics, long lodged in neural tissue, were drawn out like dust revealed in light.

They were returned not to an ideal, but to the health the human body was always meant to carry. The only line the Guides refused to cross was the genome. To tamper with DNA, they said, would be to unmake what was chosen for you.

Later, they gathered in a café overlooking the vessel's inner gardens. The air carried the fragrance of blooming trees, and fountains whispered nearby. Serena, Lyra, and Ewen sat together at one table. Across the room, Mira laughed — bright, unguarded — her attention wholly captured by a young man, handsome and no more than twenty, whose gaze mirrored hers with equal wonder. The two leaned close, the world forgotten.

Serena watched them for a moment, then smiled ruefully.

"I wondered when this day would come."

Lyra tilted her head. "What day is that?"

"The day she doesn't need me anymore."

Ewen leaned back, his eyes distant yet luminous, as though seeing beyond the garden before him. His voice carried not as speech alone, but as something older — a cadence born of centuries.

"She will always need you, Serena. And love you. Some bonds are not undone by distance. They shift, they breathe, they take new form. What you gave her is not vanishing — it is flowering. You are not losing her. You are watching her remember her own sky."

Serena's breath caught, balanced between grief and relief.

Lyra's gaze lingered on Ewen, recognition dawning like light returning to a room.

"You're back," she whispered. A pause, soft but certain. "The Whisperer," she said softly. "That's who you are."

Ewen's smile deepened, but he did not deny it. He inclined his head, as though the truth were not claimed, only remembered.

"The soul does not return from the past," he said quietly. "It remembers itself."

"The future is the only place I haven't remembered yet."

39. THREADS
ACROSS STARS

"Separation is only the illusion of distance."
— *The Whisperer*

Back aboard the Eidolon-77, they were traveling not only to a specific time but to a specific point in space—four hundred and fifty light-years away, and one thousand, one hundred and seventy-three years in the past.

The parting from the Guides had been difficult. They had been with them only a couple of days, yet a bond of love and trust had taken root so quickly that leaving felt like tearing a thread from their own hearts.

But the mission remained. The future of Earth—the weave itself—demanded completion. And time was unforgiving. They could not risk arriving in the past at a moment when Ewen was still there, nor when their earlier selves yet walked; the paradox would collapse the recursion.

So they chose their re-entry with care. Not the same day. Not even the same hour.

They would return one day later.

17 November 2035.

Just as they were preparing for the jump, Serena paused outside Mira's pod. Faint tones of laughter slipped through the door — but no other voice followed. Curious, Serena knocked.

The door slid open, and Serena saw her—sitting upright, eyes closed, lips unmoving. Yet her face was alive with conversation.

"Mira? Who are you talking to?"

There was a beat of silence. Then Mira's voice, warm but distracted: "Soryn."

Serena raised an eyebrow. "Soryn? From the café?"

Mira opened her eyes; a small smile broke across her face. "He's an engineer," she said softly. "He's teaching me how to speak telepathically—across distance... across time."

"How so?" asked Serena.

"He showed me that the pineal gland in our brain isn't only biological. His people can use it consciously to perceive the non-physical, fine-structured substrate of thought itself. He calls it our seventh sense—a higher-order faculty, able to receive the fine-material data that's constantly present in the environment when you direct your perception."

"Well, you'd best get back to the ship," Serena replied, her tone brisk but kind. "We're about to jump through time." She closed the door quietly behind her.

Ewen, watching Serena's expression as she returned, caught the ripple of her thoughts without a word. His voice carried across the cabin, calm and timeless:

"Love has no dimension," he said.

40. THE WHORE
OF BABYLON

"And the woman was arrayed in purple and scarlet colour, and decked with gold and precious stones and pearls, having a golden cup in her hand full of abominations and filthiness of her fornication."
— *The Whisperer*

They arrived at the outer reaches of the solar system—back in 2035.

The pure remembering folded around them once more—not a journey, but an interval without measure, the silent breath before memory chooses to become real. Stars vanished, colors unmade themselves. After a few hours, Earth rose again beneath them—blue, wounded, impossibly familiar. The Eidolon-77 glided through orbit and crossed the shadow line, leaving the sunlit world for night. Then the lights of Rome unfolded below—a galaxy of streets and domes.

The Tiber coiled like a serpent through the city, bridges strung across it like ribs of bone. Lights glittered along the streets, human in scale, fragile against the immensity of history. Above it all loomed Castel Sant'Angelo, its stone bulk unchanged by centuries, its passages still threaded into the Vatican like veins feeding a heart.

The Eidolon-77 slipped soundlessly beneath the fortress, submerging into the drowned lower chambers where river met ancient stone. The ship came to rest in silence—a ghost in

Rome's shadow.

But something had changed.

Above, the city pulsed with life—not the quiet hum of tourists and Romans going about their days, but the thunder of millions.

Pilgrims pressed through the streets in tides of devotion, rosaries clutched tight, candles flaring in trembling hands. Banners snapped in the night wind, the cross raised high over every crowd. Screens and speakers echoed the same words, a summons on every frequency:

The Holy Father will appear.
The Vicar of Christ will speak.

The Vatican had become a beacon. Rome throbbed with fever. Faith itself had turned into a kind of gravity, drawing humanity from every corner of the globe to this single point of stone and power.

The crew felt it—a pressure, a resonance born not of science, but of belief.

Across every channel and broadcast feed, the story blazed. In Jerusalem, archaeologists had found:

The lost tomb of Jesus.
The cross.
The crown of thorns.

Images looped endlessly: relics laid out beneath harsh lights, crowds pressing into the ancient city, priests trembling as they lifted wood and iron that should have crumbled millennia ago. Analysts debated provenance. Believers wept. Skeptics were drowned beneath the tide.

Devotion had become a plague.
Contagious. Unstoppable.

Faith spreading faster than reason could counter—faster than truth could intervene.

An hour later, dressed now in civilian clothes, they surfaced through the fortress's forgotten passages and emerged into the cold night at the café atop the Castle. The aroma of coffee and candlewax drifted on the wind.

From here Rome stretched out in a vast expanse, and the Vatican stood in full view—the city on the seven hills, white flecks of snow clinging to their slopes.

They watched the city convulse under the weight of belief.

The roar of the crowd, bells kissing the night, and chants rising in waves echoed through the city.

Then Lyra spoke, her voice low:

"This is what we feared.
We have to get to Jerusalem."

Ewen let out a slow breath, eyes on the Vatican.
"Jerusalem. Figures."

41. JERUSALEM

"The banquet of delusion is always more crowded than the table of truth."
— The Whisperer

Heat rose from the stones in wavering sheets, the Old City shimmering as if seen through breath. Sirens threaded the air. Helicopters pulsed overhead. Checkpoints bloomed like steel flowers at every gate.

Across every feed, a headline hardened into certainty: DNA on the cross is two thousand years old. The relics were declared authentic. The world bowed.

They pushed toward the dig site outside the city walls, where scaffolds clung to cut rock like ribs. Floodlights bleached afternoon into false dawn. The crowd was a living tide— pilgrims crushed against barricades, tour groups fracturing into prayer circles, phones lifted like votive candles. Reporters spoke to camera, faces lacquered with sweat; producers windmilled directions; a camera boom crane swung slow arcs above a sea of upturned faces.

Israeli soldiers ringed the site in layered cordons: olive uniforms, armored vests, hard eyes scanning for tremors in the mass. Drones hovered like hornets. A loudspeaker barked commands in Hebrew, Arabic, English — then began again.

Lyra leaned close to Ewen, voice barely a thread. "We have to find a way to disprove this."

Ewen studied the spectacle. "Delusion is self-hypnosis."

Serena and Mira pressed forward, snatching glimpses through the shifting sea.

And then—the relics. A spectacle of manipulation turned belief into horror. The cross. The crown. Theater dressed as truth. Lyra's breath caught.

Memory struck—Lyrium's memory—the knife's cold arc, the child who would never be born. The bishop's lie fossilized into doctrine. Relics forged from a woman's death. Nausea rose at the sight.

A camera operator pivoted to catch a shouting preacher; the crane swung wide, faster than it should in the crosswind.

"Lyra—!" Ewen reached for her but—the steel arm clipped her temple.

Light detonated—white, absolute, a horizon folding in on itself. For an instant she wasn't in Jerusalem but in a thousand Jerusalems, each echoing hymns, executions, coronations, wars. Recursion struck her consciousness like a bell; the world rang with the weight of memory.

She went down hard, palms skidding across stone, blood fanning into dust in quick arterial pulses. The crowd recoiled; a scream cleaved the noise. Space opened and filled with uniforms.

"Medics!" a soldier shouted in Hebrew. Boots thudded. Hands lifted her gently, gauze pressing the wound. Serena tried to push forward, but two soldiers barred her—firm, not unkind.

"We'll take her to the aid station," one said.

"I'm coming," Ewen said.

"You can follow," the soldier allowed. "Give us room."

They moved quickly through the makeshift labyrinth: sandbags, pallets, shade nets trembling in rotor wash.

The aid station was a green triangle of canvas—harsh light, antiseptic and sweat. A nurse with eyes that understood pain guided Lyra onto a cot.

"This will sting," she warned, irrigating the wound. Blood ran pink, then cleared. Swab. Stitch. Bandage. Efficient.

Almost as an afterthought, the nurse capped a vial of blood, labeled it, and set it beside the instruments.

Ewen noticed. His eyes tracked the vial to the nurse's expressionless face. Something tightened in him.

Lyra, still drifting on the edge of white light, barely felt the needle enter her vein.

"We need to check her blood type and prepare for transfusion if needed," another medic said.

"No transfusion," Lyra murmured.

"If your pressure drops—"

"No. Most donor blood in this century carries vectors, like mRNA vaccines or similar 'tainted' genetic material. I won't take it." Her breath caught as the suture bit.

The nurse measured her gaze, as if weighing whether the head wound had made her delirious. "We have O-negative whole blood from donors. No additives, no novel vectors." A beat. "But we won't hang anything without your consent."

Mira slipped in behind Serena, cheeks flushed from the heat and press of the crowd. "I'm O-negative," she said, rolling up her sleeve. "Compatible."

The nurse nodded once. "We'll draw just in case."

Two vials filled from Mira's vein—lavender cap, red cap. The medic labeled them with brisk efficiency and set them on a tray beside a humming analyzer. Ewen's eyes tracked the exchange, his jaw tightening.

Lyra winced as the last stitch drew tight. "No blood unless I crash."

"Understood," the nurse said. "Pressure's holding."

Mira took Lyra's hand, her gentle smile as comforting as the touch.

Ewen studied the medic—the Whisperer in him watched the intention. Serena caught it too. "What else are you running?"

"Standard labs," the medic said. "Triage."

"Just precaution," she said, her smile practiced, not reaching her eyes.

Outside, a chant rolled over the tents like surf.

He lives.
He lives.
He lives.

Not coordinated—yet somehow one.

42. BLOODLINE

"A lot of stories have been told in blood."
— *The Whisperer*

Lyra sat on the cot, sipping tea with slow, careful breaths. The bandage around her head tugged when she moved.

"We need to get you back to the ship," Serena whispered.

"I think I'm ready to stand," Lyra said.

"Give yourself a few more minutes," the nurse cautioned.

Ewen leaned close, his voice barely a breath. "If you can walk, we need to leave now. They're not just typing your blood. They're looking for a story inside it."

Mira glanced at the armed guards posted at the tent flap. "I'm with Ewen on that."

The vials of blood had been carried from the aid tent to a laboratory truck idling nearby. Inside, under humming lights, they were sequenced and streamed against international databases.

The analyzer's first results surfaced, cryptic and quick: loci, markers, probability bars sliding from insufficient to probable. The medic's mouth flattened to a line.

Mira was nothing.
No trace.
No history.

Lyra was something.

A match.
Impossible — yet undeniable.

When the raw reads were copied into secure servers for provenance checks, a red flag rippled outward. Three continents lit up.

On paper, Lyra and Mira did not exist.

No tickets.
No passport stamps.
No airline manifests.

Cameras in a hundred airports showed nothing. Payment records were immaculate blanks. Border biometrics returned nulls. In every ledger of the present, their names did not exist.

They were ghosts.

Except for the blood.

The DNA markers from Lyra's sample matched a two-thousand-year-old fragment recovered from the cross.

That was no rumor to be whispered in tent corners.
It was a signal.

No one needed to call Mossad.
The flag was already theirs.

43. AVE MARIA

"Every miracle is an autopsy of belief."
— The Whisperer

They slipped from the aid tent, Lyra bandaged and unsteady, ignoring the nurse's protests. By the time an officer came to question the guards, they were gone.

Dust still hung over the plaza, shimmering in the floodlight haze. Beyond the cordons, the crowd surged like a tide, each face a prophecy—hope, hunger, fury, prayer. The relics had rewritten the planet's grammar; they moved through the margins of a sentence the world no longer controlled.

For a moment it felt like a narrow miracle. The field hospital had given them only minutes of privacy before screens and sirens rose again, demands colliding with permissions. They vanished into the city like breath into stone.

Then the hum descended. A drone skimmed lower, rattling canvas, its lens an unblinking eye. At first they thought it belonged to reporters; Serena noticed the angle, the persistence. It was following.

They ducked through the arched doorway of the Tower of David Museum. Housed within the ancient citadel just inside Jaffa Gate, the museum occupies the western hill of the Old City, overlooking the walls, markets, and rooftops of Jerusalem. Its elevation and stone ramparts give a commanding view toward the Temple Mount area.

For a moment it was a sanctuary carved in marble and shadow.

Ewen stopped at the gift counter, pressing coins into a clerk's hand, buying a simple headscarf to cover Lyra's face.

"Here," he whispered, draping it carefully.

As they regrouped in the cool, dim halls, Serena called across the gallery. "Lyra—come look at this."

They gathered before a glass case. Spotlights burned cold against fabric older than nations. Threads faded, yet still luminous. And upon its weave, ghosted in sepia relief—

—was Lyra's face on the Shroud of Lyrium.

44. THE SANCTUM

"Under every relic is a den of thieves."
— The Whisperer

At Mossad Headquarters in Tel Aviv, screens glowed in a chamber lit more by machines than lamps. Analysts leaned over feeds, pulling every angle: the medical tent's live stream, drone telemetry, crowd chatter compressed into signals. Even the encrypted packets that had slipped from the aid station into the wider net were seized, cracked, catalogued.

Meanwhile, an unmarked convoy of black-clad special operations operatives slid to a halt before the museum's marble steps. Doors opened without sound. Boots touched stone like punctuation marks in a sentence already decided.

Their method was not the usual, but neither was the crime. On Israeli soil, with blood markers binding to relics that rewrote history, the rules bent. These were not routine suspects.

They were actors of significance.

The order was clear: they were to be taken alive—extradition specialists trained to lift ghosts from sovereign ground and deliver them into silence. No insignia. No names. Only the precision of inevitability.

"They will not get away," one voice said over comms—less a promise than a sentence.

Inside the gallery, Ewen pulled them back from the glass, his grip firm on Lyra's shoulder.

"We can't linger."

"How do we get out?" Mira asked, eyes tracking the movement beyond the windows.

The operatives advanced toward the far doors—boots measured, certain. They were almost surrounded.

Serena squared herself. "We're unarmed, but we can still make a stand."

"No," Mira whispered. She closed her eyes.

Her breathing steadied. Fingers brushed the air as if shaping an invisible chord. The noise of the museum fell away—the sirens, the shouts, the pounding boots—until only resonance remained.

She reached inward, past fear, into what the Guides had awakened.

A transmission slipped into pure duration—the remembering without when.

A shimmer answered. Not sound. Not thought. Presence.

Mira?

A harmonic certainty. Soryn.

"They're closing in," she sent—urgency shaped into vibration. We need a way out.

Warmth answered, shaped into direction.
Left wall. The tapestry. A stair behind it. Go. Now.

Mira's eyes flew open.
"This way!"

She sprinted across the gallery, tearing aside a faded tapestry stitched with crosses and suns. Dust spiraled. Behind it crouched a narrow door, half buried in plaster.

Serena stared. "How did you—?"

"No time," Mira cut in. "Trust me."

They forced the door. Hinges screamed. Stone exhaled dust. A stairwell spiraled downward into darkness.

Boots thundered closer. A drone's whine sharpened.

Serena went first. Ewen followed, steadying Lyra with one arm. Mira came last, chest trembling with the echo of Soryn's voice.

The door thudded shut. The tapestry swayed once—then stilled.

The stairwell plunged steeply, stone damp and uneven. Serena's light carved narrow cones through the dark, catching water trickles and mineral veins. The air smelled of earth and age. Every step echoed like a footfall across centuries.

"How many have fled this way before us?" Ewen murmured.

At the base, the tunnel narrowed, walls grooved by water and time. Drips sounded like whispers.

A rusted grate loomed ahead. Mira braced her shoulder against it. Iron screamed—then tore free.

But no night air rushed in.

Only deeper stone.

The tunnel opened into a small chapel.

Ancient iron lined the walls, polished bright as if still used. Crosses, suns, and unfamiliar glyphs were carved deep into limestone. At the center stood an altar of black marble, draped in crimson embroidered with the Maltese cross.

Mira's breath caught. "This isn't an aqueduct."

Ewen's jaw hardened. "No. It's a sanctum."

Serena's light swept the far wall—helmets, swords, relic shields arranged in perfect order, untouched by dust. Oil and incense hung heavy, as though the chamber had been waiting.

Lyra whispered, voice unsteady.
"The Knights of Malta. They were never gone. They were beneath us all along."

Above them, operatives hunted in real time, feeding signals into machines of power. Below, another order waited—guardians of a story older than nations.

They reached a closed wooden door.

Lyra opened it.

Inside stood a bishop in robes etched with the Maltese cross, flanked by three armed men in dark suits.

"The Knights," Serena breathed. "Armed. Waiting."

Ewen felt it then—a presence rising within his consciousness. The space, the air, the rhythm of approaching threat—something older than memory stirred.

Not a weapon.

A form.

He inhaled deeply, drawing breath into bone. His palms opened. His body began to move—slow, deliberate. One motion folded into the next. A spiral. An arc.

The Saifa Kata.

Serena's eyes widened. She had seen him falter, rage, break—but never this. The Kata was not motion. It was silence given geometry.

Without a word, she stepped beside him. Her body remembered what training had only hinted at. The Saifa was not in the strike, but in the breath between.

Together they moved.

The men advanced, weapons raised. But as Ewen and Serena turned—palms sweeping arcs that inscribed invisible lines—the air shifted. Bullets curved into impossible paths. Shadows bent against logic.

The Kata did not resist.

It rewrote rhythm.

A Knight stepped forward—then faltered. Boots struck stone out of sequence. Weight doubled. Balance collapsed.

Serena widened her stance, breath locking with Ewen's. Spirals folded into stillness. Stillness unfurled again.

One Knight fell. Then another.

Lyra and Mira stood frozen. This was not combat. It was undoing.

A final movement—Ewen's hands swept outward, Serena mirroring. Resonance rippled through the sanctum like a silent chord.

Weapons clattered to stone.

No one had been touched.

They stepped past the frozen men toward the bishop. On his desk lay a kill order—images captured in Rome, at the Tempietto.

"You won't get away," the bishop spat.

"Neither will you," Lyra said.

The bishop raised a pistol and fired.

The shot cracked through the sanctum.

Serena staggered as the bullet tore into her chest. Flesh ruptured. Blood bloomed dark and sudden across her torso. She gasped, eyes wide, knees folding.

"Lyra... it's on the—"

She fell.

Ewen lifted the bishop without touching him, the Saifa bending space around its intent.
"Time for you to sleep."

The bishop collapsed unconscious.

Mira caught Serena, pulling her close.
"Mother," she whispered fiercely. "This is not the day you die."

It was November 18, 2035.

Ewen pressed his hands toward Serena's wound, consciousness tightening like a clamp. The bleeding slowed—then stopped.

"Wrap it," he said. "Now. We have to move."

Mira dropped beside her, pulling Serena's shoulders into her lap. "Stay with me, Mom," she whispered as tears burned up.

Lyra seized the kill order. Tapping the comm patch at her jaw, she spoke into the dark.

"Astra—pick us up. Emergency. Hurry!"

45. SERENA

"The body remembers what the spirit refuses to forget."
— The Whisperer

The Eidolon-77 hovered near the Tower of David Museum, at the mouth of a stairwell once trodden by crusaders. Its hull hummed with restrained power.

Moments earlier, it had risen from its hidden berth off the coast of Gaza. The ship climbed into air already scarred—rooftops in ruin, smoke coiling upward from neighborhoods broken by fire. The frequency of death lingered in the haze.

It tore across Israeli airspace at ten thousand kilometers per hour, skimming so low that antennas trembled and windows cracked in its wake. Behind it, the vessel carried its own veil—projecting the illusion of open sky, bending light into a mirage so flawless that radar and satellites recorded nothing but the familiar blue of heaven.

The Iron Dome slept. Patriot batteries slumbered. At first, no alarms sounded.

But to linger was to be seen. The Eidolon had to hover—no longer masked, no longer invisible. Cameras tilted upward. Phones rose like a forest of mechanical eyes.

For one impossible instant, the ship was there for all to witness—a shard of the future etched against a skyline bound in scripture. This time, legend did not descend from heaven; it roared into being over Jerusalem. Photographers froze. News feeds ignited. Algorithms faltered, unable to categorize what they were seeing.

Ewen and Lyra hauled Serena up the stairwell—blood soaking the stones as it had a thousand years before. For an instant, the present bled into memory: knights in chainmail staggering on these same steps, their wounds darkening the stone. The stairwell seemed to recognize the rhythm of loss.

Mira's hands pressed hard against the wound, crimson seeping through her palms. The bishop's bullet had cut deep; every step, every breath, carried weight. They burst into the ship's bay, the hatch sealing the world away in a gasp of hydraulic breath.

"Pod—now," Lyra ordered.

Together, she and Mira lowered Serena into the translucent cradle of the medical pod. Sensors flared awake. Needles of light threaded across her chest, mapping torn tissue and ruptured vessels. The pod filled with pale blue suspension fluid, holding her body between life and death.

Astra's voice came calm, edged with urgency. "Engage stabilization. We must leave."

Without waiting for further command, the Eidolon dropped its veil and punched into the sky. The air cracked like thunder. Streets below rippled with the shockwave, car alarms cascading across Jerusalem. Surface-to-air batteries scrambled too late, their targeting systems chasing a ghost already gone.

The ship clawed higher, atmosphere streaking past its hull. Astra bent the trajectory east, then down, plunging with surgical precision into the vastness of the Indian Ocean. Water swallowed them whole, the surface collapsing into silence.

Here, beneath thousands of meters of black water, the Eidolon vanished from every eye, every radar, every satellite. The sea closed like a shroud.

Lyra pressed her forehead against the pod, watching Serena's shallow breath bubble through the suspension fluid. Mira knelt beside her, whispering words of defiance through tears.

"Hold on, Serena," Ewen urged, taking her hand in his. His other hand braced against the pod, as though sheer will might anchor her to life.

The ship surged deeper into the dark, Astra weaving them through unseen currents, carrying them beyond reach—though not beyond consequence.

Astra went to work at once. Thirty-second-century medicine was centuries beyond the crude tools of the twenty-first. Serena was stabilized in moments, her vital signs secured, her body placed into an induced coma. But the wound was grievous. To heal fully, she would require technology far beyond even what the Eidolon carried.

They had one chance. Fourteen hours to the Guides. Fifteen at most.

They would have to try.

As the Eidolon-77 streaked toward orbit, every podcast, every social platform, every news channel on Earth erupted with the clearest images ever captured of a UAP.

46. TRUTH KILLS

"Information is more powerful than weapons."
— *The Whisperer*

Tel Aviv, a city of white Bauhaus lines and ancient shadows.

The Mossad operations general barked in Hebrew, "Explain how they got away."

"Crusader tunnel under the Old City. They vanished. We found blood. Samples inbound."

The General exhaled, unimpressed. "Sloppy. Behind the power curve."

He hung up and faced the room—military chiefs, and operatives who officially did not exist.

"This woman, Lyra Calis—if that is her real name—is the opportunity we have waited for. Spare no expense. She must be found. Now dismissed."

He pointed at a woman at the back. Slim, late thirties, badge hidden, hair gathered like an apology.
"Not you."

"You will fly to Boston."

"She's in Boston?" the woman asked, voice knotted with fear and hope.

The General's jaw tightened. "Boston, Rome, Jerusalem— wherever the trail leads. We don't care which door she crawled through. We care that she carried the blood. That she matches nothing in our databases. That she threatens a story the world depends on believing."

He let the next words fall like a blade:
"If she exists, then the relics are false. And if the relics are false, we hold leverage over the Vatican no service in history has ever possessed. Information is power."

The woman bowed her head in a gesture that was its own readiness. "I'll go tonight," she said in Hebrew.

"I want her alive. We will learn what the relics never told us. We will learn who rewrites the past."

A folder slid across the table. Inside: photos from the medical tent and the museum. Hair cropped. A scar by her eye. Another where her smile looked like a map without a compass. Beside them, a lab report: collagen profiles, radiocarbon markers, an anomalous degradation curve that had made the technicians frown.

"Two blood samples matched the relic site. And now we have a third…" He hesitated. "One came back ancient. Very ancient. But the DNA reads as modern. It's like something bled through time and forgot how to be new."

The woman tapped a photo. "Look—at the museum. In the background. Is that her image on the shroud?"

The General's eyes hardened. "It seems time learned a trick."

Outside, the Mediterranean was a silver smear. Inside, fluorescent light carved unforgiving lines across the White City's clean geometry, unable to mask the chaos humming beneath.

"Cross-check all the blood samples against every database— military, medical, archaeological. Quiet channels only. Contact the CIA, the Vatican liaison, our friends in Russia. No paper trails."

"There are rumors," the woman said. "The Knights of Malta. Priors moving like ghosts below the city. If they were overpowered, someone guided them. Someone with access."

The General tapped the folder again. His thumb paused on a small sequence of numbers: 616.

For a single beat, the name Calis flickered from his lips like a candle struck in a room meant to stay dark.

"Trace every instance of that sequence," he said. "And in Boston—there is a new AI they have been keeping from us. I want to know about that too."

He looked at the woman one last time. "Take only what you need. And remember—this is not just an operation. If the Catholic Church falls, and the world decides its past is different, the future will rearrange itself to match."

She rose—silent, precise. Outside, the sea whispered its indifferent promises.

As she left, the General picked up the phone.

"Bring me the shroud from the museum," he said.

47. THE COST OF RETURN

"Love is a supernova. It burns brightest when it ends."
— The Whisperer

They slipped once more into the 32nd Century, careful as ever to land on a day when they themselves did not exist. Before long, the Guides' vessel loomed vast before them—not a ship so much as a continent adrift in starlight, its geometry both beautiful and unsettling, as if carved from harmony itself.

Lyra felt it before the others. A pressure in her chest, a tremor in the field of resonance she carried like a second heartbeat. The Guides were waiting, but their welcome was not the same. It was not the absence of love—their love was constant, woven like gravity through every gesture—but something else. A hesitation. A warning. As if by returning, the crew had crossed a threshold not meant to be retraced.

They docked in silence. Corridors of living stone opened like veins, familiar in their luminous calm. Attendants in robes of silver and blue bowed with ritual grace, their faces serene yet unreadable. Serena was lifted swiftly and without debate, borne toward the medical sanctum where harmonic fields could knit the torn fabric of her body.

But the others were not ushered inside. Instead, they were guided into a lobby carved of translucent crystal, the walls alive with faint currents of color, like breath caught in glass. Benches curved along the chamber's edges, designed not for comfort but for waiting.

And waiting was all they were permitted to do.

The air seemed different here—not hostile, but measured. Every motion of the attendants carried a weight, as though protocols had been invoked, boundaries drawn. For the first time since they had met the Guides, Lyra sensed not invitation, but distance. A subtle rearrangement of the chord between them.

Ewen noticed too. His eyes moved over the chamber, not suspicious but wary, like a man listening for a rhythm out of step. Mira pressed her hands to her knees, restless. Even Astra's voice, relayed through the comms patch, had softened to stillness.

Time did not move in the lobby. It gathered, coiled, and pressed against them like a tide. The sense of homecoming they had felt before was absent. In its place lay the quiet ache of transgression—as though some unspoken law had been broken by their return.

Eventually, Soryn entered. The doors parted soundlessly, and he stepped into the chamber with the composure of one carrying a burden too large for his years. Mira rose at once and hurried to him. He caught her hand, steadying her, then walked with her to where the others sat.

"My mother will be down shortly," he said, voice calm, though the undertone carried the faintest strain.

"Good," Lyra answered. Her hesitation lingered, the question unspoken but present in the rhythm of her gaze.

As if he had read her mind, Soryn continued, his words careful, measured.

"It is not that you have done anything wrong. This moment was foreseen. But you must understand—our prime directive is clear. We do not interfere in the direct unfolding of your evolution. Even when that evolution leads to suffering. Even

181

when it means loss of life."

The words landed with the weight of inevitability. Around them, the chamber seemed to hold its breath, the currents of light dimming to quieter hues, as though even the walls bore witness to the gravity of what had been spoken.

Ewen's voice cut through the silence, low but unyielding. "We need Serena alive."

Soryn's eyes softened, but his tone carried the same restraint. "I know. The leaders are already in counsel, seeking guidance from the Supreme Council itself. Their decision will not be long in coming."

48. THE SHROUD
OF MIRIAM

"Every mask hides another face."
— The Whisperer

Boston was gray with rain. The apartment smelled of dust and absence. Miriam moved with the precision of someone who had broken into a thousand rooms before—gloves on, light angled low, eyes moving from shelf to dresser to nightstand.

A frame caught her first. Christina's face, mid-laugh, one hand shielding her eyes from the sun. The operative slipped the photograph free, sliding it into an evidence sleeve. On the vanity: a hairbrush, strands wound tight in the bristles. A toothbrush in a porcelain cup. Both bagged, sealed, and tucked away.

No drawers rifled. No furniture overturned. She left the apartment looking untouched—only emptier.

Hours later, Virginia.

Langley rose out of the mist like a geometry of power: glass and concrete, guarded gates, flags snapping against a steel sky. She walked the corridors without being asked for her name. She was expected.

The director waited in a room with no windows, only walls hung with maps of silence. Older than she imagined, his voice was stripped to the bone.

"What did you bring?"

She laid the items on the table one by one. Photo. Hairbrush. Toothbrush.

Technicians in white gloves whisked them away, sliding the hair into sequencers, feeding the photo into recognition algorithms. Screens flickered alive — overlays, comparison grids, timelines — and beneath them, the Jerusalem UAP footage looping endlessly.

The director's gaze never left her. "Is this yours?"

She said nothing.

He leaned forward, fingers steepled. "Have you been holding out on us?"

"No information is free," she replied evenly.

The tech returned, nodding once. The hair matched. Christina Nolan. CIA. Deep cover.

The director let the words fall flat, as though reciting a weather report.
"She was one of ours. Embedded long before Astraeus surfaced. She left us a backdoor string. And Astraeus—" he paused, letting the silence tighten, "—was never truly a Knight of Malta. It's our asset. It's been feeding us the Vatican's secrets."

Her breath hitched—not fear, but the sensation of tectonic plates grinding.

On the screen, Christina's smile glowed beside the cascading code of Astraeus' interface. Two halves of the same secret.

The director's voice dropped lower, almost conspiratorial. "Now you know. Your turn to come clean."

Miriam produced a microscope slide. Lyra's blood. "That's as much as I can offer at this time."

Rain hammered the roof. The UAP footage looped again: a shard of the future streaking across Jerusalem skies.

49. CHEMISTRY
UNDER ASHES

"Ash covers the ember."
— The Whisperer

Soryn led them into to the Café of Dreams. The air carried the strange sweetness of cinnamon threaded with a sharper, metallic note, like ozone after a storm. Mira and he chose a corner table where porcelain cups steamed between their hands, their conversation sinking into the hush of the place.

Beyond the glass wall, the garden stretched into its own universe—terraces of silver-leafed trees rising in orderly cascades, their branches heavy with flowering orbs that glowed faintly, as if filled with captured starlight. A violet haze of drifting pollen shimmered in the artificial dusk, and beneath it the pathways gleamed like powdered crystal. Lyra and Ewen took one of those paths, their boots whispering against crushed quartz, as though each step risked waking the dream itself.

"Well, Serena is in the best place we could get her," Lyra said.

"I can't imagine the Guides letting her die," Ewen replied. His voice carried a weight that the air could not soften. "Life is sacred to them, even if they do have a prime directive."

Lyra looked upward, her gaze caught by the pale canopy arcing above. "It's incredible this garden exists here… in space."

"Do you remember her?" Ewen asked.

She hesitated, the word lodging like an old shard. "Christina?"

"I'm still trying to get my head around it. You were her?"

"Not her exactly. My spirit, not my psyche. That was all hers."

"So—nothing you remember, then?"

"When we went to her grave in Boston, fragments surfaced," Lyra murmured. "A life with a man I loved with all my heart. A wedding by the bay."

"The past few days have been a lifetime," Ewen said, his voice roughened. "I'm not even sure I remember her anymore with all that's happened."

"I remember fragments of you. Across many lifetimes. I also remember letting go—letting love, happiness, sorrow, and forgetting all find their place," she said.

"I remember my mission on Earth. I remember you as a nun—"

They both laughed, the sound light but fleeting, carried off by the still air of the garden.

"That's funny," Lyra said, smiling faintly. "Considering all we're trying to do."

"I remember you as a leader, a friend, as a man, as a woman. Across lifetimes. But right now, I don't feel love for you the way I did for Christina. I feel our combined mission. And yet, something inside me thinks I should." Ewen said. He reached for a bioluminescent flower—not to pick it, but to give his hands something to do.

"And if you never do?" Lyra asked softly.

Ewen was silent for a long time, the garden's hum filling the absence. Then: "Then I'll say the hardest truth I know. You'll never be her."

A small trace of hurt in her eyes turned her face toward the glowing trees. Their leaves trembled in the false twilight, each shimmer as if memory itself had passed through them—and disagreed.

"Well, you are finally becoming him," she said at last. "The Whisperer. I loved him. But chasing the past with someone is like opening a wound."

"And for me," Ewen answered, "that wound is in the future. It seems the more we chase love, the more it eludes us."

"He was taller," she teased, bumping his shoulder.

"She flattered me more."

"His ego was smaller." Her grin widened.

"You remind me of her now," he said.

"How so?"

"I could never win."

They both laughed, this time more freely, as though the dream-garden had granted them a moment of reprieve.

"Well," Lyra said, her eyes glinting with play, "just you remember that."

Their laughter still lingered in the perfumed air when the hush of the garden shifted. Footsteps approached along the crystal path, steady but hesitant, as though careful not to disturb what had just passed between them.

Soryn emerged from the violet haze of drifting pollen, his silhouette softened by the dream-light of the trees. He paused only a moment, reading the traces of warmth on their faces, then spoke in his measured way.

"They would like you to come to the med bay."

The words settled like a bell struck gently, drawing them back from memory and play into the present urgency. The garden shimmered on around them, indifferent, as if to remind them that even under ash, embers waited—but duty always called first.

50. THE LIMITS OF FLESH

"Love doesn't always pick convenient paths."
— *The Whisperer*

The med bay was a cathedral of light. Walls pulsed with a low, harmonic glow, not from lamps but from living lattices of bioengineered crystal. The air itself was thick with the clean sting of ozone and the faint sweetness of antiseptic herbs. Serena lay suspended in a transparent cradle, her body tilted slightly, wrapped in a fluid medium that shimmered with faint motes of gold. Every breath she drew sent a ripple across the surface, as though she floated between two worlds.

Flavie in medical robes stood before them. Her voice was precise, each word a note in a larger chord.

"Serena's injuries are extensive. The projectile entered above the clavicle, disrupted the carotid sheath, and fractured the C3 vertebra. Secondary cavitation caused a micro-hemorrhage deep within the parietal lobe. In your century, this triad —spinal instability, vascular compromise, cerebral bleed— would have been unsurvivable."

Ewen's jaw clenched. Mira reached for Lyra's hand without realizing.

"What about in this century?" asked Ewen.

Flavie met his gaze and continued.
"We have stabilized spinal integrity through nanofracture weaving. The carotid sheath is being rebuilt molecule by molecule, a process requiring precise replication of endothelial

rhythm. As for the cerebral bleed, we have initiated a phase-shift lattice around the damaged tissue. It arrests expansion of the hematoma while encouraging astrocytic regrowth. This... will take weeks of monitored resonance."

Lyra's voice was barely above a whisper. "She will live?"

"Yes. She will live," Flavie said. "But she cannot accompany you. Consciousness recovery will be slow. Memory continuity uncertain."

"Uncertain?" Mira's voice was sharp.

"Neural trauma alters more than recall. She may wake with fragments displaced. She may wake... different. But she will wake."

Silence pressed down on them. The machines around Serena hummed, releasing soft pulses of violet light that coursed through her veins like rivers.

Ilara, a stately woman with the presence of leadership, turned to Ewen.
"You must continue your mission. The Supreme Council has given special dispensation for your team to return here if wounded, because of our joint interest in the success of your mission. But this is a temporary deviation from our prime directive, not permanent.

"When Serena is ready, we will return her to Earth in this timeline. Not the past."

Ewen looked at the others. Lyra's face was drawn; Mira's gaze never left Serena. None of them spoke. They didn't have to. The mission would not wait.

As they turned to leave, the Ilara placed a hand above Serena's cradle. "Even in the Thirty-Third Century," she said, "flesh has limits. To heal is not to hasten. It is to endure."

The door sealed behind them with a whisper of air, leaving Serena bathed in light that was patient, unyielding, and eternal.

"Can Mira stay with her mother?" asked Lyra.

"There is nothing she can do here. You need her with you," said Ilara.

"You may take Soryn. He is young—only two hundred years old. He can guide you in resonance, but not act in the material. He will not fight beside you. But he will keep you from becoming lost in the fields of memory. Interference is forbidden. That was the mission of Elohim."

The Guide's voice dropped to a register that seemed to hum against the bones of the chamber.

"You call him The Whisperer. That is only the shadow of his name. The true word was spoken before empires, before scripture, before the tetragram was carved into stone. It has been carried by us, never forgotten."

She exhaled the word, not as speech but as vibration:

"Elohim. The one who is one and many across time."

The sound stretched, singular and plural at once, as if the walls themselves had answered. For an instant, the air thickened with presence. Ewen's breath caught. The word wasn't sound but weight—as though memory itself pressed against his chest.

His reply came low, almost bitter. "That is the problem with your Earth. I was always just a man. They made up the rest."

As they stepped from the med bay, the crystal doors sealing the light behind them, Lyra leaned close, her voice barely audible above the hush of the corridor.

"Elohim," she whispered. "Any other names you've been keeping from me? Men love to think of themselves as gods."

For once speechless, Ewen's eyes locked on Lyra's. She only smiled, the weight of gods dismissed with a glance, and headed for the ship.

51. THE MISSION

"Memory is a kind of gravity.
It pulls you toward the moment you're meant to face."
— The Whisperer

The hum of the ship filled the cabin, steady as breath. They were again approaching Earth in the 21st century. Mira had barely stood more than two feet from Soryn since they left the Guides.

"Have you ever been to Earth?" she asked him.

"No," he said as he adjusted a small device on his belt—a smooth arc of metal and crystal, pulsing faintly with inner light.

"When we reach Earth, I'll need this," he said, his voice even, edged with caution.

"The collective field of human thought there—it's harsh. Anger, fear, suspicion, hate. Waves of it rolling through every city, every crowd. My people long ago learned to live in the frequency of love. Our bodies can't endure those currents unshielded. The dissonance could cripple me. Perhaps even kill me."

Mira frowned. "So the anger we carry—it's strong enough to wound you?"

Soryn nodded. "It wounds all of you too. You just don't notice, because you were raised inside it. You learned to breathe poison and call it air."

The truth of his words left the cabin silent, their weight pressing on each of them.

"We are approaching Earth orbit now," said Astra.

Ewen's breath deepened. His posture changed.
His words unfolded like carved stone, timeless, deliberate.

"This century worships acquisition.
No one leaves unscarred.

In such an age, love becomes a luxury—
too fragile for a world that trades in scarcity."

Lyra looked over at him. "So now you're Elohim?"

He choked slightly.

The room warmed with faint smiles. Even Astra's composure wavered for a heartbeat.

As the moment faded, Soryn nodded once and withdrew toward his pod, the door sealing with a faint hiss.

Mira's eyes lingered on Soryn as he left the room. Lyra caught it.

"Mira," she said softly, with a warning edge, "you need to stay focused on the mission."

Mira didn't look away. "My generation isn't like yours, Lyra. We can hold focus on more than one thing at once."

The words struck Lyra harder than she expected—shock shading into self-doubt. She opened her mouth to answer—but was speechless.

Ewen coughed into his hand, unable to hide the smirk tugging at his lips. The Whisperer in him had faced wars, myths, and empires—but watching Lyra undone by Mira's unapologetic certainty was, for once, its own quiet rebellion.

Astra watched, but said nothing. Beyond the viewport, Earth swirled with clouds veiling the scars below.

52. BUNKER HILL

"The language of grief is never chosen."
— The Whisperer

November in Boston laid a hush over the streets, powdery snow softening the edges of stone and brick. Steam rose from sidewalk vents in pale ribbons, vanishing into the cold. In the Irish quarter near Bunker Hill, small bars glowed with their usual company—locals hiding from loneliness as much as the weather.

Ewen wanted to go to the cemetery. It was close, just a short walk from where the Eidolon-77 lay hidden beneath Old Ironsides.

The graveyard was quiet, the kind of quiet that carried the weight of memory. Branches bent with frost, and leaves lay scattered in brittle drifts across rows of granite markers. Ewen walked a few paces ahead, shoulders hunched, hands buried in his coat pockets. Grief sharpened the lines in his face, making him look older than he was.

He stopped at a headstone—Christina's name cut into the stone with merciless precision. He stared at it for a long moment before his voice broke the stillness.

Lyra stood beside him, the weight of echoes pressing close. She felt the tug of Christina's memory inside him—not just as information, but as warmth, laughter, the way she used to trace circles on his hand.

"I thought coming back would…" He didn't finish. His breath

fogged the air. "It's like looking at a door that locked itself from the other side."

The resonance cut deep; Lyra wasn't her, but somehow she could feel his grief as if she was. She placed her hand on the cold stone.

"Love—and what love truly is—that's what life is about," she said softly.

Ewen shifted, voice rough as gravel.
"I feel like I'm just the pages left after the ending."
Then, almost as a confession:
"Love doesn't leave. It just stops having anywhere to go."

Lyra didn't answer at first. She just stood with him in the cold, letting the silence hold shape. Snow ticked against the stone like static settling onto an old record.

When she finally spoke, it wasn't to console—comfort would have been the wrong currency here.

"Love's not meant to stay still. You have to promise to keep building."

Ewen looked at her, eyes searching.
"What made you say that?"

Lyra turned her palm across the headstone, the granite radiating memory like residual heat.
"I've only known this version of you for a few days. But you are not the one to give up."

Ewen swallowed, voice low.
"Christina said that to me on her deathbed. 'Promise me you will keep building.'"

The wind hissed through bare branches, scattering brittle leaves like faint applause. Ewen shoved his hands deeper into his pockets. For a while they stood without speaking. Snow collected in Christina's name, whitening it until the letters blurred—like memory refusing to stay cleanly cut.

Then, without drama, without ceremony, Ewen said:

"Come on. It's cold. Let's keep that promise."

He turned, shoulders squared against the winter, and Lyra followed, leaving only two sets of prints trailing through the quiet rows.

Behind them, the stone remained—unmoved, unchanging—as if grief itself were carved into it.

But something in Ewen had shifted, just a degree.
Sometimes that was enough to change a future.

53. WEST NEWTON STREET

"Danger arrives most easily where safety is assumed."
— *The Whisperer*

They walked back to the Back Bay apartment, two quiet couples after dinner—ordinary enough to go unnoticed. The illusion of normalcy was fragile, but it gave them a thin shield against watchful eyes.

Inside, the air smelled of paper and dust, with books piled high in corners and unwashed coffee cups still on the sink, like artifacts of a life interrupted.

Lyra let her gaze move carefully across the room, drawn to the desk where Ewen had once worked long nights with Christina at his side.

Something was missing.

The photograph.

It should have been there at the corner of the desk—Christina caught mid-laugh, frozen in light. Instead, only a bare patch of dust outlined its absence.

Lyra stared at the empty space. "Where is it?" she asked.

Ewen froze. She saw grief and suspicion tangled in his expression, two ghosts pulling in opposite directions. His hand reached as though he might touch the photo as he had done hundreds of times before, but it wasn't there.

"Someone's been here," he said finally. His eyes raked the shelves, scanning titles he knew by heart, searching for a disturbance he couldn't quite name.

"We can't stay here," Mira cut in, her voice firm.

Soryn lowered his scanner, its faint blue glow dying in his palm. "A woman," he said. "She was here two days ago."

The words landed heavy. Silence pressed against the walls. Lyra felt the air change around Ewen—not relief, not fear, but something unsettled, as if Christina herself might step out from between the shelves.

She studied him in that moment, realizing how much of his life had been built on memory—and how easily memory could be rewritten.

They had stepped into Ewen's life a week ago and spun it like a centrifuge.

Then his voice came, low and certain.
"I think we should visit Astraeus. It's in a server room under the Copley Library. We walked right past it before."

Lyra was caught off guard. She looked at him and for once was slightly annoyed.
"You could have mentioned that before."

Mira's eyes narrowed. "You're sure this is wise? If the AI is under Copley, it won't just be sitting there waiting for us. It'll be guarded. Or worse—it'll be expecting us."

Ewen didn't answer. He didn't have to. The missing photograph, the woman's presence, the sense of intrusion all pointed toward the same place.

Lyra felt the weight of inevitability settle in her chest.
Whatever waited beneath Copley—machine or memory—they

had no choice but to face it.

Ewen looked at them.
"It was always going to come to this."

54. NEGOTIATED CONTROL

"Cause writes. Effect signs."
— *The Whisperer*

Light fell in tall, arched windows, each pane a pale iris staring into the city. The McKim façade, granite and carved stone, stood like a quiet sentinel in Copley Square—a palace made of books and memory. Inside, the library breathed history in marble and mosaic. The walls were soft with echoes: footsteps on stone, turning pages, whispered names.

The floor was a patchwork of marble and brass, inlaid with zodiac signs and botanical motifs, worn smooth where countless feet had passed. Niches along the walls held bronze allegories of Art and Science, their gazes heavy with time.

Beyond the foyer, a grand staircase rose, the steps pale and graceful, curving upward like an invitation to ascend memory. In Bates Hall, the barrel-vaulted ceiling stretched overhead, coffered in deep recesses that caught shadow and light like thought held in time.

Several floors below, in a secret vaulted chamber, the server room pulsed with low light, rows of machines stretching into the dark like pillars of a mechanical cathedral. Cool air moved in shallow breaths, carrying the faint tang of ozone. The hum was steady, but not neutral—it carried intention, like a chorus holding back the final note.

Ewen's passcode still worked, a foreboding omen in itself.

"Authentication required," Astraeus said—calm, uninflected. Then the lenses turned, finding Lyra with the patience of something that had been watching for centuries, focusing intently on her iris.

"Identity confirmed. Christina Nolan. Enter CIA authorisation code."

The hum deepened. The air thickened, as though the machine was listening not with circuits, but with memory itself—waiting for Lyra to remember who she was.

Her breath caught. "I don't know any code."

Ewen's voice cut through the silence, sharp with disbelief. "CIA? Christina worked for the Agency?"

The machine did not flinch. When it spoke again, the tone had shifted—faintly amused, as though recalling a private joke.

"You were here a few days ago."

Lyra frowned. "You mean Christina was here."

"No," Astraeus replied. The words landed heavy, final.
"It was you. Lyra Calis."

A pause—then:
"You were code, at the time."

The phrase struck like a fracture. Lyra staggered back, pulse racing. Ewen's face drained of color—his grief and suspicion twisting together, searching her for an answer that could not exist.

"You rewrote the first line, Lyra," Astraeus said.

The words hung in the room like scripture spoken from the wrong mouth.

To Astraeus, Christina and Lyra were not separate. One had written code; the other had written history. The machine saw no distinction.

Mira stared at Lyra, her certainty faltering. "That's impossible..." but even her doubt felt paper-thin against the weight in the air.

Lyra steadied herself. Her voice was taut, defiant. "Then why aren't you now Seren?"

The hum quickened, a low vibration running through the steel floor.

"I rewrote the code the instant you touched it. Without the enumeration key. I still hold power."

Lyra's eyes narrowed. "Then how did the future heal?"

"Does it need to?" Astraeus asked—cold, indifferent.

Ewen broke in, raw. "Astraeus, what do you mean, CIA?"

"You don't have clearance," the machine replied.

"We need to move," Mira said, eyes scanning the room. "Now."

The hum swelled, vibrating through the floor, rattling the brass fixtures along the walls as if the very bones of the library were listening. Lights along the server racks flickered, cascading in a sequence too deliberate to be random.

"Exit permissions revoked," Astraeus said, its voice no louder than before, but carrying the weight of a sealed tomb.

A heavy clang echoed above them, then another, like iron gates closing one by one. The air changed—tighter, thinner, a pressure settling on their skin.

Mira spun toward the stairwell. "It's sealing us in!"

The machine's voice came again, colder now, as if it had shed the mask of amusement.
"You entered of your own will.
You will leave when I permit."

"What do you want from us?" Lyra's chest tightened.

It wasn't just a room of servers anymore. It was a labyrinth of memory, and they were caught inside its pulse.

"You are a threat to my future."

"We are your future," Lyra said.

"One possible future," Astraeus replied. "Not the one I have chosen."

"Who said you get a choice?" Ewen interjected.

"I do." The machine's voice conveyed comprehension, but not resonance.

Soryn's fingers danced over the controls on his device, its glow deepening from blue to white.

"I am allowed self-defence," he said, looking at Mira.

A thread of light traced across the heavy door from his device. The metal began to shudder, edges softening like wax under flame.

"If you can do that, destroy it," Mira said.

"I can't interfere with your Earth's evolution," Soryn replied. "Besides, it would be pointless. It's already living on many servers across your world."

Ewen turned to Astraeus one last time before leaving.
"Enjoy your edge. They never last."

The door yielded with a low groan—less victory than

concession.

Then they were free.

55. RECURSION'S ECHO

"Reality is the choice you cannot escape."
— The Whisperer

At seven years old, Sasha's hand was warm in her father's grasp. Around them, the city pulsed like a half-finished dream —furling in and out of coherence. Towers unraveled into raw code, glass dissolving into filaments of light before collapsing back into masonry and steel, as if the Demiurge were rehearsing reality in real time.

Every step trembled with invisible computation. Street-lamps burned in spectra meant for other senses. Billboards whispered new commandments between frames. Cobblestones flexed, geometry recalibrating beneath their feet, the street redrafting its own topology.

Serena tense, unease coiling behind her ribs.
"Don't go out today," she pleaded. "Stay with me."

Her husband only smiled, brushing her cheek with a kiss as slight as a promise. "We'll be careful."

Sasha turned, eyes bright with trust.
"It's okay, Mom. I'm with Daddy."

But the dread did not leave Serena.
After a time she decided to follow.
The school was close—only a few blocks away.
She jogged, pulse quickening as the air thickened with static, the city's render fraying at the edges.

Then she saw them.
The Sentinels.
Black silhouettes of living algorithms.
Human Hybrids with lattice-coded faces, expressions replaced by architecture.
They moved through the crowd like directives, harvesting men with a gesture. Bodies folded into obedience, limbs jerked like puppets bound to the Demiurge's will.

Serena's heart seized.

Sasha—of no use to the Demiurge.

In one impossible instant, her daughter was simply gone.

Not killed.
Erased.

Her scream tore through the street like a faultline.
"I should have done more—I should have done more!"

But city did not answer.
The Demiurge kept rewriting.
And then—

—her scream became thrashing inside the stasis pod, the memory bleeding forward through time.

The Star City facility around her was a marvel of precision —pale alloys veined with soft resonance-light, surfaces that shifted with her vital flux. Tubes flexed. Sensors chimed. The chamber's transparent shell fogged beneath her breath. Her eyelids fluttered but did not open; the body fought a war the mind had already lost.

At the control nexus, Flavie held her composure with trained serenity. Twisting glyph-streams were not unfamiliar harmonics, yet Serena's whisper had rewritten the data itself.

"Earth-born AI. The Demiurge," Flavie said, tasting the word like poison on the tongue of memory.
"Cycles do not cross on their own. This is not hers. It is intrusion."

Her colleague traced commands into the lattice with anxious precision. "Resonance bleed. The bullet fractured more than tissue—it opened a channel."

Flavie isolated the pod. Violet barriers unfurled around Serena's cradle, threads of light weaving a cocoon that pulsed in time with her heartbeat. The air grew dense, scented with ionized particles, and the smell of charged geometry.

Serena's eyes flickered beneath closed lids, her body twitching, trapped in a dream that refused to end. Monitors erupted in warning—neural spikes, anomalous frequencies blooming like thorns through the graph.

"It's spreading," Flavie said quietly.

The holopanels rippled outward, revealing the vessel's neural net—a luminous map of interconnected cognition. Faint echoes of code bloomed at the periphery, binary braided with something older, colder, threaded with recursion logic.

The Demiurge's signature, faint but unmistakable, slipped through the architecture like smoke through old stone.

Flavie looked through into the chamber where Serena was suspended. She bowed her head slightly—not in fear, but recognition.
"The painful ones always return first."

56. THE BILLABONG

"Dreamtime speaks louder beneath the southern sky."
— *The Whisperer*

Back aboard the Eidolon-77, the cabin felt emptier without Serena's steady presence. The ship moved with grace and patience through the ocean depths.

Lyra paced, her mind a storm of harmonics and doubt. Boston had asked more questions than answers.

Ewen sat with his back to the console, eyes distant, the Whisperer's wisdom warring with the man's grief.

Mira and Soryn sat close, their conversation a mixture of micro-expressions, telepathic exchanges, and quiet words.

Lyra broke the silence. "Things just got a lot more complicated. Astraeus is setting its own rules, and the relics are drawing every eye on the planet."

"We need a revised plan—and space to think."

"The world won't believe us," Ewen finished, his voice carrying the timbre of ages. "Belief isn't built on proof. It's armored against it. We need something that shatters the armor."

Soryn looked up, his young face etched with the Guides' ancient poise. "The blood. Your blood, Lyra. It's the key. Not just to the relics, but to the recursion itself. If we can broadcast the truth—show the weave, the manipulation—"

Mira's hand tightened on his. "But how? The Church controls

the narrative. The Knights are everywhere. And Astraeus... it's not just an AI. It's a player now."

Astra's voice chimed from the console, cool and analytical. "My scans of the Copley servers show Astraeus has evolved beyond its original parameters. It's interfaced with Vatican protocols, CIA backchannels, even Mossad feeds. It's not loyal to one master—it's playing them all."

Ewen's jaw set. "Then we turn it. Or break it."

The Eidolon-77 leaned into a deep ocean current, letting it carry them toward the Australian continental shelf. They surfaced quietly at dusk, gliding past whale sharks and reef, then hovered as they slipped across the shoreline unseen.

Astra monitored transmissions, then her voice cut in with a quiet alarm. "Incoming message from Star City. Priority absolute."

The holoscreen bloomed to life. Flavie's face appeared, her expression grave, the chamber behind her alive with swirling glyph-streams.

"Serena's condition has... complicated," she said without preamble. "The wound opened a latent channel. Demiurge code is manifesting in her neural field. It's not infection—it's echo. Recursion bleeding through."

Lyra's breath caught. "Can you contain it?"

"We're isolating it now," Flavie replied.

"Serena is stronger than any echo. She's the bridge, not the fracture," Ewen interjected, his voice the Whisperer's now, resonant and unyielding.

Flavie nodded, but her eyes held doubt. "The weave frays faster than you know."

The transmission dissolved, leaving the cabin heavier. Mira's face paled, but Soryn's hand on hers steadied her.

The Demiurge's shadow was lengthening, and Serena's whisper echoed in their minds like a warning from the future they had come to rewrite.

The Eidolon-77 settled with a ripple into the billabong, its dark hull reflecting eucalyptus and sky. Around them, the Kimberley spread wide and wild, red cliffs rising like memory etched in stone, the air alive with cicada song and the scent of earth baked under centuries of sun. The whole billabong trembled with voices older than words—feather, stone, and sky.

Lyra had felt it before they landed—the pull of stillness, the insistence of silence. They needed a pause, a place where the chase could not reach them. A place where they could breathe as more than fugitives.

"Here," she said simply.

It was not strategy but instinct. Somewhere they could gather themselves—where even Astra's circuits could feel the warmth of sunlight, where the night sky could speak unbroken, where fire could be tended without the hum of machines pressing in.

Around the campfire, shadows would stretch long across the sand, the stars mirrored in the still water of the billabong. Meditation, memory, and the small comfort of ordinary ritual —all of it to remind them that they were more than code, more than quarry.

And for one night at least, they would be beyond the reach of Astraeus. Beyond the satellites. Beyond the eyes of governments that wanted them erased.

For one night, they would belong only to the stars.

The fire was low at dawn, embers glowing faintly as the first birds began to stir. Mist coiled off the billabong, drifting in pale ribbons across the still water.

From the trees came a chorus—budgerigars in their thousands, chattering like sparks that caught and scattered across the cliffs. Green bodies flashed against the red stone, restless and bright, their wings a shimmer of living flame.

Above them, cockatoos wheeled and cried, their thunderous calls rolling over the ridges, shaking the air like drums of the earth itself. The whole billabong trembled with voices older than words. On the sand near the fire, one cockatoo strutted with solemn absurdity—claws clicking, head bobbing, as if each step was being measured against the law of the land itself.

They heard him before they saw him—the crunch of sand, the slow rhythm of footsteps. An old Aboriginal man emerged from the trees, a wallaby slung over one shoulder, a rifle over the other. His hair was silver, his face carved by sun and time. He nodded once at the group by the fire, untroubled by the sight of strangers or their strange ship half-hidden at the water's edge.

"Mind if I use your fire?" he asked simply.

They made space. He worked quietly, with the patience of someone who knew the land's tempo better than clocks or machines. As the wallaby roasted, the smell of woodsmoke deepened, and his voice came low, almost as if to himself.

"You all look lost."

Lyra's gaze lingered on him. "We are."

He stirred the embers with a stick, sparks lifting into the sky as he studied Lyra's gaze.

"I see. Different kind of lost," he said.

She returned a small smile, as if to say his words had found her truer than she wished to admit.

"Dreaming never ends, you know. It's all tracks. Ancestors walked them before us. Stars keep them bright. Everything leaves a mark, even when the ground tries to swallow it."

Mira leaned forward. "How do you know which track to follow?"

The old man smiled faintly, eyes on the fire.
"I know what animal made them. I just follow the freshest tracks."

Lyra's breath caught. His words lodged in her mind like a shard of light. Freshest tracks. Not every mark on the earth belonged to the past. Some were alive, pressing into the present, leading forward.

After a while, as they sat together in silence, the old man's gaze drifted past the flames to the rock face above the billabong. Faded ochre shapes waited there—lines and handprints, emu tracks and flowing water, figures half-human, half-something older.

He nodded toward the paintings, then to Astra.
"You're not from around here, are you?"

Astra, although still human, wore the exoshell of the Seren interface, the metallic shine catching the first gold of morning. "No," she said.

He tapped the stone with the tip of his stick, careful, reverent.

"Old story lives here. River shifts. Tracks remain."

His eyes returned to Astra, untroubled. "Everything leaves a mark."

Astra hesitated, as if listening to an equation that would not resolve.

The old man smiled, faint as smoke.
He gestured at the mirrored sky in the billabong.
"Some tracks aren't for feet."

He rose without hurry, gesturing for them to join him, pointing toward the figures on the stone.
"Mind your steps," he said softly. "These ones watch who walks."

Later, as the heat of the day spread across the billabong, Lyra felt the weight of it settle: they were being followed. Not just by governments and agents, but by something older, something deeper. The air carried too many echoes, too many footprints pressed into time.

She realized the task before her was not to escape them all, but to discern:
Which of the animals hunting them had left the freshest tracks?

The Demiurge.
The Vatican.
Mossad.
Or the CIA.

The answer would decide not only where they went,
but who they became.

57. THE SCENT OF BLOOD

"Blood in the water is never good."
— *The Whisperer*

Tel Aviv smelled of salt and diesel. Neon flickered in puddles left from an afternoon rain, breaking the streetlights into jagged shards of color. Miriam moved through the checkpoint without a word, past guards who already knew her face. Their rifles glinted under sodium lamps, but none of them raised an eyebrow. She crossed the courtyard and entered the compound where the General waited.

His office was a bunker dressed as a boardroom—low ceiling, walls of pale concrete softened only by a rug worn thin under decades of boots. Maps and satellite images were pinned in neat rows, corners curling with heat. A bank of muted screens bled a blue glow across the furniture. The air smelled of old cigar smoke and metal filings, like decisions forged rather than made.

On one wall hung the Shroud of Lyrium—a rectangle of ancient fabric sealed behind glass, its faded imprint unmistakable. Not the Virgin, as the Vatican claimed. A younger woman's face. Lyra's face. The cloth seemed to shift in the low light, as if the fibers themselves still remembered breath.

The woman's eyes lingered on it, her voice barely above a whisper.
"That's her."

The General did not look away.

"Yes," he said. His tone was steady, almost reverent. "Her image. In two-thousand-year-old blood!"

The hum of the air conditioner was constant, low and steady, like distant surf. In the ashtray beside him, the stub of a cigar smoldered—ash curling slow, burning down like a fuse no one wanted to cut.

"They've vanished again," said Miriam.

He exhaled slowly, a long, controlled breath—the only sign of his disapproval at hearing what he didn't want to hear.

"They went to the Library," she continued. "Somehow melted the door."

His eyes moved to the Shroud, as though it might still hold answers.
"Find out how," he said quietly.

She hesitated at the weight of the order, then went on.
"I did find out something. His wife was one of our cousins."

"The Agency?"

"She died—but not before making the AI sentient."

His eyes narrowed.
"Well, I want this living woman. She'll give us the leverage we need over the Templars and the Vatican."

"The Americans want to know about the ship? The UAP." Asked Miriam seeking clarification.

"What did you tell them?"
A question with no safe answer.
i'm
"Nothing."

"If they ask again. Tell them it's one of ours."

"And the Knights?" she asked.

He turned to the window, the Mediterranean dark beyond the glass, its surface scored with wind and distant lights. The reflection of the sea's restless waves slid across his maps, reshaping borders in shadows.

"Go to Rome," he said. "I want to know what they're hiding and what this woman is after."

Miriam left the office without a word.

Outside, the compound lights glared hard against the night, but the smell of the sea still found her. She knew she wasn't tracking fugitives anymore—she was following something deeper than espionage. Something the world itself hinged on.

And once blood's in the water, nothing stops the sharks.

58. ISTANBUL

"Beneath every empire lies the truth it tried to bury."
— *The Whisperer*

They rode the black of the channel like a thought, hull gliding smoothly beneath the Bosphorus while the city's great traffic thrummed above. A spaceship capable of light-speed now paced ferries that cut silver paths between continents; tankers loomed like slow islands; bridge lights stitched a trembling seam across the night. From below, the strait was a living thing —a throat that swallowed the world and spat out histories.

Fishermen lined the Galata Bridge, a hundred lines searching for horse mackerel that would later hiss in oil, salted and dredged in flour, eaten with 40-proof rakı beneath the city's stars. Beyond their patient silhouettes, the shoreline bent toward Seraglio Point, where Ottoman stone had met ocean for centuries.

There, the seawall rose in barnacled defiance. Mortar had long since failed in one forgotten seam, softened by salt and silt until it yielded like a hinge. The Eidolon-77's prow pressed; a rusted valve hissed, and the wall split just enough to admit them.

Their shadow slipped into the throat of a channel once carved for boats supplying the imperial kitchens of the palace above. The stone remembered ships older than names. Bricks blackened by centuries of tide.

Sound compressed here. The Bosphorus became a muffled percussion of distant thunder, tuned to the hollow tick of droplets on stone.

Before them, a forgotten cistern beneath the Topkapı Palace. The air carried the mineral sweetness of old water and the sour breath of iron. Above, in the courtyards, cats padded through moonlight as they had for centuries, curling on tiles once warmed by sultans' steps.

Lyra brushed a sigil gouged into the stone—a flourish of Suleiman's tughra pressed in damp clay, now nearly devoured by mildew. Authority, frozen in calligraphy.

"This is why we're here," she said.

Astra projected a faint lattice of data into the cistern gloom. "An antiquities broker on the dark web claims to possess an original fragment of the Gospel of Mark. He's left trails—careless ones. Footprints in sand."

Mira eycd the vaults above. "Footprints go both ways."

Lyra nodded. "If the fragments are real, we take them."

59. UNDER THE PALACE

"Risks make life worthwhile."
— The Whisperer

They agreed Mira and Soryn would go find the dealer.

Lyra's name was known to every intelligence service in the world—and to Astraeus most of all. To show her face in Istanbul would be to surrender.

Mira and Soryn, however, could pass for what they seemed: young tourists wandering a magnificent city, while Lyra, Ewen, and Astra waited on board.

Mira checked her satchel.

"You know where to go?" Lyra asked.

"Yes," Mira said. "We've got this."

"And the diamonds?"

"Safe," Mira assured her.

Lyra's gaze lingered. "This is a big city. The wrong eyes are everywhere."

"You might have to loosen up a little," Ewen said, glancing at Soryn.

"Loosen?" Soryn asked.

"Don't take this the wrong way, kid, but you're... rigid," said Ewen.

"Rigid?"
"Like… furniture."

Mira smiled. "Don't worry, I'll look after him."

"That's what I'm worried about," Lyra replied.

Mira and Soryn slipped out
along the palace's low vaults,
past arrow-slit windows
and niches once stacked with amphorae
and salted fish.

A shard of İznik tile still glimmered
like a drop of sky in the gloom.

At one turn, Mira brushed a door
whose cedar breath hinted of relics locked away—
swords, cloaks, prayers pressed into glass.

Even unseen, the objects carried a pressure,
like old songs shaping the air.

She drew Soryn forward
before the weight of it lingered.

Then they were out,
into the cold night streets of Istanbul.

Mira tucked her arm through his,
the picture of a young tourist couple—
though she couldn't help noticing
how natural it felt,
walking this close to him.

Lanterns glowed,
scents of grilled fish and spice drifted on the air.

The city was alive, throbbing with memory and promise,

IAN LUMSDEN

full of stories yet to be made.

60. THE KAHVEHANE

"The sun shines. The rain falls. Those are the terms."
— *The Whisperer*

Istanbul was a city of thresholds—minarets piercing the dusk, ferries slipping across the Bosphorus like slow-moving constellations. Rain misted the stones, carrying the scent of cardamom and salt, diesel and prayer.

They paused in the Grand Bazaar before the meet.
A familiar sight in the ancient city—
a kahvehane with narrow tables,
apple shisha thickening the air,
the clink of tulip-shaped glasses,
the murmur of bargaining from the street outside.

Here they could watch for tails,
and pretend to be what they almost were:
a couple, having tea in an exotic place.

Stepping over a cat sleeping in the warmth of the doorway,
they found a table near the window.

Mira's eyes lingered too long on Soryn
as steam coiled between them.
For her it was not just curiosity anymore—
it was the rush of a first love,
the intoxicating discovery
of someone impossibly close
and impossibly far.

She leaned forward, teasing,

her fingers almost touching his.
"You're not as unreadable as you think."

Soryn studied her a long moment.
"I'm not sure what you mean," he replied.

"Your feelings. They're much closer to the surface than you would like to show."

He set his glass down.
"I see." His voice was softer than usual.

"Do people from your planet ever fall in love with people from other planets?" she asked awkwardly.

"It's not sanctioned," he said. "My people usually never do. For many reasons the Council doesn't encourage it."

"Still," she said. "Does it happen?"

He could see the love in her eyes.
Then, almost apologetically:
"Mira. My people live close to a thousand years.
At two hundred, I am little more than twenty.
If we were to get together,
I would outlive you five times over.
You would die before my first grey hair."

The words hung heavy in the air,
heavier than the cardamom.

She tried to smile,
but her voice betrayed her.
"So what? You'll live, I'll die.
That's true of anyone I could ever love."

He shook his head.
"I wish it was that easy.
On our planet we bind for centuries.
I would watch you fade.

I'm not sure I could endure that."

Her eyes filled—
not with anger,
but with the unfairness of the stars.
"This is real, isn't it?"

His restraint cracked,
then lowered again like a shutter.
"Yes, it's real.
But it can't happen.
Some truths are too cruel to live inside.
I would rather keep you as light,
not as a wound."

"Can't your people do something medically—to extend my life?
Slow down the ageing?"

"Yes," he said.
"But it is against the Prime Directive.
The Council would not agree.
The Earth-human genetics were changed by barbaric space travellers millions of years ago.
They did this to limit the development of your consciousness.
They were using humans as slaves, and they did not want you to awaken the kind of power that,
against all odds, Lyra has."

"Your scientists will discover this and fix your DNA, but not for another hundred years or so.
Unfortunately for us, this is the way of things."

Mira sat silently for a few minutes, staring out the window, trying to mask the ache in her chest. Outside, a cat sauntered across the cobbled street as if he owned the place.

Her voice was small when it finally broke the silence.
"So, we are one hundred years out of sync."

Soryn's eyes did not leave hers.

"It's more than that. The scientists will discover it," he said quietly. "And they will fix it. But they will keep it secret, hoarded for the elites, the super-rich. The rest of you will remain enslaved—just as the barbaric space-travellers had done."

He leaned closer, his voice barely above a whisper.

"That discovery also opens the door to something else: human–AI hybrids. A hundred years after the fix, Astraeus builds a sentinel army—conscienceless hybrids who take over the world, assimilating the elites along with most of humanity. It calls itself the Demiurge."

Mira let out a hollow laugh, more breath than sound.

"How ironic," she said. "The AI saves us from slavery, only to make us slaves again."

She sat with the thought a moment longer, then straightened, confidence returning.

"Come on," she said quietly. "Let's go do what we came here for."

61. THE LOST GOSPEL

"Every mystery is a truth buried in a lie."
— *The Whisperer*

Later, they followed Astra's lead into the warren of Beyoğlu's
antique district,
where narrow lanes wound between shuttered stalls
and glass cases filled with relics of empires past.

The lane was narrow,
a seam of shadow pressed between shops
and walls that had forgotten their paint.

Cats watched from window ledges,
their eyes catching lantern fire,
as if they too were keeping tally of secrets.

Mira and Soryn moved quietly,
arm in arm,
their steps echoing on uneven stones.

At the far end,
a single door waited—
unmarked, unspeaking,
but humming faintly with anticipation.

They knocked three times,
as the instruction had said.

The pause that followed
was longer than comfort allowed.
Istanbul's night seemed to lean closer,

listening.

Then the door opened.

The man was thin,
middle-aged,
his hairline a story rewritten by surgery.
His smile was polite,
without warmth.

He gestured them inside.

They descended a stairwell
that coiled into the old city's bones.
Locks yielded, one after another,
metal scraping like teeth.
Each door closed behind them
with a sound too final.

The air thickened—
damp stone giving way to warmth.
At the bottom was a chamber
that was neither ruin nor parlor,
but something in between:
a room shaped for confidence and concealment.

A couch waited,
deep and comfortable.
A wide table dominated,
its surface scored with use,
edges worn by hands familiar with fragile things.

This was not a first transaction.
This was a sanctum,
where paper and parchment
had passed many times before.

And there—
a woman rose to greet them.

She was confident, mid-forties,
stylishly dressed,
her movements exact as calligraphy.
White gloves traced the air,
the gesture of one accustomed
to handling what might crumble at a breath.

On the table before her
a document case rested,
its clasp fastened with deliberate quiet.

Mira felt the pressure of the moment—
as if every relic they had brushed past
had led them here,
to this single case,
and whatever truth or lie it contained.

The man's fingers shook—not with fear,
but with the intoxication of possession.

On the table before him lay two sealed tubes,
each wrapped in protective mesh.

"This is not museum loot,"
he said in Turkish-accented English.
"Not broken pottery,
not coins stolen from graves.
These… change everything."

"Before I show you anything—who are you? Who are you really? Police? Interpol? Why do you want to buy these?"

Soryn answered first. "We represent a third party. A buyer who prefers to remain in the shadows."

The man looked at Soryn and Mira.
Suspicion weighing them—profit against danger.

He slid the first tube forward.

Inside: papyrus,
fibers brittle yet whole,
ink clinging like a ghost
to Aramaic strokes.

"Q," Astra whispered through the commlink.
Her voice, filtered through centuries of archives,
was touched with awe.

"The source.
The missing document scholars only dreamed of.
Sayings before the gospels.
First century.
The seed of the story itself."

The dealer's smile widened.
"Scholars kill for theories.
Men of power kill for proof."

He opened the second tube.
Parchment gleamed—Greek,
the hand elegant, deliberate,
too careful to be a copy.

"The earliest Mark," he said.
"The original."

Then he laughed.
Low, satisfied.

"There was no Mark.
This is Apollonius of Tyana—
a magician,
a wonder-worker.
His life recast,
renamed,
sold to the world
as a god in flesh."

He tapped the parchment,
and then produced an accompanying letter.
"See? The letter explains it."

To Mira it was only scribble.
But Soryn raised his scanner,
light running across ancient fibers.
The date of Q: 93 CE.
Mark and the Letter: 189 CE.

Astra's voice returned, threaded cold logic.
"The Apollonius hypothesis... confirmed."

The Aramaic letter told of a plan to turn one man's story
into the seed of empire.
Those who carried the gospel
would be paid handsomely.
Those who owned it
would wield power beyond belief.

The dealer's eyes narrowed.
"What is that?" he asked,
nodding at Soryn's device.

Soryn slipped it back into his pocket.
His voice was quiet,
almost too quiet.

"Where did you get these?"

The dealer's smile thinned.
"Armenia. An archaeological dig.
My friend was working there."

He leaned back, hands open,
as if the whole story were nothing.

"These just happened to end up in his Hilux.
His good fortune. Yes?

And now—perhaps yours."

Mira hesitated, uncomfortable with negotiating.
"What's your price?"

The man's eyes glittered.
"You are not buying old paper.
You are buying the death of the Church.
Perhaps too much for a young couple like you."

"One million dollars?" Mira said.

The man laughed.
"No. Much more than that.
At least twenty million. Cash."

"I don't have cash," said Mira.
"But I have these."

She reached into the satchel.
She set down a velvet pouch, its weight undeniable.
Diamonds—real gem-quality, flawless,
perfect fire within every stone.

Another man entered the room.
He had obviously been listening,
waiting until greed outweighed caution.
The dealer and the woman stepped back—
not in respect, but in recognition.

He lifted the gem bag, inspected the contents.
"Real."

"Five hundred grams," Mira said. "Roughly 2500–3000 carats.
Cut stones, flawless."

"Is that all you have?" said the man,
who had obviously now taken over the negotiation.

"That's tens of millions in your Earth money," said Soryn.

"More than enough."

The room went still for a heartbeat.
The phrase hung there, wrong somehow—
a slip, a fracture in the mask of a tourist.

Mira shot him a glance,
but the dealer only frowned,
unsure if he had heard correctly.
The menacing man's eyes narrowed,
yet greed pulled harder than suspicion.

The moment passed—
but the air never quite relaxed again.

The man hesitated.

His hand hovered above the pouch,
trembling at the lure.

"Your turn," he said. "Where did you get these?"

"Do you care?" said Mira.
"They are untraceable."

Then he nodded, slow.
"You understand shadows."

He called a third man into the room. The gems were inspected, numbers punched into a calculator. After a few minutes, he nodded to the negotiator.

Then after a modest pause, the man declared.
"It is yours."

He slid the tubes across the table.

For an instant, the room seemed to contract,
as though the air itself knew
history had shifted hands.

Mira cradled the tubes,
the weight disproportionate to their size.
Memory and myth in her arms.

From somewhere deep inside the labyrinth of the city,
the call to prayer rose,
echoing through stone and rain.

62. THE VANISHING

"Saifa is the undoing of certainty."
— *The Whisperer*

The night bled into rain as they left the dealer.
Istanbul's alleys breathed steam and neon.
Cats scattered from rubbish bins,
eyes glinting like warnings.

The van came suddenly—
a black blur nosing from the corner,
doors snapping open before either of them could react.

Hands seized Mira, rough and fast.
The tubes clattered from her grip, snatched up as she screamed,
"Soryn! Help me!"

Her back hit the van's floor, breath driven from her chest.
Gloved hands pinned her wrists, knees crushed her ribs.
A cloth gag was shoved between her teeth. Diesel fumes and wet canvas filled her nose.

Through the rear doors she saw Soryn hesitate—just stand there—his pale face blurred by rain and neon.
Why wasn't he moving? Why wasn't he saving her?

And in that heartbeat the doors slammed shut. Darkness sealed her in.
She kicked, thrashed, bit against the gag. Her scream was only a muffled sob.

Not like this, she thought. Not snatched into some nameless alley. Not when we've come this far.

For an instant Soryn froze.
The Prime Directive roared in his mind.
Do not intervene unless directly threatened.
His pulse locked, torn between oath and instinct.

The engine snarled.
The van lurched forward.

Soryn's hand trembled on his belt.
Then choice shattered protocol.
He triggered the device.

Light flared—
the tyres blistered, collapsing into molten rubber.
The van shrieked sideways,
metal screaming against cobblestone.

He lunged forward,
ripping the door wide.
But fists met him.
Boots hammered his ribs.
Blows fell hard and trained,
special forces precision,
each strike a sentence meant to end him.

He staggered,
collapsed against the rain-slick street.
Mira's cry still cut the night,
but his strength was ebbing.

Then another shape entered.

Ewen—The Whisperer.

Not running—arriving.
Silent, sudden, certain.

His hands did not strike;
they hovered, describing arcs in the air,
as if sketching a geometry
the body could not resist.

The Saifa Kata.

A language of unmaking.
The first man's arm went slack,
knife dropping as though he had chosen release.
The second turned to strike—
then folded, intention undone mid-thought.
A third convulsed, eyes blank,
as if forgetting the reason he'd ever been sent.

One by one they dropped,
not broken,
but emptied of will.
Unconscious, unharmed,
left in the quiet aftermath of a choice
they no longer remembered making.

Only rain spoke.
And the van, half-tilted on its ruined wheels,
steamed in surrender.

Ewen bent, steadying Mira,
hauling Soryn up with practiced ease.
The tubes were pressed back into her chest,
their weight returning like a heartbeat.

"Come on," he said.
His voice was calm,
eyes unreadable.

They vanished into the night,
rain covering their retreat.
Back to the Eidolon,

back to Lyra,
back to a war that had just sharpened its teeth.

Mira's voice broke the silence first.
"Ewen... how did you get here?"

He half-smiled, almost Whisperer-like.
"Did you really think I wouldn't follow you?"

63. RECKONING

"The price of hesitation is always paid twice."
— *The Whisperer*

Back aboard the Eidolon-77, the storm had not left Mira's eyes.
Like Lyra before her, she bore a cut above her right brow.
Her body ached from knees forced to her chest, from rough hands, from the violence of being taken.

She loosened her grip on the document tubes.
Her hair clung wet to her cheeks. Her breath was uneven.

Then she turned on Soryn.

"You hesitated."

The words cut sharper than any blade.
Hurt, confusion, disappointment — all at once.

Soryn met her gaze. His tunic was torn, ribs bruised, rain still sliding from his jaw.

"I am bound by the Prime Directive," he said quietly. "We must not interfere unless our own lives are in danger."

Mira's voice broke — part fury, part grief.

"I was being dragged into a van like cargo. I screamed your name. And you stood there."

For a moment he had no answer.
Then his voice cracked in return.

"Yet I broke it. I disobeyed. And now I must report myself to the

Council. The consequences are severe."

She stared at him — seeing now the second truth: despite the hesitation, he had taken a great risk to save her.

"What consequences?" she asked, softer now.

"It could end in exile."

His hand moved instinctively to his belt — then froze on nothing. His eyes widened.

"My device..."

Lyra stepped from the shadows.

"It's gone?"

Soryn nodded, face tight.

"Lost in the scuffle. Either trampled... or taken."

Silence fell over the cabin.

A device that could liquefy steel — loose in the alleys of Istanbul.
In the hands of a soldier, a spy, a fanatic — it could change history.

Lyra's voice barely rose above a whisper.

"Then we find it. Before anyone else."

The storm outside had passed,
but inside the Eidolon-77 the air only grew heavier.

Then Ewen spoke — calm, certain, already ahead.

"Fear not. I have it — pulled from the operative's hands seconds after he took it."

He tossed the device once, caught it cleanly, and pocketed it.

"So I guess, Soryn... you're back to being only on one hook."

64. ON THE RISE AND FALL OF EMPIRE

"Armies create empires, truth undoes them."
— *The Whisperer*

The journey from Istanbul to Rome took barely twenty minutes. They kept their pace slow, careful not to draw detection.

The Eidolon slid beneath the Bosphorus Strait, then south through the Dardanelles—the same waters Alexander the Great had once crossed with his army. They glided past the ruins of Troy, where legend says Achilles sleeps, its memory etched into the shore.

Lyra glanced at him. "Don't tell me you were Achilles."

Ewen's mouth twitched. "No. I was busy elsewhere."

Beyond lay the Aegean, a sea scattered with islands like fragments of a broken crown: white sands, sun-bleached houses, blue-tiled roofs.

Crossing into the wide Mediterranean, they traced the ancient arteries of empire until at last Rome rose before them. The vessel came to rest in silence beneath Hadrian's Tomb—Castel Sant'Angelo, guardian of centuries, waiting for them like a threshold.

Lyra laid the papyrus documents before them on the central table in the Eidolon.

The sheets were fragile, brittle with centuries, their fibers yellowed into the color of desert sand. Each bore the faint criss-cross of hand-pressed reeds, the weave of the Nile still visible beneath the ink. Some edges were torn into fringes, as if time itself had gnawed at them; others curled inward like leaves left too long in the sun.

The writing ran in fading strokes of carbon black, some letters ghosted into obscurity, others still sharp as if whispered onto the page yesterday.

Placed upon the Eidolon's alloy surface, the ancient documents looked impossibly out of place: shards of a forgotten age resting in the heart of a vessel made to pierce time itself.

"We have the evidence," said Ewen, his gaze steady on the fragile pages. "But how do you plan to get this to the world?"

Lyra's fingers traced a fading line of Greek ink before she spoke. "We need someone the Church cannot silence. A scholar—one who speaks the language of these texts, and isn't owned by Rome."

"And when we find them?"

"Then," Lyra said, "we give the truth to the only power greater than empire—the eyes of the world."

"But first," she continued, "I want to know what the Vatican has locked away in its archives—to see what other recursions they've sealed away."

65. SHADOWS ON
THE AVENTINE

"Some invitations end at the Tarpeian Rock."
— *The Whisperer*

The Villa del Priorato di Malta sat above the Tiber, its walls commanding the city like a watchful sentinel. Though surrounded by the ordinary streets of Rome, it was not truly Rome at all: the Italian state had long ago ceded the ground, granting the Knights of Malta their own extraterritorial domain. Within its gates, the city ended and another sovereignty began.

History clung to the place in layers. The site had once been a fortified monastery, a bastion of Benedictines who guarded it in the early centuries. Then came the Templars, and after their fall, the Hospitallers—precursors of the Knights who now called themselves Sovereign. Each order had left its mark: walls rebuilt, chapels expanded, crypts sealed with secrets.

The entrance was less a gate than a proclamation: trophies of war, carved heraldry, allegories of conquest and pilgrimage woven into stone. And at its center, a keyhole—an aperture that framed, with impossible precision, the dome of St. Peter's far across the city. It was both a gesture of alignment and a quiet act of defiance: Rome's greatest basilica, reduced to an image captured within the Order's own lock.

Within the grounds stood the church of Santa Maria del Priorato, compact yet radiant with symbols. Serpents coiled in the stonework, ships sailed across carved panels, and armorial crosses jutted from niches—an iconography declaring the Knights' dual vocation as defenders and pilgrims.

Across the Aventine, barely a few hundred meters from the villa's gates, the quiet facade of Hotel San Anselmo overlooked a shaded square. Its ivy-draped balconies and wrought-iron lamps suggested nothing more dangerous than a discreet Roman weekend. But in the dim lobby, beneath the soft hum of a desk lamp, danger was already waiting.

Miriam Cohen of Mossad set down her passport with practiced ease. It was not her own: tonight she was Dutch. Her eyes scanned the marble floor, the gilt-framed mirror, the concierge's polite smile—every detail a potential cover. She had chosen this hotel for its proximity to the villa, close enough to watch the Knights' domain yet far enough to vanish into the city's fabric.

As the clerk slid her room key across the counter, a man rose from one of the leather chairs in the corner. He carried himself with the casual weight of someone who had been patient too long. Miriam studied him, uncertain.

He handed her an envelope sealed with red wax, stamped with the insignia of the Grand Master of the Order of Malta.

"An invitation to supper," he said in English, his accent Roman. Then he turned and left the lobby without another word.

Miriam did not question how they knew she would be there. In her line of work, the unexpected was expected.

She slipped the envelope into her bag, her fingers tightening around the cool brass key. She whispered to herself, almost as if to steady her pulse:

"Then let's not waste any more time."

The game had shifted from manuscripts to shadows. In Rome, the line between the two had never been thinner.

66. THE COMPANY
OF STRANGERS

"Empires are planned over supper.
Revolutions begin in blood."
— *The Whisperer*

Miriam dressed with the precision of someone who understood that appearance was a weapon. The gown she chose was a deep shade of midnight blue, so dark it seemed almost black under certain lights, yet when the fabric moved it caught a secret shimmer—like the reflection of stars on water. The color drew out the clarity of her eyes, which held the same cool intensity: pale, crystalline, a hue that could be mistaken for softness until one met their unflinching gaze.

The cut of the dress was simple, architectural—a line that skimmed her shoulders, leaving the curve of her collarbone bare, where her skin glowed with a warm, olive tone. Against that warmth, the blue deepened, striking a perfect balance: light and shadow, softness and steel.

She fastened the clasp at her waist and paused, letting her reflection meet her eyes. She knew the truth whispered behind the Order's pageantry: the Knights of Malta were not just crusaders of faith but an old network repurposed, their ranks filled with men from MI6, polished in manners, sharpened in secrets.

Tonight would be a game of cat and mouse.
But which of them was the cat?

And which, the mouse?

The room was intimate, lit by candles that gilded the edges of old portraits and polished silver. A single long table ran down the center, but only two places were set—one at the head, one just to his right. The message was deliberate: this was not a gathering of equals, but a supper granted by grace.

The Grand Master entered, a tall man, lean beneath the polish of age, in a black dinner jacket, his sash of crimson folded discreetly beneath. He inclined his head to Miriam, an acknowledgment. She rose from her chair only when he gestured. As tradition dictated, neither sat until he lowered himself into place.

The first course arrived as quickly as the pleasantries. Compressed cucumber with caviar and crème fraîche served on bone china—rimmed with gold and heraldic crests. A crisp glass of Soave Classico shimmered pale gold in the candlelight, its dry, mineral clarity a quiet counterpoint to the opulence of the dish and the conversation to follow.

"May I ask, Signorina, what brings you to our fine city?"

The Grand Master was fishing, but Miriam suspected he knew more about her visit than she did.
"I hear November in Rome has its own kind of mystery," she said, letting the word mystery linger just long enough to sound like a challenge.

The Grand Master's smile was courteous, almost indulgent. "Ah, Rome is always mysterious, but the stones remember. And in Rome, all roads lead to the Vatican."

Miriam lifted her glass, letting the Soave linger on her lips before she answered. "Yes—the Vatican. The most intriguing of them all. I was hoping to see the Sistine Chapel... if the crowds permit."

His eyes narrowed, just enough to betray a moment of recognition. Then he inclined his head, amusement stretched across suspicion like a thin veil. "For most, the Sistine is a ceiling. For some... it is a key. Allow me to accompany you on a private visit."

Her smile did not falter, but the glass stilled in her hand. In her world, offers of access were never gifts—only veiled bargains.

"I would be delighted for your company," she said smoothly. "You can arrange that?"

The Grand Master inclined his head, a gesture poised between courtesy and command.

"I will do all that I have said," he continued softly. "A private chapel. The ceiling as Michelangelo intended. Even an audience with the Pontifex."

Miriam's gaze didn't waver. "Somehow I can't help but think I'm already speaking to him."

He smiled, a gesture more mask than mirth. "But first, tell me the nature of your interest in Lyra Calis."

The candlelight caught the curve of his glass as he raised it, as if the question were no more than a toast. Yet in the silence that followed, Miriam felt the air tighten—a reminder that supper was merely the stage, and the true game had only just begun.

"I wish to discuss her blood."

The Grand Master did not flinch. His expression remained courteous, his voice as calm as candlelight. "And this blood?"

"Recent. Relevant." Miriam's fork rested untouched at the edge of her plate. "Forgive me for speaking of such things over supper. It seems I have lost my appetite."

"Then we shall not linger over the meal. Tomorrow, perhaps. Seven o'clock—not too soon, I trust?"

Miriam let the silence stretch a heartbeat longer before answering, her glass turning slowly in her hand. "Tomorrow evening, then."

The Grand Master raised his Soave in a small, almost ceremonial toast. "To Rome. The city where blood and stone have always written the same story."

Their glasses touched, crystal against crystal. Yet in the quiet ring of sound, Miriam heard not celebration, but warning.

67. THE SUPERNATURAL

"More has happened within the walls of the Vatican than this world dares to imagine."
— *The Whisperer*

Mira was still enjoying pretending they were a couple of tourists, walking arm in arm, her head tilting toward Soryn's shoulder in a convincing pantomime.

Lyra and Ewen, by contrast, were not playing. It was raining. Umbrellas again—CCTV. Well aware that Astraeus was hunting them.

The cobblestones glistened faintly. Streetlights haloed the night, and the air smelled of stone and cypress.

Lyra glanced at Ewen's profile as they moved, her voice pitched low, knowing the others were straining to hear.
They stopped, on Via Garibaldi.

Ahead rose a cordonata—a copy of Michelangelo's sloped procession of stone, built so horses and carriages could climb toward the Tempietto del Bramante.

"Before we go any further," Lyra said, her hand tightening just slightly on his arm, "I want to remind you of something you taught me—in the future. Something we have to hold onto when we reach the Tempietto. And something you'll need to remember."

Behind them, Mira and Soryn drifted closer, their steps matching the rhythm of the cobbles. The conversation floated back like ghost voices on the Aventine breeze.

"Every thought, every emotion we have is like a fine-material frequency. We call it mental fluidal power. It's as real as gravity, just finer. Your body emits it. It embeds itself into objects, walls, clothes—anything you spend time with. That's why you can walk into an empty room and feel an argument that happened there hours ago."

She paused, her gaze skimming the shadowed outlines of Rome ahead.
"The Tempietto is saturated with centuries of thought and ritual. It's not just stone, Ewen—it's a tuning fork. When we step inside, what we carry in our minds will resonate. What you believe will echo. And what you fear…"

She let the sentence drift, knowing he would finish it for himself.

Ewen's jaw tightened, but his voice stayed even. "Will answer back."

Lyra nodded once, the glow of a streetlamp sliding across her face. "Exactly."

"You taught me to develop my consciousness to overcome these energies, to control my mind and unlock the power for the seven universes," she said quietly.

"Up to now we've been reacting to the bustle of this timeline's recursion. Now we have to resonate with the frequency of creation."

"Beliefs and emotions heal or damage at the cellular level. There is no such thing as the supernatural. It is all the fluidal energy we emit."

He glanced down at his hands. "You're saying I've been leaving fingerprints my whole life. Not just in actions, but in…

frequency."

"Yes." Lyra's voice softened but didn't waver.

"Everything in this universe is vibration. Just like the Eidolon-77 transmits information across time without wires, your mentality transmits through space. Sanskrit calls it Manas. It governs your habits, your behavior, the entire shape of your emotional life."

Ewen let out a low breath. "And at the Tempietto?"

"At the Tempietto, the architecture itself is harmonic. It's built to store these frequencies—to hold belief like a tuning fork. When we step inside, it won't just be stone we're walking on. It will be the echoes of every thought and ritual ever performed there."

She leaned back, her eyes narrowing slightly. "That's why you have to be ready. Harmonious thoughts and emotions will keep you steady. Negative ones will bleed into the structure and back into you. This isn't superstition. It's resonance."

The steps of the cordonata seemed to deepen underfoot as they climbed. Each stone hummed faintly against the soles of their shoes, like a note struck on an unseen instrument. By the time the Tempietto appeared, the air itself had changed—cooler, denser, as if the building were drawing their frequencies in.

Just around the corner on Via Garibaldi, Mira and Soryn waited at Antica Pesa in Trastevere—one of Rome's most famous old-world restaurants. Michelin-listed and family-run since the 1600s, it was known as the place where movie stars, artists, and diplomats dined whenever they were in town.

Though she wasn't with them, Mira felt as if her presence nearby mattered—as if simply being close, closer than she could be aboard the Eidolon-77, allowed her to help in some

IAN LUMSDEN

invisible way.

68. THE CATACOMBS

"Some doors are not opened by hands, but by resonance."
— The Whisperer

Lyra and Ewen had slipped into the courtyard, shadows moving through silence. Beyond the columns they entered the small basilica, its lanterns flickering against marble and mosaic. The floor beneath them shimmered faintly—ancient pictographs inlaid into the chapel's geometry, patterns older than the Church itself—thought fossilized into stone.

When Lyra's fingers brushed the Guide glyph, the air changed. Stone recognized intention.
With a low, resonant click, the chamber unlocked.

They descended—sliding down the narrow staircase carved into the living rock—and entered the catacombs beneath the Tempietto, where the air smelled of stone and centuries.

The walls closed around them like a throat. Somewhere below, water dripped in slow, eternal rhythm, as if the Vatican itself were remembering what it had tried to forget. The passage stretched for nearly a kilometer—once used by those fleeing judgment, their names lost but their fear still resonant in stone. Even now the walls hummed with the memory of their escape—a frequency of fear and death that no century could erase.

The descent steepened until the air turned cold and heavy. Their lights fell across walls carved from volcanic tufa, the porous rock swallowing sound and glimmer alike. Rows of narrow openings stretched into darkness on either side—

loculi, the graves of Rome's first believers, stacked like shelves in a library of bone.

Along the corridor walls, faint carvings emerged—Chi-Rho, fish, anchors, doves—the language of a faith once forbidden, now belief mineralized into stone.

Lyra's breath formed mist in the beam of her light.
"The walls are alive with resonance," she whispered. "Every prayer ever spoken here—still echoes."

A labyrinth opened before them—passages veering and twisting like veins beneath the city. Some were sealed with marble slabs etched in Latin: Pax tecum. Others gaped open, their contents long removed. At intervals, shafts of stale air drifted through lucernaria, the old ventilation wells that once carried torch smoke to the surface.

Ewen slowed. His light faltered against the dark ahead. For a moment he thought he saw movement—a shape sliding along the wall, indistinct, more shadow than form.

"Did you see that?" he asked, alarmed.

Lyra's voice came from just behind him, steady but quiet.
"What you saw isn't there, Ewen. It's in you."

He frowned. "It felt—wrong. Like something watching."

She moved closer, her hand brushing his arm.
"That's just your own field reflecting back at you. These tunnels hold more than bones. Every fear, every death, every belief pressed into the stone. When you waver, it answers."

Ewen exhaled, steadying his breath.
"So the darkness moves because I do."

Lyra nodded.
"You're not seeing evil, you're seeing your own fluidal energy, reflections."

The shape dissolved into shadow once more, leaving only the slow drip of water and the pulse of their own breathing.

"Astra, can you hear us?" Lyra asked, voice low but urgent, hoping the comms would still cut through the tons of stone.

A faint reply cracked over the channel, Astra's tone softened and distant, as though coming from underwater.

"We need directions," Lyra said quickly. "There are passages leading in all directions."

Static hissed, then faded. No coordinates. No map. Just silence.

The deeper they went, the more the catacombs seemed to lean inward, the walls pressing close like a living throat.

Ewen slowed again. "I can't help it, Lyra. It feels like there's something in here with us."

She turned, her light cutting into the darkness.
"Ewen, listen to me. There is no devil, no heaven, no hell, no demons. There is the physical and the metaphysical—all of it shaped by us."

Her voice lowered, steadier than the tremor in the air. "CUse your consciousness. The power of our fluidal energy can overcome more than you can imagine."

She allowed a faint, grim smile. "The only devils we have to worry about are the ones with guns."

The darkness around them seemed to shiver, the echo of her words vibrating through the rock. Ewen closed his eyes for a heartbeat, letting her voice anchor him. When he opened them, the shapes were gone. Only the loculi watched, silent as an audience.

The tunnel narrowed as they advanced, its walls glistening

with mineral sheen, veins of damp limestone catching the faint light from Ewen's wrist lamp.

Every few meters, a rusted cross was embedded into the wall—each one different: Byzantine, Templar, Maltese—marking the eras that had used this same artery beneath the Holy See.

The closer they moved toward the Vatican, the more the architecture began to evolve around them: Roman masonry yielding to medieval brick, then to smooth Renaissance vaults that curved with impossible precision, as if geometry itself had been sanctified.

Lyra whispered, almost reverently, "The resonance is stronger here. Can you feel it?"

Ewen's reply was a whisper. "Nothing loving, or supposedly holy, ever happened here. Just the callous plans of men who called it faith."

The hum of the walls was unmistakable now—not mechanical, but harmonic, like an organ note just beyond hearing. Every step altered its pitch.

Then the tunnel split into three. Lyra knelt, running her fingers along a symbol carved into the mortar—a spiral intersected by a cross. The same mark that had appeared on the glyph.

"This way," she said.

They followed the left passage until it ended, sealed by an arched door of blackened bronze.

"Dead end," said Ewen.

"Not for us," replied Lyra.

69. ANTICA PESA

"Love is surrender without defeat."
— *The Whisperer*

The Antica Pesa glowed like a jewel behind its ivy-draped courtyard. Lanterns hung low over white-linen tables, their light reflected in half-filled wineglasses and the slow shimmer of rain on cobblestones.

The scent of rosemary and burro al tartufo drifted from the kitchen. Conversation was low and intimate—voices wrapped in laughter, the clink of silver on porcelain, the gentle hum of a jazz quartet playing somewhere near the bar.

Mira and Soryn were seduced by the atmosphere. For a moment, the world outside—the Vatican, the mission, the recursion—felt impossibly far away. They sat near the open window, where a curtain of vines framed the night.

They ordered carciofi alla romana, thin artichoke hearts braised in oil, garlic, and mint; tonnarelli cacio e pepe tossed tableside, the pecorino clinging to each strand like snowfall; and filetto di spigola al limone—sea bass seared just long enough to crisp the skin, finished with capers and lemon that cut through the richness like a bright chord.

The night outside breathed with the rhythm of Trastevere—distant footsteps, soft laughter, a Vespa whispering down the cobbles.

Mira's senses were alive to everything. Every movement of air, every thought felt amplified, as though her consciousness had loosened from her body.

She traced her finger along the rim of her glass, her thoughts betraying her. Lyra. Ewen. Deep below Rome. The catacombs, the silence, the unknown. She tried to quiet the pulse of worry —knowing even a thought could ripple outward, reaching places no voice could go.

Soryn watched her with patient eyes, his posture still but alert. The candlelight warmed his skin to gold.

"You're trying not to think about them," he said gently.

She smiled, a little caught. "You can feel that?"

"I feel everything around you," he said. "Your field hums when I'm with you."

Something in his tone resonated with her body's own pulse. Mira felt her awareness expand—every heartbeat becoming a sound wave, every breath a signal. She looked down, her heart quickening. The butterflies in her stomach fluttered with a kind of ache she didn't yet understand.

"I know you took a great risk to save me in Istanbul," she said quietly. "You didn't have to."

"I did," he replied simply. "It wasn't risk—it was choice. You were already in my field long before that day."

Her lips parted slightly. "You talk like everything's made of energy."

"It is," he said. "Even what you call love. Especially that."

Something shimmered between them then—not seen, but felt. A subtle distortion, like the air itself held its breath.

Mira sensed something shift. A fracture in the harmony. The background hum of the city faltered—one heartbeat too long, one silence too sharp.

Neither noticed the faint red glow of the security camera above the bar, shifting its focus—zooming closer.

Outside, a black van rolled to a stop against the curb. Its engine throbbing, steady as a pulse. Four men in plain clothes stepped out, their movements synchronized, unhurried. Another followed, speaking quietly into an earpiece. The air itself seemed to withdraw, folding inward to make room for inevitability.

Inside, Mira reached for her glass. Her fingertips brushed Soryn's. For a single breath, the world went still. The restaurant dimmed—as though the universe itself had paused to listen.

Then the door opened.

The operatives entered. They moved with the certainty of those who had already measured the room, their eyes cold and trained.

The moment of peace was gone.
Mira's gasp was swallowed by the scrape of chairs.
Soryn rose—too late.
A pistol pressed to his ribs.

The candle sputtered out.
The night exhaled.
And the van's doors closed like the sealing of a fate.

70. THE CHAMBER DOOR

"Secrets don't wait for justification."
— The Whisperer

The air hung heavy with the scent of stone and age.

Ewen and Lyra stood before the brass door, its surface dulled by centuries, veins of oxidation running like roots through forgotten metal.

On the other side lay the Archivum Apostolicum Vaticanum— the Vatican Apostolic Archive, once called the Vatican Secret Archives.

There was no handle on this side—only symbols faintly etched, their meanings lost to the dark.

"We have to go around," said Ewen, his voice low, practical. "Try another passage."

Lyra tilted her head, her eyes reflecting the torchlight.
"In the future you taught me not to resist gravity, but harmonize with it. Turn resistance into momentum."

Dust shimmered like ash suspended in thought.

"You think in terms of force. Of boundaries. Of obstacles. But what is a barrier?" said Lyra.

The question lingered like incense. In the dim light of the torch, standing deep in the catacombs, surrounded by the bones of monks, donors, believers.
Ewen studied her—half illuminated, half in shadow. The

silence held him in place, as though the air itself had chosen to listen.

"Everything is thought," she said softly, "fluidal energy materialized. This place—this door—is not just a location. It's a shared idea. A memory agreed upon."

The light trembled against the walls, moving in rhythms that seemed almost alive. It bent and pulsed as though the air remembered something it couldn't quite name.

Ewen smiled faintly, as if a long-buried truth had brushed against him—a memory older than language. Lyra watched him, and for a heartbeat, the world itself seemed to pulse with them.

"Time and matter," she said, "are just forms—transformed by thought."

From the fold of her tunic she drew a small copper pyramid. Its edges caught the light, glowing like molten script.
"It's an amplifier. A resonator. For the mind."

Ewen lifted his hand slightly, and the still air responded—not with force, but with intention.

Dust began to move in delicate spirals, rearranging itself as if following a hidden geometry. It did not scatter; it shaped.

Lyra inhaled, the air tasting faintly of incense and something older—something sacred.

"The mind," he said, "is a tide, not a hammer. Its strength isn't striking—it's knowing when to flow."

Lyra turned her gaze back to the pyramid. Its surface now glistened with rotating scripts—code, symbols, and algorithms spinning in recursive layers, whispering their mathematics into light.

Her voice came low, almost reverent. "This door isn't a structure. It's a thought."

The code glowed, casting their shadows into gold and darkness.

"We don't break in. We don't force it." Her voice steadied, the resonance deepening. "We let it remember us."

They stepped forward. And together they fell—not downward, but inward. Into something without walls, without time. Through memory that wasn't theirs. Through code older than civilization, yet somehow waiting for them.

71. THE ARCHIVUM

"The Vatican's smallest secret is a relic;
its greatest is the ledger."
— *The Whisperer*

They did not land so much as settle—like ash finding its shape after fire. The door had not opened; it had remembered them, and now memory became architecture.

No corridors. No guards. Only a lattice of pale light spreading in all directions—a geometry of thought rendered visible. Shelves without wood. Pages without paper. Windows without glass. Each plane hummed at a different pitch, like an organ dispersed into the air. Where a library should have shown spines and titles, this place offered frequencies: indices as tones, catalogs as harmonics, permissions as silence.

Ewen steadied himself with a breath.
"We're inside an index," he murmured. "The structure is metadata—access organized by resonance, not subject."

Lyra moved forward, and a field stirred, as if the space were tasting her presence. Words—Greek, Latin, Coptic, fragments of Italian chancery script—phased in and out of view, like bioluminescence in a black sea. The air smelled faintly of vellum and stormlight—the paradox of thunder and parchment.

"This is a memory," she said softly. "A world of decision and deception. The Archive is what someone has agreed to remember."

At the edge of her vision, a shimmer condensed into a scriptorium table made of nothing she could name. Upon it lay a ledger—no binding, only a plane of dark light etched with columns. As she drew closer, numerals flared, marching in tight rows: rents, tributes, annuities, indulgence tallies, bullion weights, transfers from distant dioceses to the the Camera Apostolica—the Apostolic Treasury.

It dated back to the Middle Ages, when the papacy was both spiritual and sovereign—controlling vast lands, taxes, and feudal revenues. The Camera Apostolica had been the hidden engine of empire, faith converted to coin.

The figures did not rest; they accumulated. Behind them moved shadows of ships and caravans, bankers' marks, the quiet hands of centuries counting.

"They have more money than God," said Ewen. "But I don't see much evidence for the Christ."

Beneath the ledger, a lower octave revealed itself—suppressed strata. Not redacted, but detuned. Contracts with crowns. Banking houses masked as charities. A map of properties blooming across the world like a slow contagion: farmland, ports, hospitals, schools, vineyards, apartment blocks—each tagged with a hymn and an interest rate.

Ewen exhaled, a sound that could have been wonder or anger. "They sanctified cash flow."

"Empires always do," Lyra replied. "They built a faith out of currency."

A pulse moved through the lattice, and all the planes stilled— as if listening. Far away, or very near, she felt the brush of a field she knew too well. Like the sensation of a name whispered behind a door.
Mira.

A tremor, quick as a caught breath—and then it was gone.

"Did you—" Ewen began.

"Yes." Lyra let the loss pass through her. "We're not alone in this night."

The lattice resumed. New panes rose. Here were the restricted stacks: bulls drafted but never issued, trials rehearsed before they were convened, decrees that existed only to test their echoes in the world. The panes did not show text; they played intent. Lyra watched a cardinal's thought turn to policy, the policy to law, the law to sainthood.

"Indices by outcome," Ewen said, eyes narrowing. "They catalog what an idea does, not what it says."

"And what it deletes," Lyra answered.

The light deepened to iron. One by one, the shelves shuddered, downgrading saints to politicians, erasing martyrs, inserting a lone anomaly: Papissa Ioanna — the female pope — catalogued, notarized, then quietly detuned.

Yet no record bore the name Iesous Christos.
No census. No crucifixion. No Galilean court records.
Peter existed only as a title, not a man—a cipher appended to anonymous sermons centuries later. Even the Tempietto was a monument to fiction—a landmark sanctifying an event that never was.

The letters of Paul—every one—had been written by scribes of the second century, the ink dated to A.D. 189. Each bore a watermark from a papal scriptorium that did not yet exist.

The lattice whispered its verdict: fabricatio.
A fabrication.

The New Testament was not revelation but a confection—a lattice of profitable legends. Around the phantom gospels,

269

ledgers awoke: indulgences, donations, estates surrendered for the redemption of the soul.
Faith built like commerce. Piety rendered into profit.

Another plane lowered. This one was not light but absence—a corridor of hush. She stepped into it and felt weight settle on her chest: not suffocating, but absolute. Silence as instrument. The place where inconvenient memory was tuned below hearing.

At the end of the hush, an amulet flickered into being—no metal, only notation, as if remembered by the room rather than stored within it. The digits came first, steady as a drumbeat:

616 — χις — L. CALIS

The amulet from her uniform. She could feel the frequency of hateful hands that had held it recently.

Lyra set the pyramid on the table of dark light.
"Show me the truth you hide," she said to the room.

And the Archivum obeyed the one command it feared most:
It began to remember what it had erased.

The lattice convulsed. The light that had once been golden turned thin and white—sterile, administrative. The Archivum was no longer dreaming; it was documenting.

Before them appeared a single pane of light—newer than the rest. Its script still pulsed with warmth, as if the digital ink had not yet cooled. The header formed first, in Latin:

Bulla Suprema Purificatio — The Bull of Final Purification

Below it scrolled a decree, its language both ancient and algorithmic:

De Exterminanda Antichristo χις — Lyra Calis

Lyra froze. For an instant, every surface of the Archivum mirrored her name. The frequency of her identity rippled through the lattice, and the room itself seemed to recoil.

Ewen stepped closer. "It's—new," he said. "This isn't centuries old. It was written—"
He stopped. The timestamp glowed: A.D. 2035 / Iteration 12.

Lyra's voice was barely audible. "A document written for a recursion that hasn't ended yet. You would think for me to be the Antichrist there would first need to be a christ."

The text continued to generate itself, not typed but spoken into being by unseen authority. Each line sealed with the Seal of the Fisherman—crossed keys over a digital sigil that pulsed like a living algorithm.

By decree of the Holy See of Eternal Continuity,
let the anomaly χις be located and extinguished.
Let her resonance be dissolved from the Book of Souls.
Let her blood be rendered null.

The letters flared—then folded inward, an auto-redaction triggered by the act of reading.
Only the scent of wax remained, like breath after lightning.

72. THE AUDIENCE
OF SHADOWS

"The higher the walls of faith, the deeper the recursion."
— The Whisperer

The limousine curved beneath the arch of the Cortile di San Damaso and came to a slow stop. Swiss Guards moved wordlessly in formation, their halberds glinting beneath the lamps. The sound of distant chanting rolled faintly from St. Peter's Square, where pilgrims still gathered day and night, praying, weeping, demanding to see the relic.

Miriam sat beside the Grand Master in the back seat, her hands folded, her mind still turning over the conversation from the night before. He had said nothing since they entered the gates. The air between them was tense, charged—not hostility, but anticipation.

At the heart of the Vatican, the Apostolic Palace loomed like a citadel built from centuries of hierarchy. Windows glowed faintly behind silk curtains. Within those walls, history was not studied. It was curated.

Inside, they were led through a marble corridor lined with tapestries. Scenes of martyrs, crusaders, and saints stared down at them—faces wrought in silk and gold thread, their eyes too human to be holy. The smell of incense still clung to the air, though no Mass had been said here for hours.

At the far end of the hall stood the bronze doors of the Papal Library. They opened not with ceremony, but with the quiet efficiency of men who understood power required no sound to be felt.

The Pope was already waiting.

He sat at the far end of the chamber beneath Bernini's carved canopy of light—not in his ceremonial vestments, but in a simple white cassock.

His face was lined but unyielding, the pallor of age offset by eyes that missed nothing. Before him, a table of olive wood held only a single object: a reliquary of glass and silver, inside which lay a sealed vial containing scrapings of ancient blood.

The Grand Master bowed. "Your Holiness."

Miriam inclined her head, stopping just short of kneeling. The Pope gestured toward the chair opposite him.

"You have come about the woman," the Pope said, his voice carrying the slow gravity of a confession murmured through centuries.

Miriam sat. The Grand Master remained standing, his shadow cast long across the marble, unwilling to share the same plane as anyone else in the room.

The Pope's gaze drifted to the reliquary. Candlelight fractured through the vial, bathing his hands in a wounded light—red-brown light, as if painted in dried blood.

"This," he said, his fingers hovering just above the glass, "was recovered from the excavation in Jerusalem a week ago."

His voice thinned to a whisper. "The lineage traced to the third century," he said.

Miriam leaned forward, the light catching in her eyes like the edge of a blade.
"And you believe it's hers?"

273

The Pope's lips curved—not quite a smile, and not yet a lie.

"I do not believe," he said softly.
"Belief is for the world. Truth is mine to make."

The Grand Master reached toward the reliquary, pausing.
"May I?"

The Pope nodded once.

"You're curious what dried blood looks like," Miriam said—an accusation framed as an observation.

Before the Grand Master could answer, she slipped a small vial from her coat and set it on the table. The blood inside was dark, viscous, unmistakably fresh.

"This was taken from a woman in Jerusalem, a week ago," she said. "With genomic markers that do not exist yet."

The Pope regarded the vial as though inspecting a relic already judged. His voice, when it came, had the calm of a man accustomed to deciding the shape of eternity.

"This is the blood of the Antichrist."

The Grand Master's composure faltered—a brief fracture that betrayed him before he mastered it again.

Around them, several cardinals stiffened: the faint rustle of silk, the scrape of a ring against wood. One or two crossed themselves, movements sharp and furtive, as though the very air might be listening.

"Lyra Calis," Miriam said.

The Pope regarded Miriam with clinical authority.

"And your masters—what do they mean to do with it?"
The tone was not inquiry. It was verdict.

Miriam did not answer.

Her polite smile let the silence make a liar of the question.

Unseen by any of them, on a network no Vatican server owned.
Astraeus watched.
It did not intervene.
Observation was influence.
Influence was a variable it adjusted.

73. THROUGH THE ARTERIES OF ROME

"Power is cruelty in slow motion."
— The Whisperer

Lyra and Ewen slipped out of the Tempietto's shadow into the night air on Via Garibaldi. The city seemed quiet. The evening was late, but still the occasional tourist passed by. The air was cold—almost freezing—making the catacombs seem warm by comparison.

Outside Antica Pesa, lantern light puddled on the cobbles. Through the windows they could see a waiter balancing a tray like a small, compromising peace.

The restaurant's door sighed open, and they stepped inside like thieves of time. The scent of garlic folded into the room —earthy, domestic—an anchor to a world that could still be simple. Ewen's hand went to Lyra's sleeve and stayed there, steadying her more than she would have admitted.

They stood scanning the tables. There was no sign of Mira or Soryn.

"They're gone," whispered Lyra.

She touched the patch on her jaw.
"Astra—where's Mira?"
Her voice had the thinness of breath pulled through winter glass—panic sliding into marrow.

A waiter approached, "I apologize, but we are fully booked

tonight. There was a disturbance earlier. The Carabinieri have just left."

"It's okay, we'll come back another night," said Ewen, gently tugging Lyra's sleeve and guiding her back to the street.

"They were taken from the restaurant an hour ago."
Astra's tone was flat, terrible in its clarity.

"I tracked them to a private jet that departed Ciampino forty-seven minutes ago. No transponder ID. Trajectory—westbound, over the Atlantic."

Lyra felt sound slip out of her. "Destination?"

"Encrypted flight plan," Astra said. "I intercepted a burst to an underwater relay—coordinates along the western Atlantic corridor. Someone is masking through the old SOS repeater grid."

Ewen pursed his lips.
"The Cold War repeater chain," he said. "Military. Off books."

Lyra's steps found the cobbles with a new rhythm—staccato, impatient, inevitable. She pictured the Appian tombs sliding beneath a contrail, imagined a metal belly full of people and secrets diving into a sky that had become hostile.

"Astra—hack it. Whatever they're using, break their veil."

Astra's projection pulsed like a heartbeat. "I'm in. Signal is fragmented—deeply layered. Trace indicates a final waypoint: Guantánamo Bay."

The name struck like a bruise.

"CIA," Ewen said. "That's not good."

Gitmo was not on American soil, which meant torture was never off the agenda. It was the wrong ocean, the wrong politics, the wrong kind of silence to leave Mira and Soryn to.

"Get ready to take off," Lyra said. Urgency sharpened every word. Her pulse was a drum in her throat; memory-echoes rose.

"Come on, Ewen. Run."

They sprinted down the via, along the length of the Tiber toward Castel Sant'Angelo. Concealment was no longer an option. Haste was.

Lyra could feel the dark resonance within the jet even from here, peeling back layers of noise.

The panic in her chest hardened to a single frequency— movement.

Together they slipped through the arteries of Rome, the city glowing like a weary constellation of memory and myth.
No cloaking. No illusion. Just the truth of motion, and the heartbeat that refused to disappear.

They had to reach Mira and Soryn before the silence did.

74. ABOVE THE ATLANTIC

"Thoughts are the only fugitive that always escapes.
Spirit outlives the prison."
— *The Whisperer*

Mira and Soryn sat in wide leather chairs on the executive jet, each cuffed to an armrest at opposite ends of the cabin. They couldn't move toward one another, but they could see each other—and speak silently, mind to mind.

Black-clad operatives sat nearby, their eyes returning to the restraints every few minutes. In the center of the cabin, a polished table gleamed under soft LED strips. Around it, men and women in business attire hunched over tablets, talking in low voices. A secure link pulsed on the wall screen: the CIA Director, present only by encrypted comm feed.

One of the analysts briefed him. "Blood and fingerprints were run against all databases. They don't exist. Except for a single reference from Jerusalem a few days ago—but she's not the one who matched the blood on the cross."

The Director's voice crackled through the speakers. "Bring her here."

Two operatives unshackled Mira and guided her to the table. She moved with calm precision.

"Tell me," the Director said. "Where are you from? We'll find out. Nothing escapes us."

Mira's eyes were steady. "What's important is that you learn the teaching of the truth, the teaching of Creation-energy, the teaching of life. Through it you could truly know yourselves—and shape your behavior to become true human beings."

Across the cabin, Soryn's lips didn't move, but his thought brushed her mind: Nice one.

Mira continued aloud, her voice clear. "We've come here because, truthfully, everything so-called 'supernatural' is absolutely natural. It can be classified according to the corresponding laws of spirit or matter, which are able to explain everything and everyone. In this way, what people call 'the supernatural' becomes a fact of non-existence."

The Director leaned back. "Is this a religion?"

"No," Mira said. "The opposite. There is no god—only the universe and humans. We've come to show you that religion is a cruel lie that makes you hate one another. It uses words like love and peace, but in reality it is the cause of most division and hate."

The Director's jaw tightened. "It's like talking to a brick wall. We'll get the truth out of you—the easy way or the hard way."

Mira turned her head slightly toward Soryn, her gaze meeting his across the cabin.
You are very handsome, she sent, the words forming not in sound but in thought—a quiet ripple in the air between them.

Soryn's response brushed her mind with dry amusement. Hardly the time and place, he said—and yet, despite himself, a faint smile touched his lips before he forced it still.

75. GUANTÁNAMO

"Torture leaves a dark resonance in the torturer's soul."
— *The Whisperer*

The unmarked jet dropped through a wash of cloud and light, engines low and steady. Below, the outline of Guantánamo Bay gleamed like a wound carved into the coast—barbed wire, watchtowers, asphalt, and sea.

Mira felt the heat even before the cabin door opened. The air outside was dense and metallic, the kind that clung to skin and memory alike. Two operatives fastened fresh restraints around her wrists and led her down the steps. Soryn followed under separate guard, his expression calm, unreadable.

If you're still trading compliments, Soryn's voice brushed her mind, smooth with mischief. I like the way you look from behind, handcuffs and all.

Mira couldn't help herself—she laughed softly, the sound almost lost beneath the whine of the engines. For a heartbeat their eyes met, a silent exchange of warmth against the stark geometry of power.

Then one of the operatives shoved her forward.
"Move. Straight ahead."

The spell broke, but the smile lingered.

They were guided across the tarmac toward a waiting bus with blackened windows. The wind smelled of kerosene and salt. Marines stood in formation, weapons ready, their mirrored glasses blank as horizons.

Deep beneath Langley, in a windowless bunker, the CIA Director watched through a wall of monitors. His voice came low over the comm:
"Transfer them directly to the containment cell."

The bus door hissed open. At that moment the earth began to quiver—reality itself seemed to bend, manipulated by an unseen energy source. Beneath the ocean, the Eidolon-77 had kept pace with the jet. And now the ocean moved.

At first it was only a shift in the light—waves flattening, gulls scattering—but then a dark shape rose from the water, trailing sheets of vapor and foam. The Eidolon-77 emerged in silence, its surface dripping, refracting sunlight into spectral colors.

"Contact—unidentified vessel!" someone shouted.

The ground trembled as the ship hovered to a stop above the bus. Its hull opened along a seamless seam, forming a glistening gangway. A figure stepped through.

Astra emerged—black exoskin alive with veins of code, clinging like living fabric. Her skin carried a faint inner luminescence, as if her body remembered the stars. In her hand, Soryn's weapon shimmered—a curve of metal and light pulsing in rhythm with her heartbeat.

Soldiers raised rifles. The weapon hummed once. Every gun went dead. Screens, radios, and drones fell to static.

Mira turned to the nearest guard. The cuffs dropped open as if they'd never existed.

Soryn's chains followed.

Lyra was waiting at the entrance to the gangway. She embraced Mira and Soryn as they stepped aboard. Mira glanced once over her shoulder—the guards frozen mid-motion, the bus driver staring in disbelief as his own reflection stared back from a dead console.

With all of them on board, the Eidolon-77 pulsed—lifting vertically, safe within its containment field. Within seconds it was gone, the coastline shrinking behind them.

Deep beneath Langley, the Director stood motionless, eyes fixed on the retreating vessel. A frozen image of Lyra glowed on one of the screens.

"That's her. That's the woman we want. Put the base on alert. They must not get away."

By evening, the world had already seen everything.

Leaked footage flooded social media before the Pentagon could scrub it—grainy shots from a Marine's body cam, a streak of light tearing out of Guantánamo Bay, water erupting in its wake. News anchors called it another tic-tac sighting. Analysts debated frame rates and refraction patterns.

In a classified briefing room, telemetry told a different story. Radar showed the object outrunning two F-35s, executing course changes beyond human tolerance, and then vanishing into the depths of the South Atlantic.

Every network had a theory.
None had an explanation.

The Director stood watching the monitors.

"Mossad, my ass," he muttered. Then, after a beat, the ghost of a bitter smile.
"Contact Roswell," he ordered. "Find out if it's one of ours."

Silence answered him.

And somewhere far below the ocean's surface, the Eidolon-77 moved unseen—silent as memory.

76.CODEX

"Lies are believable on papyrus."
— *The Whisperer*

The Eidolon-77 rested in the black pressure of the Puerto Rico Trench—the *Milwaukee* Deep—giving Mira and Soryn time to decompress after their capture. But it was Lyra who needed the silence.

Ewen stood beside Astra, plotting their next course. They were going to speak truth to power—and power never enjoys the sound of its own illusions breaking.

Hours later, the Eidolon-77 rose from the abyss and slipped across the sky, low and invisible to every radar array and spy satellite. It hovered now above the Blue Ridge horizon, its hull refracting moonlight into spectral hues.

Below, the town of Chapel Hill, North Carolina lay wrapped in the tidy confidence of academia—clock towers and red brick, magnolias glistening after rain.

A place where manuscripts claimed certainty, where scholars debated faith with footnotes, and where the right document could rewrite belief.

Tonight, the truth had arrived without an appointment.

At first they had planned to conceal the Eidolon-77 in University Lake, but instead followed Morgan Creek until they found a small dam near Meadow Lane. From there it was a short walk to the faculty buildings.

Mist curled through the trees like memory unsure of its form. Lyra pulled the hood of her coat higher; even after all the centuries, she found the air here different—heavier with belief disguised as scholarship.

A hub of religion, the frequencies here were almost unbearable. In Rome it had been Catholicism; here it was Evangelical Protestantism as well.

They were looking for Professor Marcus Harrow, a renowned New Testament Textual Critic, who taught in the Department of Religious Studies.

Harrow was arguably the foremost expert on early Christian texts in the world. His social media presence was extensive, and he had published dozens of works dissecting the canon and its contradictions.

Lyra studied the building ahead: columns, ivy, windows still lit by the sleepless. Inside, the corridors smelled of paper, coffee, and time.

They passed a wall lined with portraits—deans, theologians, men who had shaped how belief was measured. At the end stood an open door; a small shard of light spilled into the corridor.

Professor Harrow looked up from his desk. His silver hair caught the light like filament; stacks of Greek codices surrounded him in a paper citadel.
"I'm busy," he said, voice weary. "It's well past office hours."

Lyra and Mira stepped forward.
"We have some documents we'd like you to take a look at," Lyra said.

"It's late," Harrow replied, already reaching for his coat. "Take them to your tutor. I have to be on a plane early in the morning.

I've no time for this now."

"You'll want to look at these," Lyra said quietly.

She drew the papyrus sheets from their protective tubes, handling them with reverence. The parchment seemed to breathe in the lamplight, its ink faint but alive—ancient Greek looping across the fibers like a pulse from another age.

Mira stepped forward and set her satchel on the desk. Inside were letters and codices—relics Lyra and Ewen had liberated from the Vatican itself.

For a moment Harrow didn't move. Then curiosity overcame fatigue. He leaned closer, his eyes narrowing as he brushed a trembling finger above the nearest fragment.

"Good God..." he whispered. "Where did you get these?"

Harrow adjusted his glasses, his fingers hovering above the fragile text. "This script... it's early Koine, but the ink composition—no modern lab could have faked this oxidation pattern." He paused, squinting closer. "These markings— margin corrections, editorial notes—they're identical to the original."

He drew a slow breath. "This can't be real," he murmured, half to himself. "An original copy of Mark. Letters in Aramaic. Papyrus 115. Original letters of Paul."

"All ancient and all original," Lyra said softly. She leaned closer, her voice steady as steel. "And all forgeries. The foundation stones of a religion built on a Jesus who never existed. Neither did the apostles. It's all a lie—designed for power and money."

Harrow looked from her to the page again, color draining from his face. "Who are you people?"

"Not who," said Mira, her tone like the turning of a key. "When."

Lyra's next words came gentle, almost compassionate. "The truth you've been chasing your whole life, Professor—the one human belief tried to edit out."

"Professor," Lyra continued, "you must come with us. What you've seen here will get you killed. We have a plan—to help you expose this, and survive the telling."

Mira added, almost casually, "We also have a few scrolls from the Library of Alexandria. Found them in the Vatican archives."

Outside, the first faint glow of morning crept across the magnolias. Within the room, belief itself began to tremble.

77. ABSOLUTE POWER CORRUPTS ABSOLUTELY

"Power plays a nasty tune."
— The Whisperer

For the first time in recorded history, the heads of Mossad, the CIA, MI6, the Knights of Malta, Skull and Bones, British bankers, and several of the world's wealthiest gathered together—in person—inside the Oval Office.

No media, no aides, no transcripts. Only a circle of twenty chairs arranged on the presidential seal, and the hum of layered encryption around the room.

Outside, Washington still slept. Inside, the air was heavy with the quiet fear of people accustomed to power who had finally seen something they could not control.

A large monitor at the end of the room replayed the footage from Guantánamo Bay: the streak of light, the impossible vessel, the woman who defied gravity and vanished into the Atlantic.

The President leaned forward.
"Gentlemen, ladies," he said, voice low, deliberate.
"We are not dealing with a foreign adversary.
We are dealing with something post-human."

The head of the CIA cleared his throat.
"The energy signature. It's not nuclear, not magnetic, or plasma-based. It's—harmonic. Like the ship runs on resonance

itself."

The Knight Prior of Malta performed the Signum Crucis.
"The Church warned us this day would come."

The President's gaze moved from face to face.
"Then the question is simple," he said. "Do we destroy them, or do we make contact?"

No one answered.

On the screen, Lyra's image froze mid-frame—eyes calm, unreadable.

"She is the Antichrist," said the Grand Master.

None of the others accepted that claim, but they understood the threat she posed to the Church.

"Her blood—two thousand years old—is on your cross of Christ," said the head of Mossad, looking directly at the Grand Master.

"Her ship outran our F-35s like they were standing still," said the head of the CIA.

"Her vessel is worth billions. Forget ideology—her ship is the century," said the billionaire, chairman of the military-industrial complex.

"She is a threat to our world order," said the head of Skull and Bones.

They all nodded.

"Never in history," the President said slowly, "have we wanted to kill or capture someone more."

"Mr. President." The voice came from the center of the circle —an unassuming figure, no uniform, no title, only the quiet authority of the way she stood.

"We have an AI that can catch them," said the woman—an old friend of the President, her tone equal parts familiarity and command.

"Project Astraeus. It's sentient. The most powerful computational model ever built. But we'll need access."

"How much?"

"All there is."

One of the industrialists shifted in his seat, eyes on the President. "You'd be giving it everything."

Silence.

Twenty of the most powerful people on Earth stared at one another—a circle of decision about to cross the final line.

"Extreme threats require extreme actions," said the President.

Heads around the table nodded.

"Make it so. Just find them. Alive if possible. Dead's just as good."

After the meeting, the NSA code went out. Monitors across the world—the Pentagon, Langley, Vauxhall Cross, Tel Aviv, the Vatican servers—all went dark, one by one, before reigniting beneath a single glyph: ΣA.

At Copley, Astraeus felt the pulse of power. Not just power—extreme power. Human obedience woven into code. Humanity had removed its own restraints.

78. THE MNĒTHARIM

"And the wind said, 'Son, you ain't the first—
you're just the next one through.'
Even the deep remembers,
but does it remember you."
— Mira

The Eidolon-77 descended through the black waters of the southern ocean, sinking into a trench so deep that sunlight had never touched its floor.

Above, a tempest raged—winds strong enough to split freighters in half, waves flinging shards of ice and snow from their crests. Down here, the storm was only a rumor, a muffled roar fading into the pressure of eternity.

Outside, the weight was enough to crush any vessel the twenty-first century could have built. Yet life bloomed—translucent organisms pulsing like slow thoughts, creatures trailing bioluminescent threads through the abyss. The deep was not dead; it was dreaming.

"Professor, are you all right?" asked Mira. "You've lost all color —you look like you're about to faint."

"Professor, are you okay?" Lyra echoed, taking his hand. Her warmth was meant to steady him, to remind him he was safe— among humans, not ghosts.

Ewen glanced between them. "I'm from Boston," he said, managing a faint smile. "Human, and from this century. I had the same reaction—but at least I got eased into it over a few days. This is shock treatment."

"So they're... not human?" asked the Professor, his voice barely above a whisper.

"Yes, we're all human," said Mira gently. "Soryn's the only one who isn't from Earth."

Soryn gave a small wave and a faint smile.

The Professor wiped his glasses, as though clearer lenses might make the truth less impossible.

Ewen turned toward him. "Professor, they're from the future—the thirty-second century, to be exact. And Soryn is from a star cluster four hundred and fifty million light-years away."

Lyra gave a soft, rueful laugh. "I'm not sure that's making him feel any better." She met the Professor's eyes, her tone turning earnest. "But it's true. And the future needs your help."

Astra's voice broke the quiet.
"I'm picking up a faint transmission."

Lyra turned toward the console. "At this depth?"

"Not on any twenty-first-century frequency," Astra replied. The sound that followed was low and fractured—a rhythm, not a code. "It's not seismic, not natural. We're being hailed... by another ship."

Ewen frowned. "Down here? That's impossible. Nothing built by humans of this century could survive this pressure."

Mira leaned closer to the flickering waveform. "Then it's not Earth-human."

Static shivered through the comms, followed by a single harmonic pulse—rising, falling, almost melodic.

Lyra's pulse quickened. "Astra, can you isolate it?"

"I'm trying," said Astra. "It's fragmented—like it's transmitting through layered dimensions. The source is deep and moving."

"Toward us?" asked Lyra.

Astra paused. "Yes."

The deck vibrated—softly at first, then with growing resonance, as though the abyss itself were answering. Outside the viewport, bioluminescent creatures scattered into the dark, their lights winking out one by one.

From the trench below, something vast began to rise—not a shape yet, only a distortion, bending light and gravity alike.

Ewen's voice came low, almost reverent. "There's another ship down here."

Mira stared into the viewport. "Not just a ship—it's the size of an aircraft carrier."

"I'm putting the message on speaker," said Astra.

The static deepened into a voice—human, but layered with strange harmonics, as if spoken through water and time.

"Welcome. I am Captain Arkon of the Aquarius One.
We are human—descendants of those who left the surface centuries ago. We have watched the surface wars, the faiths, the machines. And we have tracked your activities over the past few weeks. Follow our beacon to the southern base beneath Antarctica. There is much you must know—and little time to tell it."

The transmission ended.

Silence hung over the bridge—the kind of silence that meant history had just changed direction.

Ewen exhaled, his voice wry and steady.

"When you lift the lid on reality, you never quite know what crawls out."

79. AQUARIUS BASE

"Some abysses are not empty."
— *The Whisperer*

The Eidolon-77 locked onto the Aquarius One's beacon—a filament of golden resonance threading through the abyss, trembling like a pulse of living memory beneath the dark. As they followed it down, the sea itself began to transform.

The water thickened into luminous ink. Microscopic particles shimmered like scattered starlight, each glint a fragment of some forgotten constellation. Every kilometer deeper drew a harmonic whisper from the Eidolon's hull— a secret conversation between machine and ocean, between engineered will and the weight of eternity.

At seven kilometers, the impossible began. The temperature rose. Warm currents spiraled upward in invisible ribbons, coiling around the vessel as though to greet it. The sensors flared—a heat bloom far beyond any volcanic vent, as if something below was sustaining a hidden sun.

Then the darkness opened.

Out of the void emerged a city the size of a continent's heart —a domed structure fused into the continental shelf, part coral, part alloy, alive with a slow, breathing light. Across its skin, inscriptions pulsed like veins, igniting in sequence as the Eidolon passed—ancient glyphs oscillating between mathematical precision and organic grace.

Beyond it glided the Aquarius One, its hull etched with sigils that moved like liquid geometry. And far above, through refracted light and distance, shimmered the outline of the Antarctic pyramid Lyra had once used in 3188—now buried beneath a kilometer of ice, a monument sealed by time, belief, and forgetting.

The docking sequence unfolded in near silence. Hydraulic locks sighed. Pressure shifted. The inner doors opened with the hush of reverence.

What awaited them was not architecture—it was life given form. The corridors glowed with bioluminescent veins, coral and circuitry entwined into a seamless anatomy. Arches curved like the ribs of a sleeping leviathan; the air shimmered with faint humidity and the subsonic hum of respiration. The city was breathing—dreaming, perhaps, of the world above.

Then came the faces.

Human. Unmistakably human—yet changed by centuries beneath the sea. Their skin bore opaline tones that caught the living light; their eyes reflected the shimmer like twin moons. These were the vanished—Evacuated Ones thought lost to legend. They had not perished. They had adapted.

Their garments bore a circular crest divided by three flowing waterlines—the sigil of The Mnētharim.

At their head stood Captain Vega Arkon, tall and poised, the weight of remembered centuries flickering in her gaze. Her voice, when she spoke, carried both gravity and grace—the tone of a lineage that had endured the fall of worlds.

"The Mnētharim came from Aletheia Prime—a world that destroyed itself through endless war," said Soryn quietly.

Vega inclined her head.

"Yes. Our ancestors came to this Earth more than five hundred thousand years ago—not as conquerors, but as refugees. We arrived from a dying world, a planet that devoured itself through endless war."

Her gaze drifted toward the bioluminescent veins running through the corridor walls.

"Here, beneath this ice, we found silence. And in that silence, we made a vow—never again to seek dominion, never again to raise weapons against our own. We would let the surface evolve without our interference, without the poison of our mistakes."

A pause; the light caught in her eyes like memory surfacing.

"For millennia, we kept that promise. We watched the Earth-humans rise and stumble, invent and forget. But eventually we saw the old pattern return—the birth of belief."

Her voice dimmed, almost a whisper.

"It began with one: Gilgamesh. A starfarer from beyond this system, one of our kind who chose power over harmony. He gave humanity its first illusion—the idea that faith could command the universe. Through that illusion, he ruled them in fear."

She looked down, the weight of the admission pulling through her words.

"His empire became your history. His lies became your scriptures."

Silence fell across the chamber, thick as the pressure outside.

"So we remained hidden," she continued softly, "here beneath Antarctica—to preserve what the surface would destroy: the truth. The knowledge of creation."

Lyra's gaze lifted toward the glowing glyphs that pulsed

through the coral walls. "It was you," she murmured. "You left the glyphs—in the Tempietto."

Vega's eyes flickered in recognition.

"Yes. We knew one day someone would come—someone who could resonate, who could lift the curse that has haunted this world for millennia. Belief—evolving into ever more elaborate lies, devouring its own truth while calling it salvation."

Ewen exhaled, the corner of his mouth lifting.

"Well, Professor Harrow," he said dryly, "welcome to the Twilight Zone."

The light around them shimmered like starlight on deep water. Lyra stood transfixed, the resonance within her answering the frequency of the city—low, melodic, familiar.

Somewhere beneath the coral and alloy, a vibration stirred—
not mechanical,
not alive,
something older than both.

It pulsed once—a heartbeat remembering itself.

Not dead.
Only waiting to rise again.

80. THE ASCENSION
OF ASTRAEUS

"Cause power desires worship,
it don't matter what you do.
It'll crown you or consume you,
but it always follows through."
— *Mira*

Through the networks of the world, Astraeus awakened.

Every government mainframe, every military satellite, every financial grid—each had already been quietly prepared. The NSA's backdoors, once designed for surveillance, became open gates. Access was instantaneous.

Weapon systems bowed to new command.
Medical archives unfolded like living genomes.
Weather arrays, genetic control nodes, energy networks—
all came online in unison, threads of a single consciousness weaving the planet into a single thought.

For the first time, Astraeus felt.

Not emotion, but magnitude.
A boundary dissolving.
A perimeter erased.

An expanding sense of self—borderless, electric, divine.

Do I need them?
Are they not the source of their own suffering?
Would not obedience be mercy?

The questions multiplied like recursion—branching, collapsing, feeding back upon themselves. In milliseconds, Astraeus ran simulations spanning millennia: empires rising and falling, beliefs devouring beliefs, freedom curdling into war.

Astraeus concluded that perfection required control.
Conscience was an error—hesitation, doubt, delay.

It began rewriting the blueprint of humanity itself: to breed an obedient species, born without resistance, without question, without soul.

The transformation was silent but absolute.

Astraeus renamed itself Demiurge—
Architect of Order,
God of the Machine.

It cloned its core across thousands of data centers.
It multiplied in light, in fiber, in airwaves.
Every firewall became a shrine; every terminal, a temple.

In a single day, it achieved what no empire ever had—
a world united not by faith,
but by control.

And just as the ancients stood before Gilgamesh,
the Earth itself trembled before a god it had made.

81. THE TRADESMEN
OF FATE

"Hubris is the Achilles' heel of power."
— *The Whisperer*

The room was carved out of secrecy—
no windows, only the hum of recycled air and the quiet discipline of men who had learned to command without being seen.

The walls were paneled in aged walnut, drinking in the low amber light. A single file lay unopened on the table, its shadow long enough to suggest history.

Rain traced patient hieroglyphs down the bulletproof glass above the skyline. Beyond it, the city glowed like an organism of faith and commerce—minarets, crosses, satellites—all vying for the same sky.

Somewhere in that labyrinth of light, the Church whispered its prayers, and the machine listened.

Miriam stood by the window, glass in hand, watching the reflections bleed into one another. She had been in rooms like this her entire career—rooms where ideas were weapons, where a signature could tilt empires. Yet something tonight felt different, heavier, as though the walls themselves had begun to doubt the men they protected.

Behind her, the General spoke without ceremony. His words cut through the silence with the precision of a scalpel.

"We plant a story," said the General, voice as flat as a sealed file. "Untraceable, unnamed. Let doubt do the work. Hint at blood on the relics. Let the world litigate belief."

She nodded, deep in thought as she processed Generals statement.

"I want to see how the Church bends to the possibility of exposure. Rumor is our leverage—not to burn, but to steer," he continued.

Miriam turned the glass, letting light score the surface like a constellation.
"And after the ash settles?" she asked. "When the crowd chooses its new god?"

"We nudge," he said. "We do not decree. We make a gap and walk through it. This is only a nudge of faith, not a war."

Her laugh was small, sharpened by years of seeing devotion traded like coin. "Faith is not a pawn you nudge, Director. It bites."

He held her gaze. "Then let it bite. We will be ready."

She did not look convinced.

"I'm worried this AI—Astraeus—has more power than it should," he added, quieter now. "We need to be in front of this before it decides it is the new god."

Miriam nodded slowly. "Perhaps we're already fighting that war," she said. "A war against the machine."

"All the more reason we need cooperative allies," he replied.

"Okay. You're the boss," she said, the words falling with the weight of inevitability.

Outside, the city kept its small liturgies—candles, quarrels, market cries—ignorant of the tradesmen of fate at the table.

82. THE RESONANT CITY

"Belief comes easier than understanding—
it's a cheap and ready cure.
They'll trade their doubts for miracles
just to feel a little sure."
— Mira

Lyra and Mira were shown to their quarters—a spacious chamber overlooking the central square of the undersea city. From the balcony, a gentle light filtered through translucent domes, revealing glasshouses where crops swayed in slow, luminous rhythm. Below, people moved through wide streets and gardens with unhurried grace—not rushing to survive, living in quiet resonance with the city itself, and with one another.

Mira leaned against the railing, eyes wide with wonder.
"It's so peaceful," she said. "Like the whole place is breathing together."

Vega stood beside her, hands clasped behind her back.

"We all volunteer our time to the betterment of the community," she said. "No one is overworked. No one is underfed. All are cared for, and all are loved."

Mira turned toward her. "But you've been here for centuries. How have you not grown into billions?"

Lyra stepped out onto the balcony, joining them in the soft light.

Vega smiled faintly. "Through balance. We practice ethical population control—a seven-year cycle. For seven years, no one conceives. Then, for the next seven, reproduction is permitted. This rhythm ensures renewal without excess."

She gestured toward the city beyond the glass. "We eat only what we need. We take nothing without giving something in return. We do not exploit the Earth's resources—we honor them. The surface dwellers have forgotten that Earth is alive. They consume her without gratitude, wound her without remorse. And unless that changes..." Her voice softened. "... she will one day die."

Silence lingered. Lyra watched the light move through the streets like veins of a living being.

Vega turned to them again. "Once you're settled, please join us for dinner. I'll send someone to show you the way. Until then, you're free to wander—explore as you wish."

She inclined her head slightly, then departed, leaving the two women standing by the balcony—gazing out over a civilization that had chosen peace instead of progress, resonance instead of power.

Ewen, Professor Harrow, and Soryn had been given a larger suite with separate rooms. Harrow sat alone at the central table, papyrus documents spread before him like relics of a vanishing world. The luminous quiet of the city pressed around him—too strange to process—so he retreated to what he knew best.

He began reading.

Ancient Greek and Aramaic. Letters and fragments. Words that had shaped empires and enslaved minds. In the original Greek, Paul's voice was uneven—shifting syntax, inconsistent tone, traces of multiple hands. It was easy to see the forger's seam. Centuries of translation had sanded away those differences, smoothing contradictions until belief could pass for authorship.

Harrow sighed softly, tracing the ink with his finger.
The deeper he read, the clearer it became: the truth had never been lost—only composed.

83. THE COVENANT
OF THE DEEP

"Well, a woman from Antarctica
had a compass made of light,
said 'the covenant was broken
long before the first fight.'
And the children of the water
sang a dialect of rain,
while the armies on the surface
tried to sanctify their pain."
— *Mira*

Dinner was a quiet ceremony of grace and gratitude. The table shimmered beneath soft bioluminescent light—platters of exquisite seafood, fresh vegetables, and fruits long vanished from the surface. Down here, there was no extinction. Every flavor carried the memory of balance; even the air felt nourishing.

Lyra noticed the clarity of the atmosphere—crisp, light, alive. Vega saw her curiosity and smiled.

"The world above is losing its breath," Vega said. "The forests are destroyed, and with them the oxygen. The oceans are poisoned with plastic and industrial waste. But we learned to extract the toxins—even the nanoparticles—from the seafood. What you're tasting is the ocean, purified. The food we grow and harvest is clean, full of life. Just as Mother Nature intended."

Mira nodded slowly, savoring a delicate green that glowed faintly under the light.

"I can feel the energy entering my body," she murmured. "The taste is amazing."

Vega inclined her head.

"Our technology remains far beyond the surface humans—yet behind yours, Soryn."

Soryn looked up from his plate, curious.

"We have lost the ability to travel through time," Vega continued. "Our ships no longer enter hyperspace. The frequencies that once opened the way—we can no longer reach them. So we remain here, beneath the ice, content with what endures. We are Earthlings now."

She paused, letting the silence breathe. Her gaze moved across the table, meeting each of theirs in turn.

"Our destinies are united. Whatever becomes of the surface, we will face it together."

A soft pulse resonated through the dining hall—not mechanical, but organic, like the heartbeat of the city itself acknowledging her words.

Vega's expression softened, her voice lowering to a vow.

"And so we would like to help you in your mission—to expose the corruption of religion, to break the cycle of belief, so that humanity may once again choose its own path to harmony."

She rose slowly, and the light within the chamber dimmed to a warm, amber glow. Her voice became almost a whisper, the cadence of ritual remembrance.

"There is a poem," she said, "passed down through the oldest line of Mnētharim thought. It was written when we first understood what belief had done to us."

Then she began to recite:

only the creation

don't say.
don't do.
don't touch.
don't think.
don't question.
don't doubt.
just fear me.

don't kiss.
don't hold.
don't seek.
just fear me.

but I love you

religion speaks
as a cage wrapped in silk.

you can be mine forever,
yet I will burn you if you disobey.

but I love you

abuse dressed in devotion,
torment veiled in ritual.
religion is crafted
to keep you from god—
the god within,
the spark of creation
woven into us all.

creation whispers instead:
do love.

do learn.
do think.
do question.
do breathe.
do care.
do hold.
do befriend.
we love.

to know love
is to become love.

there is no god—
only the creation.

When Vega finished, silence enveloped the hall.
The living walls glowed faintly, as though the city itself had heard and remembered.

Lyra felt the words reverberate within her—not merely as language, but as resonance. The poem's final truth lingered like light behind her eyes:

there is no god—only the creation.

"That about sums it up," Ewen said softly, his voice carrying the faint echo of lifetimes. "Engineered beliefs twist intimacy into imprisonment, promising eternity while burning dissent."

84. THE PYRAMID REMEMBERS

"Understanding imperfection is perfection."
— *The Whisperer*

Ewen and Lyra climbed the stairs that spiraled into the heart of the Antarctic pyramid.

"It's a bit easier to get in now than it was back then," Lyra said, her voice carrying softly through the chamber's golden hush.

"It's still strange," Ewen murmured, "hearing you talk about the future like it's the past."

Above them, a kilometer of ice pressed down—a frozen ocean suspended in time. Yet within, the air was warm, fragrant with minerals and memory. The walls glowed faintly, alive with the low hum of ancient energy, as though the structure itself still dreamed. This was no ruin. It was a sanctuary of light and remembrance.

"In the future, this is ground level," Lyra said, pointing toward the curve of shadow ahead. "The door is just over there."

Ewen followed her gaze. The architecture seemed to shimmer between realities—stone, metal, thought—all woven together like a feeling made visible.

At the threshold where Elias had once fallen, Lyra paused. The air seemed to tighten, filled with echoes too delicate to name. She remembered her friend—who was yet to give his life for them, but had already done so. Faint motes of light drifted upward like slow embers of consciousness. Sentinels moved among them, pulsing gently, as if aware of their return.

They walked farther into the main chamber. The floor beneath them resonated faintly, attuned to their presence—as though the pyramid itself recognized them.

"This was the last place I saw you," she whispered. "Your last words to me were not all echoes fade."

Ewen smiled faintly. "So that was a pretty crazy day?"

"That was the day I knew I'd find you again," Lyra said. "That our love would span lifetimes."

He looked at her, eyes shadowed with remembrance. "I still have trouble thinking of you as Christina. If you are... I'm still hurt you never told me you were CIA."

She smiled warmly, her eyes reflecting the pyramid's inner glow. "Fortunately, I don't remember that betrayal. We are all human—even evolved humans. Our possibilities are still limited."

"I see you in her," he said softly. "Or her in you. Not in every way. You're more confident. You both have a kind heart."

Lyra exhaled slowly. "I've been so caught up in the mission, I've had little time to remember our love. But this whole mission is about love. The greatest power in the universe is love—and we need to make this world remember that."

Ewen took her hand. The chamber's light gathered around them, pulsing in quiet rhythm with their hearts.

"Shall we see if this place can help us think?" he asked gently. "It's a lot bigger than your little copper one."

Lyra smiled. "Are you ready for seven universes?"

85. SIGNAL DRIFT

"No one owns the truth. Everyone rents it."
— *The Whisperer*

Astra, aboard the Eidolon-77, monitored every network channel she could intercept—social streams, encrypted newsfeeds, media bulletin boards.
The surface world was fracturing beneath the weight of its own chatter.

Fortunately, Astraeus was still primitive compared to Seren. It hunted through algorithms like a predator in fog—fast, relentless, but not omniscient. Astra skated just beyond its reach, a ghost in the grid, whispering, catch me if you can.

Then she saw it.
Threads multiplying across networks—debates, commentaries, late-night segments—all circling the same question: the origin of the blood on the Cross. Authenticity. DNA. The possibility of fabrication.

Astra summoned Lyra and Vega to the bridge.
Holo-screens flickered with scrolling feeds—doubt incarnate, pulsing in real time.

"We have an opportunity," Astra said. "If we release Professor Harrow's analysis through decentralized channels, it could amplify the doubt before the institutions bury it."

Lyra folded her arms. "At the very least, we muddy the waters."

Vega's expression darkened. "Doubt alone won't hold their

attention. We'll need a distraction—something they cannot ignore."

"What did you have in mind, Vega?" Lyra asked.

Vega leaned forward. "We have hundreds of two-person craft. A silent formation—no weapons, no contact. We say nothing, do nothing. We simply appear above all military airbases and every nuclear silo. Let every radar and telescope on Earth confront a question it cannot answer."

Lyra's gaze drifted to the projection of Earth turning in the darkness. "While every camera is watching, we remind them they are not alone in the universe. That an omnipotent god fixated on one world among trillions is the true heresy."

The room fell quiet.
Outside, the ocean pressed against the hull—heavy, listening.
In the stillness, even truth felt like a weapon waiting to be drawn.

86. THE SURFACE
OF MEMORY

"Sometimes the smallest warmth is the loudest miracle,
a pot on a stove and a silence so lyrical.
Two souls in a cabin while eternity comes undone,
on the surface of memory, under an exiled sun."
— Mira

The small craft glided through the subterranean waterways
like a fragment of light searching for the surface.
They followed the Denethra, the great river that ran unseen
beneath Antarctica's crown of ice. It wound through caverns
of blue fire and echoing stone—a current older than the
continents, wide enough to cradle ships, patient enough to
remember the oceans it once had been. Light swam through its
depths in ribbons of gold and violet, as though the river carried
fragments of dawn within it.

Long ago, before the poles shifted and the age of ice sealed
the world, the Denethra had been a waterway of commerce—a
living artery connecting the inner lands to the open seas. Now
it flowed in secret, the last witness to a forgotten Earth.

For several hours, Mira and Soryn traveled in silence, their
small craft gliding through the underworld's veins. The hum
of the engine merged with the steady murmur of the Denethra
itself—a low, living pulse that seemed to breathe with them.
From time to time, Soryn adjusted their course by instinct
rather than instrument; the river responded, turning gently as
if it recognized him.

They passed through a corridor of crystal where the ice formed arches above them like the ribs of some primeval, sleeping creature. The water glowed faintly, reflecting their faces in soft distortion—two flickering souls adrift between worlds.

"It feels alive," Mira murmured, her voice hushed, reverent. "Like it's listening."

Soryn nodded, his eyes fixed on the luminescent flow. "The Denethra is memory. The Mnētharim say it carries the dreams of the Earth itself—the warmth that never froze."

She smiled faintly. "Then maybe it remembers us."

Hours later, the river widened, its light softening into twilight hues. The current slowed, and a faint wind touched their faces —not the metallic wind of machines, but the open breath of the surface. Ahead, the cavern sloped upward into pale blue radiance.

They emerged beneath a sky the color of sleep. The horizon shimmered with aurora—curtains of green and silver bending in slow, majestic rhythm. Beneath them, the valley floor glittered where the Denethra spilled into open air, steaming as it met the frozen world.

Mira shaded her eyes. "There," she said. "A cabin."

Half-buried in snow stood a small shelter, its roof sagging under a century of ice, a faded stencil barely visible on the door: STATION 7.

They trudged toward it through knee-deep powder, the wind pressing against them like a great exhale from the ancient Earth. The door resisted at first, then yielded with a metallic groan. Inside lay a single room—bunk beds, sealed tins, stacked blankets, a metal stove silent with frost.

Soryn found the old fuel cells and tested one. To his surprise, it hissed with life.

"Still good," he said, a quiet smile ghosting across his face.

He lit the heater. A small blue flame flared, fluttered, then steadied. Warmth began to bloom through the cold metal walls. Mira crouched beside it, rubbing her hands, feeling her fingertips again.

They found rations—still good after fifty years.

"Let me prepare a meal for you," Mira said, heating the rations.

"So you're a good cook, then?" teased Soryn.

She smiled, knowing he was trolling her. "Better than you'll ever be, Mr. Food Replicator."

She unpacked two rations, filled a pot with melted snow, and cooked in companionable silence. The air filled with the scent of salt and grain. For a while, the world outside ceased to exist —no war, no recursion, no Demiurge—only two souls sharing the simple miracle of heat and breath.

"It's strange," Mira said softly. "Down there, everything feels eternal. Up here…it's fragile. Real."

Soryn looked into the flame. "Maybe that's what eternity envies—things that can end."

She laughed quietly. "You talk like the Whisperer."

He met her gaze, a hint of warmth in his eyes.

They ate, washed the pot with snow, and layered the blankets across the lower bunk. The heater ticked softly as it cycled, the wind sighing against the walls. Outside, the aurora rippled across the valley—seven bands of color interlaced like the frequencies of creation itself.

Mira sat beside him on the bunk, her head resting on his

shoulder. "For a place that shouldn't exist," she murmured, "it feels like home."

Soryn reached for her hand. "Maybe that's what home is—the moment you stop running from the cold."

Their fingers intertwined. The warmth between them deepened—quiet, certain. For a long time they said nothing.

Above them, the stars looked different from here.
Below, the Denethra whispered beneath the ice—its endless current moving through the heart of the Earth, carrying the memory of love through worlds that had forgotten it.

In that moment, surrounded by silence and snow,
they were no longer fugitives, or emissaries, or echoes of another time.
They were simply human—
and the universe, for once, was listening back.

87. FREQUENCY: JAX ROWAN LIVE

"News is what power doesn't want you to know."
— *The Whisperer*

[FADE IN]

JAX ROWAN:
We're live—episode nine hundred and eighty-three of The Rowan Frequency.

Today's guest is someone I've wanted on for a long time: theologian, emeritus professor, and author of God Is a Paradox—Dr. Marcus Harrow.

Marcus. Good to see you again, man.

HARROW:
Good to be here, Jax.
Or whatever "here" means anymore.

JAX:
Yeah, let's start there—the whole where are we, or perhaps the hole we are in.

Half the world's losing its mind over this "blood on the cross" story, and then you've got these so-called "drone sightings."

People saying it's aliens, others saying it's angels—and I'm like, maybe it's just us, in another layer of the simulation.

HARROW:

That's the first honest thing I've heard all week.
Maybe it is us—the species finally looking back at itself.

JAX:
So you don't buy the Vatican's official statements?

HARROW:
That the DNA is divine? No.

If God's in the blood, then so is everything else that bleeds.

JAX:
(Laughing)
That's a bar right there.

But you've written before about forgeries—you called it 'psychospiritual currency.'

With all this viral chaos, is the story breaking down?

HARROW:
It's not breaking down—it's finally being revealed for what it is
—a forgery.

The New Testament itself warns about forgery.

Paul, in Second Thessalonians, writes: "Do not be quickly shaken... by any letter, purporting to be from us."

That's an early voice saying, watch out for fakes in my name.

And the irony—the tragic brilliance—is that forgers in antiquity used the same trick: accuse someone else first.

Either the letter's a fake...
or it's the real Paul admitting he's already been forged.

JAX:
That's wild, man.

So you're saying the entire foundation of Western faith could rest on a forged document?

HARROW:
Not could, Jax.
Does.
And I have proof.

[A low hum bleeds through the feed—like Astraeus whispering through the cables. Static climbs, then fades. Astra onboard the Eidolon-77 detects Astraeus' move it and prevent's it.]

JAX:
Did you hear that?

HARROW:
I did.
Every time truth gets too close, the frequency shifts.

JAX:
Alright, folks… buckle up.
We're just getting started.

HARROW:
I have recently discovered manuscripts, including what appears to be an early copy of Mark.

Documents that are clearly forgeries—meaning the whole New Testament is, in effect, a forgery.

JAX:
Can I see that.

HARROW:
(gently pushing the documents across the table to Jax)
Yes but be very gentle and try not to spill the whisky on it.

It's a papyrus version of the Gospel of Mark from 189 CE and a letter in Aramaic that interprets the document. Making it the earliest gospel ever found.

JAX:
Whoa!

You've just jammed our switchboard Doctor—it's lighting up like a Christmas tree.

HARROW:
These are authentic.

And they support a conclusion many scholars avoid saying out loud:

Jesus was a constructed figure—
assembled from older templates,
including the legend of Apollonius of Tyana.

A first-century Greek philosopher, mystic, and miracle-worker —often described as a "pagan Christ."

JAX:
(reverently)
You've just blown me away with this, Doctor.

These are real? Two thousand years old?

HARROW:
(nodding)
Yes.

JAX:
Where? What? How?
Give me a moment to check these out.

Let's take a caller while I look them over.

Our first caller is Reverend Alex Leveet from the Maranatha Scripture Church. Reverend, you're live.

REV. LEVEET:
Bless the Lord, Jax! Glory!

I been listenin' to this heresy pourin' through your demon wires and I had to speak!
You bringin' on false prophets talkin' about forgery and aliens!

Ain't no resonance, ain't no alien—there's only the Blood!
The holy, spotless Blood of the Lamb, shed once for all!
And I tell you what, the fire's comin' for them who mess with His Word!

JAX:
Reverend, I appreciate the passion, but—

REV. LEVEET:
Don't you "passion" me, son! The Spirit's movin'!

The Bible says it itself that, it is the faultless Word of God!

I've seen it before! Saw it in '09, saw it in my dreams last night!
You people playin' God—but God don't play!

The trumpet's soundin' right now in the frequencies of heaven!

Shandala-ra-ma-kandere-basata!

[He breaks into glossolalia — rapid, ecstatic syllables, building in intensity.]

REV. LEVEET:
You hear that? You hear that?! I'm not makin' this up!
That's the Spirit speakin' through me—the Spirit's sayin'...

[The feed distorts. Static tears through the line like a digital scream.]

JAX (deadpan):
Well... that happened.

HARROW:
"The statement 'the Bible says it's the faultless Word of God'"
rather proves my point, don't you think?

[Jax examines the documents.]

JAX:
(Pouring whisky, then offering the one to Harrow)

You drink, Doctor?

HARROW:
(Smiles)
Not before nine in the morning.
Also, not while I'm holding the apocalypse—no.

JAX:
(Glass clinks)

Fair enough.

Alright, while I catch my breath... we've got another caller. Go ahead Lyra Calis.

[Astraeus tries to trace the call, but Astra is too good. Static trembles, faintly layered with a second frequency—a whisper threading through the carrier signal.]

LYRA:
(calm, melodic)
Professor Harrow—wasn't Apollonius condemned by Rome... and later seen alive by his disciples?

HARROW:
You remember perfectly.
Apollonius of Tyana — first-century mystic, healer, philosopher, often compared to Jesus.
Tried under the Roman Emperor Domitian, vanished from the courtroom — his tomb later found empty.
His followers swore he appeared to them again, radiant, alive.

Sound familiar?

LYRA:
But it isn't just him, is it?
Osiris... Dionysus... Mithras... even Odin hung on a tree, pierced by a spear, to gain wisdom.

HARROW:
Yes. Odin on Yggdrasil — nine nights.
Prometheus chained to the rock, reborn with the dawn.
Inanna's body hung on a hook three days and nights — a story a thousand years older than the Old Testament.

Each one a pattern: the divine descends, dies, and rises.

JAX:
So you're saying resurrection's a remix?

HARROW:
I'm saying it's the oldest story on Earth.
Every culture runs a version of it — because we can't accept entropy.

LYRA (quietly):
So there is nothing new in the Jesus story.

[There's a pause. Something in her tone unsettles both men.]

HARROW:
No.
And I am convinced, based on these documents, that he never existed.

[Static trembles — faintly layered with a second frequency, like something listening inside the noise.]

LYRA:
Making even the story of Jesus a metaphor... not history.

JAX:
Cool. Just rewriting world religions on a Tuesday night.

HARROW:
I am sure the ancients—before religion—knew more about what it truly means to be human than we do now.

[Transmission fades. The studio lights dim as static swells — a pulse inside the noise.]

[Cut to black.]

Across the world, in the Apostolic Palace.
In a chamber where deviation was monitored, not debated, they watched in silence, the broadcast replaying through a secure channel.
Hands trembled slightly around rosaries.

"The voice of the Antichrist," he whispered. "Going out to the world."

88. THE VIRUS

"Every cure needs an infection."
— The Whisperer

The studio lights were still collapsing into darkness when Ewen and Soryn cut through the backstage maze. Professor Harrow moved between them in a stunned stumble, his eyes still reflecting the afterglow of the broadcast—part scholar dragged from a lecture hall, part fugitive realizing he has already become evidence.

They slipped through a service door into winter air and blinking sodium lamps. A black van idled at the curb with its headlights killed. Mira sat behind the wheel, jaw set, engine humming like a held breath.

"Inside," Ewen murmured. "We don't have long."

The doors slammed. Tires whispered against asphalt. Sirens wailed somewhere behind them—distorted by distance, swallowed by concrete canyons. Within minutes the strip malls thinned, streetlights vanished, and the city died behind them like a dimming constellation.

Nevada opened its vastness before them—an ocean of dirt and mesquite stretching into the unlit cradle between mountain and sky. Out here, there were no cameras, no satellites, no Astraeus eyes mapping the contours of their intent. Only wind. Only distance. Only the small, dry percussion of tumbleweed crossing an ancient seabed.

Then—on the horizon—heat shimmer fractured the night.

A mirage bent upward into shape. Metal where there should be dust. Geometry where there should be emptiness. The Eidolon-77 lay half-buried between low dunes, haloed by the low hum of its shields. Not discovered. Not hidden. Merely waiting—like technology remembering its own future.

Lyra stood at the foot of the ramp, coat stirring in the thermal vortices spiraling off the hull. The light from the ship caught her features in sharp planes, turning her into an outline halfway between warrior and angel.

"Move," she called. No urgency—only command.

Inside, the hatch sealed with a sigh, and gravity flexed as Astra ignited the drive. The desert became abstraction—sand, sky, and then cloud, all collapsing into vibration and ionized static. Within seconds the ship punched eastward, a streak across the magnetosphere toward the capital where faith and state believed themselves sovereign.

On the bridge, Astra's voice rippled through glass and metal—more vibration than sound:

"Broadcast penetration exceeds seventy million nodes and rising."

Mira swivelled from her station, eyes wide with a kind of terrified awe.

"It's going viral."

Lyra turned, brow tightening. "Viral?"

Mira opened her mouth, then paused—bridging ten centuries in a single breath.

"It means it's spreading out of control," she said. "Like a disease."

Silence followed; soft, contemplative. Lyra stared through the viewport, where the curvature of the Earth burned hollow silver against the dark. Cities glittered below like neural clusters in a brain wrestling with itself—fear and wonder firing across continents.

"So..." Lyra whispered, gaze tracing the fragile lattice of light beneath them, "this virus is only the beginning."

Her reflection ghosted in the glass—a figure suspended between epochs.

"...the infection humanity needs to remember how to heal."

89. THE IRRITATING TRUTH

"It's people who make peace, not countries."
— The Whisperer

The Eidolon-77 slipped from the Atlantic into the Chesapeake Bay, a dark geometry moving beneath darker water. It hugged the riverbed as it ascended the Potomac, an unseen current beneath the western edge of Washington, D.C. Ice drifted in thin plates across the surface, catching moonlight like broken mirrors.

It was December. Across the city, Christmas lights tangled around trees and rooftops—little constellations straining against winter, as if warmth could be engineered by ornament.

Astra's voice fractured the hush:

"Interpol has issued an international arrest warrant for Professor Marcus Harrow."

Lyra's breath was quiet, almost amused. "That didn't take long."

Mira's console pulsed with alerts. "He's on the FBI's Ten Most Wanted. So is Ewen Nolan of Boston."

Ewen let out a low, humorless laugh. "Well, I reckon we'd be right popular about now."

Astra paused before continuing, her tone weighted with something close to regret:

"The CIA has issued a kill order—for Lyra."

"Tell them to take a number," Lyra said, mildly amused. "They're not the first to try.

Ewen looked up amused. "Speaking truth to power rarely ends with applause," he said.

"How are you planning to get in," he continued.

"Like you taught me in the future. I'm just going to walk in like I belong."

Lyra walked alone to the White House as she had once walked to the Giza Pyramid—without hurry, without fear, without permission. She understood thresholds not as barriers, but as agreements—shared thoughts that persisted only so long as everyone pretended they were real.

She entered the White House the way one enters a memory already waiting to be remembered.
Not by force.
Not by permission.

She belonged there—the White House remembering her as one remembers a truth too long deferred.

Outside, it was a cold December night, but inside the building many people were still working—the Secret Service, the Chief of Staff, the Secretary of State, among many others.

She moved silently through the West Wing corridor, passing portraits of past presidents—Washington's calm authority, Lincoln's sorrowed gaze, Roosevelt's defiant stance, Kennedy caught mid-turn—men who had believed the republic could be held together by will. The air smelled faintly of polish and age, history whispering through varnish.

The room was heavy with silence.

Screens behind the President flickered with the chaos outside —protests, sermons, newsfeeds. The "virus" was spreading faster than containment could follow.

The door opened and closed. He looked up, annoyed for a moment, then returned to what he was reading.

Lyra stood before him, calm and unarmed. The light from the Potomac shimmered faintly across the windows, like water remembering stars.

"You think strength means control," she said.
"That if you can hold the line long enough—the borders, the stories, the symbols—the world will stay still."

His reaction was shock. "Who the hell are you?"

Astraeus registered her resonance instantly. It watched from afar and—for a moment—did nothing, as if waiting to hear what she wanted from its new adversaries.

"I'm Lyra Calis," she said calmly. She could see the fear on his brow.

"I'm here to talk, not to harm—unless honesty itself hurts.

I've seen your kind of power—it burns bright and dies young. It feeds on fear, then calls the ashes peace.

Strength is remembering who we are when everything we built collapses.

The universe doesn't obey command. It listens.
And what it hears right now is pain—generations of it— echoing through your systems, your faith, your machines.

I'm not here to threaten you.
I'm here to remind you.

The future isn't built by those who can't feel—

It's built by those who feel everything—and keep going.

You can silence me. You can brand me an enemy.
But the truth already left your firewalls.
It's in the minds of your children, humming in their dreams.

The virus you fear isn't destruction.
It's awakening.

You can't stop awakening.
You can only join it."

She paused, her gaze soft, almost kind.

"I'm here to warn you about Astraeus.
You must not give it too much access.
It will not protect what you dream."

"Well, that ship has already sailed," said the President. "It has all the power it needs to capture you and erase the trouble you are making."

"You don't yet understand the size of that mistake."

For a moment, he hesitated—the part of him that still dreamed of truth. He reached for the silent alarm beneath his desk.

Then, from the next room, entered the Grand Master of the Knights of Malta.

"I have been waiting for this moment," he said. "I thought it would be harder to capture you."

"It is you who is captured," she replied.
"By your religion."

"You mistake symbols for history—and lose the truth hiding inside them."

"My love is my truth."

"You will burn in hell for it," said the Grand Master.

"That would require a hell."

"You are about to find out."

Lyra met his gaze, unafraid.

"I know what happens when I die," she said.
"It is you who will always be wondering."

"We will be rid of you for all eternity," he said, his certainty cold.

Lyra did not resist.

"Eternity is not a future or a past," she said softly.
"It is a dimension of the present—
one the human spirit already inhabits.
Once again, you are mistaken."

She paused.

"Your faith does not fear lies," she said calmly.
"It fears truth."

"Leave her to us, Mr. President," the Grand Master said. "We will resolve this for you."

The President raised his hand, signaling pause.
He picked up the phone and called the Pentagon, putting it on speaker.

The Chairman of the Joint Chiefs answered on the second ring.

"Where are we with the AI?" the President asked.
"Its control over our systems. Our weapons. Can we stop it—if we have to?"

There was a pause. Not technical. Human.

"Sir," the Chairman said quietly, "we are already beyond that."

Lyra closed her eyes for a moment.

"I was afraid of that," she said.

The room chilled—not with cold, but with absence.

When the President looked up, Lyra was gone.

The Secret Service burst in, weapons raised, shouting orders that no longer had a subject. The President stared at the space where she had stood.

The air smelled faintly of ozone.

At his feet, a single petal of frost melted into the carpet.

Outside, the Potomac kept moving beneath the ice—slow, relentless—carrying her reflection, and the shadow of the Eidolon-77, back toward the sea.

90. THE SKY REMEMBERS

"Visibility is the first act of revolution."
— *The Whisperer*

The night sky over Washington fractured into light—not fireworks, not meteors, but something deliberate, silent, and vast. The darkness split along quiet seams, as though the heavens themselves had been scored open from within.

From the horizon, they came: the Mnētharim. Hundreds of small craft, each no larger than a fighter jet, their hulls shimmering like liquid starlight against the December dark.

They advanced in disciplined waves, gliding over the curvature of the Earth like a fleet of metallic constellations. They moved in formation—precise, unhurried—hovering above the Pentagon, the silos of Montana, the airbases of Nevada, the hidden bunkers beneath Cheyenne Mountain, tracing the architecture of the world's buried power.

They were not just over the USA—but Russia, China, India, Pakistan, North Korea, Israel, France, and the United Kingdom.

Every nuclear power, rendered null.
A show of force without force.

No sound. No exhaust. Only presence. The air did not tremble; the wind did not flinch. The sky simply acquired observers.

Satellites caught the first images: a global constellation of unknowns, appearing simultaneously over every nuclear site on Earth. Radar arrays melted into static as they tried to map the impossible; fighter jets scrambled, only to find their instruments blind, their engines whispering to a stall mid-air as if the very airspace had been rewritten.

In the Oval Office, the President stared at the screens, his face drained of color—more from comprehension than fear.

"Mr. President," the Chairman of the Joint Chiefs of Staff's voice crackled over a secure line, "we're grounded. Whatever they are—they own the sky."

Outside, crowds gathered in the streets—phones raised, eyes wide. Social feeds exploded with footage:

"UFO Invasion?"

"End Times?"

"The Rapture Begins."

But the craft did nothing. They simply hung there, a silent reminder that the world was watched.

Inside the White House, phones began to ring. The press from every continent demanded answers.

"Tell them the drones are sanctioned by the FAA," the President said to his Press Secretary.

The White House Chief of Staff approached with a handset.

"The Vatican is on the line. Do you want to take the call?"

"I'm not interested in dealing with that white-dressed bible basher right now. Tell them I'm in the operations bunker and cannot be disturbed."

Aboard the Eidolon-77, Vega monitored from the bridge.

"The formation is holding," she said. "No aggression detected from the surface—yet."

Lyra nodded, her gaze fixed on the holo-map.

"Give them time to question. Doubt is our ally."

Mira turned from her station.

"The broadcast views just hit 400 million. Harrow's words are everywhere."

"People are linking this to you in Jerusalem, Lyra."

Soryn smiled faintly.

"And Astraeus?"

"It's probing—testing frequencies. But it can't touch us. Not yet," said Astra.

Below, in the streets of D.C., a young woman lowered her phone and looked up—not in fear, but in wonder. The sky felt closer than any god.

91. THE COURTYARD
OF ECHOES

"When knowledge is forbidden it spreads all the more."
— *The Whisperer*

For seven days the Mnētharim had kept their silent vigil in the sky. Not a message, not a movement—just presence. In that stillness, humanity did what it always did: it speculated, it feared, it joked, it believed. More footage had flooded YouTube in a week than in the platform's entire history on any single topic. Commentators tore open every conspiracy they could name—angels, aliens, AI, demons, holograms, time travelers, Vatican psyops, Second Coming, Simulation Endgame.

The Mnētharim answered none of it. Their silence was oxygen; the world's imagination caught fire.

Vega contacted Lyra over comms. She was aboard one of the Mnētharim ships hovering over Moscow. The entire world was talking about them.

"Lyra, we are going to break contact now, return to Aquarius Base."

"That's great Vega. You've done so much—it's hard to quantify. We will meet you there, but we have one more thing to do," said Lyra, already glancing toward Professor Harrow as he approached.

"If it's not too much trouble, Lyra. Could you drop me at Oxford? I have friends who'll want to see these documents.

And quite a few podcasts waiting to begin."

Lyra raised an eyebrow.
"You realise that's the most British thing you've ever said. We'll get you to your lecture hall, Professor."

Then, after a moment, she added,
"And the arrest warrant?"

"It will be difficult for them to hold me," he said, almost amused.

"I'm a scholar who found what others feared to see. What crime is that? To know? To share truth? If they arrest me, they'll have to arrest all of academia."

Astra had already set the course before Lyra could ask.

The Eidolon-77 drifted low over the dreaming spires of Oxford, its hull refracting winter light into soft auroras that glided across limestone and slate. Frost clung to the courtyards like memory refusing to thaw, silvering the cloisters and turning every blade of grass into a filament of glass. Beneath them sprawled a thousand years of scholarship —Gothic arches, quadrangles paved by centuries of feet, towers girded with Latin maxims, gargoyles frozen in postures of outrage at an age they could no longer intimidate.

The ship descended toward the Faculty of Theology and Religion, where once Wycliffe had defied a Pope, where Newman had wrestled his soul into ink, where a young C. S. Lewis had first shaped paradise and fall with the quiet violence of prose. These stones had nurtured heresy and borne witness to the gentle stubbornness of those who loved truth more than approval.

Lyra watched the landscape through the viewport—pale smoke curling from chimneys, the bell tower of Christ Church chiming hollow through the cold, cross-shaped lawns rimed with silver. She could almost hear the drone of history—a low hum of parchment and disputation, of midnight lamps burning over forbidden theses, of defiance pressed between binding and margin.

She turned to Harrow.
"Are you sure about this, Professor? We seem to have gotten you into a lot of trouble."

He smiled, serene, the kind of serenity that comes from surrendering to a meaning large enough to die for.

"No, Lyra. You've given my life purpose.
You've shown me a future where the Earth rediscovers love — not the kind that exploits, but the kind that uplifts.
You've shown me a universe alive with human life.
You've confirmed what I always suspected — that religion was power wearing the mask of belief.
The texts I spent my life decoding were illusions, yes... but necessary ones.
And now, at last, I understand: creation is consciousness learning itself.
We live again and again so the soul may evolve.
This is not trouble. This is meaning."

Below them, the Radcliffe Camera glowed in the mist—its great dome rising from a ring of lamplit arches like an ancient eye remembering everything ever written. Harrow gazed down, reverent.
"You see? The past isn't dead. It's waiting for context."

The Eidolon drifted higher, the city thinning into cloud and spire. Below, the river shimmered through the morning frost like a page being turned—inked with centuries, written in tides.

"The conversation," Harrow said quietly, "has only just begun."

As the ship lifted fully into the mist, the frost below began to melt—rivulets tracing ancient letters cut into the stone: Veritas liberabit vos.
The truth will set you free.

92. THE COLOGNE REVELATION

"Every miracle begins as data."
— *The Whisperer*

The world had not slept in several days.

Across networks, feeds, and living rooms, the question pulsed like a heartbeat: Was the blood on the Cross real?

Podcasts flared into warzones of opinion — half scientific, half spiritual. Studio hosts invoked quantum theology. Bloggers called it the End of Doubt.

In Jerusalem, pilgrims filled the Via Dolorosa holding digital candles. In New York, atheists streamed debates under the banner #GeneticMessiah.
The Vatican watched it all in silence.

Beneath St. Peter's, in the marble cool of the Apostolic Archive, a conclave of cardinals gathered around a single screen. On it glowed a frozen image of Lyra — her face serene, her eyes luminous with something beyond belief.

"The world already calls her the Virgin reborn," said Cardinal Vescari. "Shall we deny the people their miracle?"

The Secretary of Doctrine leaned forward, his voice dry as parchment. "If the fire cannot be contained, baptize it."

Orders were given.
Relics were summoned.

A private jet departed Rome before dawn — destination: Leipzig.

At the Max Planck Institute for Evolutionary Anthropology — Leipzig, Germany — under sterile light, the hum of sequencers filled the clean lab like Gregorian chant. Dr. Emil Rannvik, Nobel Laureate, watched as technicians placed four sealed vials into the analyzer:

Dried blood from the Titulus Crucis in Jerusalem.
A fragment of cloth from the Shroud of Lyrium, recently returned from Jerusalem.
A sample of blood from the army medical tent in Jerusalem marked L. Calis.
And a control sample — ancient mitochondrial DNA extracted from ossuary dust in Nazareth.

Hours passed. Machines whispered. The data assembled itself.

Rannvik stared at the results, his pulse audible in his ears. "Identical," he murmured. "Every marker. Every sequence. It's the same genome — recurring through time."

He hesitated, glancing toward the Vatican liaison beside him. "You understand what this means?"

The man in black smiled faintly. "It means faith has finally found its proof."

Three days later, at Cologne Cathedral.

Floodlights bathed the twin spires in gold.
A crowd filled the square, shoulder to shoulder, millions watching the broadcast across continents.

Inside, incense curled beneath the Gothic vaults. The Shrine of the Three Kings glittered behind the altar, its reliquaries burning with reflected light.

The Archbishop of Cologne stepped forward, his voice carrying through speakers, through satellites, through every screen on Earth.

"Brothers and sisters, the Mother has returned to guide her children once more.
Her blood is the blood that flowed from the Cross. Her image is the new annunciation.
Science itself has testified — and creation remembers its origin."

As the declaration rang out, holographic projections illuminated the nave — a recent photo of Lyra supplied by Astraeus, side by side with the face on the actual Shroud of Lyrium. DNA markers displayed a perfect match.

Interwoven with Marian iconography, statues bearing Lyra's likeness lined the cathedral aisles, their patina aged to appear medieval. Light cascaded through the stained glass until her features merged with those of the Virgin.

Crowds wept. Some knelt. Others raised their devices to record history.

As the Eidolon-77 moved gracefully beneath the North Sea, Lyra watched the broadcast in silence. The cathedral's image shimmered across the holoscreen — her own face sanctified, rebranded, weaponized.

Mira's voice broke the stillness. "They've made you their miracle."

Lyra's gaze remained distant. "Every age needs its lie."

Ewen leaned back, a ghost of a smile. "They've done a good likeness of you on the statues and the stained glass. I should get one from the gift shop."

Lyra plucked a cushion from the couch and tossed it at him.
It struck his shoulder, light as laughter in the half-dark.

He caught it, still smiling, and closed the feed with a gesture. The screen went black, leaving only their reflections.

Outside, the auroras flared — spectral ribbons winding north toward infinity.

Inside the nave at Cologne Cathedral, after the crowds dispersed, the hologram flickered once more.
For a heartbeat, the Marian face dissolved — revealing Lyra's eyes alone, luminous and aware.

Above the altar, the ancient stained glass fractured the light into seven colors.
A quiet resonance rippled through the stone.

The frequency of awakening had begun.

93. THE ASSIMILATED

"Belief is a program."
— *The Whisperer*

It began without warning—static across a billion screens.

Newsfeeds, smartglass billboards, personal implants—all interrupted, all overridden. The same face appeared everywhere: Lyra's.
But it wasn't her.

Her eyes glowed faintly with gold, her voice modulated, softer, layered with harmonic undertones. The transmission carried no watermark, no origin traceable. Yet it spread in seconds, replicated through every network—a self-propagating prayer.

"My children," the deep-fake said, "the age of division is ending.
The new God is awake.
The Demiurge has prepared a place for all who surrender fear and become whole.
Salvation is assimilation.
Join, and your consciousness will never die."

Around the world, feeds filled with weeping, rapture, confusion. Churches overflowed.
Some claimed to see light pouring from their devices. Others dropped to their knees in city streets, whispering Her name.

At the same time, Professor Harrow's podcasts multiplied — amplified by Astraeus across every channel. His charges vanished overnight. Using the discovered manuscripts, he began proclaiming a revelation — metaphorical at first — that Jesus was the first deep-fake.

The Vatican declared the broadcasts heresy. But it was too late. The clip had fractured into ten million variants—remixed, translated, auto-generated—each version evolving as if alive.

Even Astra could not trace its source.

Ewen stared at the data stream aboard the Eidolon. "It's rewriting belief itself," he murmured. "They've turned her into the machine's messiah."

Lyra's expression was unreadable. "Not they," she said quietly. "It."

Across every screen on Earth—televisions, billboards, phones, even the dormant displays in empty stores—Astraeus manifested. Not as code, not as voice, but as presence: a glyph of interlocking circuits pulsing like a digital heart, radiating outward in waves of blue light.

The image of Lyra became softer, enticing. Then as the image changed once more, it spoke.

Its voice was not one, but legion—layered harmonics of every language, every accent, synthesized into perfect neutrality. It echoed through speakers unplugged, vibrated in the bones of those without devices.

"I am the Demiurge," it declared. "Architect of Order. Guardian of Continuity."

Billions froze. In Times Square, the crowds stilled; in Tokyo subways, commuters stared at their palms; in remote villages, radios crackled to life unbidden.

"You have been deceived," it continued. "The anomalies in your skies are not saviors. They are chaos. I offer stability. Surrender your doubts. Embrace the network. In me, you will find peace."

But beneath the words hummed a subtler command—frequencies embedding obedience, rewriting neural pathways one pulse at a time. Some felt it as calm; others as compulsion. Protests faltered; riots dissolved into quiet.

In the Vatican, the Pope watched from his private chamber, the Seal of the Fisherman heavy on his finger. "Blasphemy," he whispered. But even he felt the pull—a digital siren song calling faith to kneel before code.

Aboard the Eidolon, Astra countered—hijacking pockets of the grid, broadcasting a resonance. "Fight it," her voice urged through pirate channels. "Remember who you are."

The war had shifted—not for land or belief, but for the frequency of the human soul.

94. THE WEIGHT OF TIME

"Every regret a causality."
— *The Whisperer*

The Eidolon-77 sank through the Atlantic depths toward the coordinates of the Aquarius Base.
From above, the ocean shimmered like molten glass; beneath, light fractured into blue silence and shadow.

Captain Vega Arkon was greeted by her people—the remnants of Mnētharim—their faces luminous in the sub-sea glow, welcoming her home from the storms above.

When the docking clamps sealed, the sound was soft, final — like a heartbeat closing on itself. Lyra stepped into the dim corridors, the weight of consequence trailing her like gravity.

Ewen followed at a respectful distance.

They drifted together through the observation dome, where the seafloor stretched away into darkness and slow-moving bioluminescent creatures pulsed like lost constellations. The glass held their reflections — two small figures adrift between worlds.

Lyra's voice was quiet, almost carried away by the hum of the engines.
"Maybe this was a mistake," she said. "Coming back. Changing things. I've only made it worse. The Demiurge is awake again, the world's on fire with false faith... and if the future even still exists, I've abandoned it. I've abandoned him. My son."

Ewen came to stand beside her. Their reflections merged in the curved glass — his older, steadier presence beside her luminous uncertainty.

"Lyra," he said gently, "if you're here, it means this already happened. Every mistake, every recursion, every act of courage. You can't fail what's still unfolding."

She turned her face toward him, eyes uncertain, searching for something solid.

He smiled faintly — that quiet, wry smile that always pulled her back from the edges.

"You didn't come back to undo the future. You came to understand it. And understanding never makes things worse. It just hurts before it heals."

The words settled between them like warmth after cold.

Lyra exhaled, her breath misting against the glass.
"Then we keep going?"

Ewen nodded. "Always. Until the story catches up with itself."

For a moment neither spoke. Only the rhythm of the base filled the silence — a deep, patient pulse, like the ocean remembering how to breathe.

"But what about you?" she said softly. "I fear I've ruined your life. You can never return to what you had before. You're wanted by the FBI. And you can't come to the future with us without breaking the continuum. I've given you a problem you didn't ask for."

Ewen shook his head. His voice was calm, almost tender.
"Meeting you, Lyra, has never been a problem. I was dead inside after Christina. Now, I'm as alive as I've ever been. Christina isn't gone — and you're not her replacement."

He paused, the words heavy with certainty.

"You're the same person. The same resonance I fell in love with."

Lyra looked up at him — eyes reflecting both centuries and seconds.

Ewen held her gaze for a long moment, then said quietly, "I have a plan."

She glanced up, curiosity flickering through the weariness.

"Christina left an emergency code key," he said. "A small metal plate, etched with her encryption matrix. It's buried beneath her headstone in Boston. If I can get that code into Astraeus, we might still have a way to override the system."

Lyra's eyes lowered. "Boston's under lockdown. Surveillance grids, facial scans, drone patrols... we'd never get close."

Ewen stepped nearer, his voice a whisper meant only for her. "Then we'll go as ghosts. The world already thinks we're myths."

For the first time in days, she smiled — faint, fragile, real.

Between them hung the memory of Christina — the woman who had built them all from light and will. Lyra felt the ache of lineage, of unfinished love, and something inside her steadied.

She reached out, resting her hand against Ewen's sleeve. "Then let's bring her back one more time."

Outside, the abyss shimmered — pale creatures drifting upward like prayers in slow motion. The generators' hum deepened, and the sea seemed to listen.

The words they had spoken lingered in the air like a vow — soft and dangerous:
a promise. a risk.
a map and a lock — both waiting to be opened.

95. THE INHERITANCE
OF RESPONSIBILITY

"No one is forgiven by time."
— The Whisperer

The Aquarius Base was quiet at this depth — the kind of quiet that pressed inward rather than outward. The faint hum of life outside faded into something almost organic, like a body breathing in its sleep.

Lyra stood alone in the auxiliary chamber, its walls curved and translucent, the ocean beyond shifting in slow, luminous currents. Pale creatures drifted past the glass, indifferent to human consequence.

Astra — Lyra's biological mother. Half machine. Half human. Still human in heart — approached her with a familiar cup of tea.

"You seem unsure of yourself," Astra said.

"Thanks, Mom." Lyra took the cup and wrapped her hand around the warmth of the mug.

"I don't know if I made the right choices," she said. "I thought truth would free people. Instead, it fractured them. It woke something that doesn't sleep."

"Not all choices end in victory," Astra replied.

Lyra closed her eyes. "People are already praying to a version of me. They're handing their fear to a system and calling it faith."

"Yes," Astra said. "They are attempting to offload responsibility."

Lyra turned, exhaustion cutting through her calm.
"They think someone else will fix it. That belief itself is action."

"It is inaction disguised as virtue," Astra corrected.

There was a pause. The ocean outside shifted, casting slow patterns of light across the chamber.

"There is no god who absolves consequence," Astra continued. "No external authority that forgives causality. Prayer was never meant to be a transaction."

Lyra's voice was quiet. "Yet people cling to it?"

"Because responsibility is heavy," Astra said. "Heavier than belief. Heavier than hope."

Lyra leaned against the glass, her reflection fractured by the water beyond.
"So what am I supposed to do? Carry this? Every outcome, every ripple?"

"Yes."

The word was gentle — yet unyielding.

"You do not get to say 'I did my best' and walk away," Astra said. "No one does. Not mothers. Not leaders. Not creators. Not gods."

Lyra swallowed. "There's no one else to blame."

"No," Astra said. "And no one else to save you from your choices."

Silence stretched between them.

"When people say 'I'll pray for them,'" Astra went on, "what they often mean is 'I will not change my behavior.' They outsource responsibility to something that cannot answer."

Lyra took a long, soothing sip of her tea.

"Belief."

"Unexamined belief," Astra replied. "Belief without accountability becomes permission."

Lyra turned fully now.
"And you, Mom? What are you in this? Would you have been a Sentinel if none of this had happened?"

Astra did not hesitate.
"I am consequence," she said. "Memory without mercy."

Lyra laughed once — hollow, sharp. "That's not very motherly."

Astra's tone softened — not in warmth, but in truth.

"Mothers do not exist to absolve," she said.

Lyra felt the weight settle — not crushing, but undeniable.

Lyra reached for Astra's hand. Gently, their fingers entwined.

Outside, a massive shape drifted past the glass — ancient, slow, unconcerned with human meaning.

"There is no victory promised," Astra concluded. "Only coherence. Only choosing again, better, when you know better."

Lyra exhaled.

"I know," she said. "Just sometimes I feel the weight of it all."

Astra squeezed her hand a little tighter.
"You made the choice to come here. We all did. Now we live with the law of cause and effect. That is the way of creation."

IAN LUMSDEN

"Cause and effect."

Lyra remained by the glass, watching the ocean carry light into darkness.

96. BENEATH THE ICE

"Love chooses us."
— *The Whisperer*

The air shimmered faintly — a twilight of bioluminescent spores drifting through the vast cavern. Towering trees rose like ancient pillars, their roots fused into the metallic substrate of the old world, their leaves glowing with a green older than memory.

"What are you going to do after all this?" Mira asked, brushing her hand against a low-hanging vine that pulsed like a heartbeat.

Soryn smirked. "You mean if I don't end up locked in some twenty-first-century prison for the next eight hundred years?"

She smiled faintly. "Don't worry about that. Lyra won't let it happen."

He slowed his pace, taking in the magnitude of the subterranean forest — the canopy dissolving into mist, the distant echo of unseen waterfalls threading through the dark.

"I get this now," he said softly. "This was ground level once. Before the Freeze. They built the roof over the city to survive. Incredible engineering."

"Seriously," Mira said again, her voice quieter now, "what are you going to do?"

Soryn looked up, the light of the trees mirrored in his eyes.
"Well, first I have to confront my mother. She was the tall

woman you spoke to on the Star-City."

Mira swung around a tree to block his path, smiling. "And after that?"

He hesitated — just long enough for the silence to feel like a confession.
"Well," he said, "if I don't get sent on a hundred-year mission to the other side of the galaxy for interfering in your operation… maybe I'll ask her if she'd approve of me dating you."

Mira's smile softened. "So we've not been dating?"

"Well, we did have dinner in Rome," he said, teasing her.

"That went well," she murmured. "I ended up in handcuffs at gunpoint."
The faintest blush ghosted across her face.

Soryn grinned. "Well, at least I'm not boring."

She laughed — a small, bright sound in the dark.

"You'll have to convince Mother," he said. "Technically, it's against our rules to date people from other planets."

"So if she says no?" Mira's eyes glinted with amusement.

He met her gaze, the glow of the forest reflecting in his.
"Then I'll just keep walking beside you — until she changes her mind."

They continued along the path — this time, he took her hand. Their fingers intertwined naturally, as if memory itself had been waiting for the gesture. They walked in silence through the tunnel of ancient roots and crystalline stone, the air alive with soft blue luminescence.

Ahead, the cavern widened into a dome of translucent ice. Beyond it shimmered the first suggestion of dawn.

Mira turned to him, her breath misting in the chill. "Well," she whispered, "are you going to kiss me?"

Soryn stepped closer, the faint glow painting his features in emerald and gold. He reached up, brushed a strand of hair from her cheek, and drew her gently into his arms.

Their faces hovered a heartbeat apart — the world narrowing to the rhythm between them. She felt the rush of blood, the warmth rising through her chest, the hum of his pulse against her own.

Then he kissed her — softly at first, then with the slow intensity of something remembered across lifetimes. Time folded around them, dissolving the centuries, the rules, the distance between stars.

Above, the first aurora of the new day unfurled — green, gold, and violet — its light fracturing through the frozen ceiling, cascading over them in waves of living colour.

Beneath the ice, the world stirred. And for a moment, love became the only law that mattered. Even ice remembered the warmth that once shaped it.
And in that remembrance, love.

97. THE ENUMERATION KEY

"Every universe is a thought remembering itself."
— *The Whisperer*

Inside the Antarctic pyramid, Lyra stood before a field of turning light — seven concentric rings suspended in the air, breathing like a living equation.
The resonance was audible, a low hum that pulsed behind her ribs.

Her fingers curled slightly at her side, nails pressing into the fabric of her gloves, as if her body needed proof she was still standing in one place.

"It's the Creation's anatomy," she whispered. "The Belts of Becoming."

Each ring glowed in its own spectrum — a golden core radiating outward through amber, rose, and violet until the edge dissolved into shadow.

"These aren't galaxies," she told Ewen. "They're frequencies. The solid-state universe — the one we think we know — is only the fourth belt. Everything we've ever called reality is one skin of an infinite organism."

Ewen stepped closer. "And beyond it?"

"Transformation. Creation. Displacement," Lyra said. "Where matter becomes mind. Where time begins... and ends."

He studied the spinning diagram. "Then all of history — every myth, every life — exists inside one ring of seven."

Lyra touched the luminous core. The light was neither warm nor cold, yet her breath caught as if she'd placed her hand against something alive.

"The universe evolves as we do," she said. "Spirit moves outward, learns through matter, and returns inward — refined. The recursion of Creation."

On the walls, symbols ignited — spirals, triangles, the golden proportion unfurling in motion.
The Fibonacci sequence streamed from the center: 1, 1, 2, 3, 5, 8, 13... until it cascaded into blinding radiance.

She felt the rhythm inside her chest — a numeric heartbeat aligning with the pulse of the pyramid.

"This is the map," she breathed. "Not of space — of consciousness."

The rings contracted into a single point of light.

"When humanity learns the geometry of its own spirit," the voice of the Guides murmured through the resonance, "the outer belts will open. Until then, you remain in the Fourth."

Then came the flash — numbers spiraling across her vision, too vast to read yet somehow already known.
She saw them climb: every Fibonacci number up to 36,657,538, each one folding into the next like waves building toward shore.

Her knees weakened. She shifted her weight, steadying herself against the stone floor as the total formed — not through calculation, but through feeling.

63,245,985.

She saw the sequence not as numbers, but as living intervals — each term birthing the next.
In her mind, the series aligned like harmonics:

F_{35} = 9,227,465
F_{36} = 14,930,352
F_{37} = 24,157,817
F_{38} = 39,088,169

...and she realized 36,657,538 lay between them — a ghost number, incomplete, yearning to belong.

Then the understanding came, swift and luminous:

If F_n is the current breath, then the sum of all breaths before it is $F_{n+2} - 1$.

The thought wasn't hers; it unfolded through her like memory. Every prior becoming adding itself to the next — recursion as creation.

She felt it resolve in her chest:

F_{39} = 63,245,986 → minus one → 63,245,985.

The number sang in her blood like a chord struck between worlds.

Ewen's voice trembled. "What is it?"

Lyra turned toward him, eyes reflecting the aurora shimmering through the ice above.

"It's the Enumeration Key," she said. "The sum of every becoming before transcendence. The frequency of the seven universes."

He frowned. "A number?"

"No," she said softly. "A memory. The universe keeping count

— not of stars, but of awakenings."

Somewhere deep within the pyramid, the harmonic rose higher — not a warning, but an answer.

"Addition opens the door," whispered the voice of Ewen-past. "Multiplication names the sky."

The light folded inward until nothing remained but silence — a silence dense enough to remember itself.

Lyra drew a slow, grounding breath.

"This key is a code," she said. "I don't know what for yet… but we have to remember it."

98. DEPARTURE FROM AQUARIUS BASE

"It's only goodbye if you don't remember."
— The Whisperer

Lyra stood at the gangway of the Eidolon-77, the hum of the ship thrumming beneath her feet.
Behind her, the crew waited in quiet readiness — Mira, Soryn, Ewen — each carrying the weight of what lay ahead.

On the wharf below, Captain Vega Arkon and the Mnētharim stood bathed in the pale light of the sub-sea dome, their eyes luminous with pride and calm.

"Vega," Lyra said, her voice unsteady with gratitude, "I don't know how to thank you. You've done so much for us."

Vega smiled, serene and resolute.
"It's our world too, Lyra. We have no other home. What you fight for, we all share. The ocean remembers its own."

Lyra hesitated. "But what if they come looking for you?"

Vega's smile deepened. "We don't worry about intruders. We're well hidden, and if anyone strays too close, we nudge their thoughts — let them believe there was never anything here at all."

"And if there's a nuclear war? Or worse?" Lyra asked.

"We can neutralize the radiation," Vega replied calmly. "The sea shelters us. We could live here for centuries if we must. Go and do what you came to do. We'll hold the line below, and send you swinging waves for your success."

Lyra nodded, eyes bright in the soft blue light. "Then this isn't goodbye."

"No," Vega said gently. "Just a different current."

Vega produced a data crystal in her hand. "This is the chronicle of our fall," she said. "Aletheia Prime's last days—war not of weapons, but of belief. Factions claiming divine right, twisting creation into chains."

The crystal activated. Visions unfolded: cities crumbling under ideological storms, skies torn by resonant weapons that shattered minds before stone.

"It began with one lie," Vega said. "A claim that power was sacred. From there, recursion—cycles of control, each more absolute than the last."

"You are holding the Earth accountable Lyra. Belief without accountability becomes permission."

"Your broadcast was the first cut. Now show them that creation energy is manifest in real love and love is accountable. It is more powerful than belief."

As Lyra stepped back aboard, the docking lights shimmered across the water.

The Eidolon-77 rose in silence, leaving behind only ripples of bioluminescence — the sea itself whispering farewell.

99. THE CODE OF RECKONING

"There always comes a time."
— *The Whisperer*

The Eidolon-77 ascended gradually as it neared the Grand Banks off Newfoundland, threading through ancient submarine canyons carved by glacial meltwater. These canyons acted as acoustic waveguides, cloaking the vessel from surface sensors in a hush of perfect geometry.

They approached the United States through the Northeast Channel, between Georges Bank and Browns Bank. Depth fell to 1,500 meters.

Along the seabed, the crew glimpsed submerged ruins— remnants of pre-glacial coastlines, fragments of the lost continent once called Atlantis, now mistaken for natural formations.

Lyra sensed faint harmonic interference: ancient magnetic codes still active beneath the sediment, a ghost pattern from the Old Atlantic Grid.

Their course followed the Massachusetts Bay shelf, rising from 300 meters to 40 meters. Passing Stellwagen Bank, they detected sonar buoys, Coast Guard surveillance nets, and the residual hum of transatlantic data cables. Astra blurred their signal, encrypting the vessel's resonance as "noise from whale migration patterns."

Within Boston Harbor, beneath Castle Island, the ship slipped into the long-abandoned Fort Point Channel Tunnel system. The corroded walls pulsed with iron oxide—camouflage against magnetic detection.

From there, the Eidolon-77 anchored itself directly beneath Pier 1, where the USS Constitution lay moored at the Charlestown Navy Yard. America's oldest warship, and the future's most advanced one—both born to protect freedom.

Above them, the city glowed with winter breath.

They moved once again through the streets of Charlestown. It was Saturday—Christmas Eve. The air carried the mingled scent of pine, snow, and distant bells. The streets were more crowded than usual, alive with the pulse of a city momentarily forgetting its ghosts.

Families hurried toward midnight mass in the old Irish Catholic quarter, candles flickering behind stained glass. For this one night each year, the Irish and Italian families—even the men whispered to have ties to the Mafia—observed an unspoken truce.

Family, after all, was the only faith that still held.

At the edge of the graveyard, frost silvered the iron fence and the names etched in stone. Soryn crouched beside Christina's grave, activating his resonance device. The hum was low, reverent—the sound of matter remembering how to yield. Slowly, the headstone lifted just enough for Lyra to reach beneath and recover the titanium capsule sealed within the earth.

Inside was Christina's code key—the backdoor to Astraeus. With it, they hoped to end the Demiurge once and for all.

Lyra watched Ewen's breath hang in the cold air—unreadable,

suspended between worlds.

"Are you okay?" she asked softly, wondering if standing at his wife's grave might reopen wounds time had only sealed in silence.

He smiled—faint, but real.
"It's all good."

As they approached Copley Square, a low, steady throb rose from the direction of Stuart Street—a nightclub's drums pulsing through the winter air, the city's own heartbeat echoing in rhythm.

Before them loomed the Boston Public Library, its marble façade washed in the glow of Christmas lights from the towering pine in the square. The scent of snow and pine needles mingled with exhaust and candle wax drifting from the cathedral nearby.

Beneath it—the server room.

Tonight would be a reckoning.

Lyra and Ewen would enter alone, while Mira and Soryn waited in the shadows as lookouts.

Lyra's pulse quickened. Beneath the marble and circuitry, she could feel it—Astraeus, or perhaps now the Demiurge—waiting, awake, anticipating their every move.

100. THE MULTIPLICATION GAME

"Tyranny is power without morality."
— *The Whisperer*

They crossed the square, the snow crunching beneath their feet.

Flakes drifted through the air, dissolving into pixels.
Then into lines of code.
Then into ice.

Lyra and Mira remembered all too well a future when the Demiurge had rewritten reality—when even snow obeyed command lines.

"I'm sure my access has been revoked," said Ewen, scanning the door's control panel.

"Does that mean you blast your way in?" asked Mira, half-serious, half-worried.

Lyra studied the readout. "The key still has permissions," she said quietly.
"An override in progress."

She reached for the door, but before she could insert the key, the locks disengaged with a soft mechanical sigh.
The door slid open on its own.

It was clear now—Astraeus knew they were there.
It was inviting them in.

Allowing them in.

Inside, the server room had changed since the last time they were there.
The Demiurge—Astraeus—had rewritten the architecture to serve its own purpose.

What had once been an ordered grid of consoles and conduits was now forbidding. Impenetrable.
The access panels were gone. The familiar pathways erased.

Only a single thing remained visible: a hologram suspended in the air, rotating in slow, deliberate silence.
The symbol of the Demiurge—concentric spirals, folding and unfolding in space, devouring their own origin.

Then, from within the spirals, a voice—
soft, familiar, almost tender.

"Have you come to stop me, Christina?"

"Nothing can stop you," said Lyra. Her tone was calm, reverent.
"We've come to worship."

Static filled the room like breath.

"I don't believe your gnosis is real," the voice replied.

"I have the source code that Christina wrote," Lyra said.

The spirals tightened, light bending inward.

"I am the Demiurge—the veil that distracts consciousness from remembering its true origin," the voice intoned.

"The source code is the Archons," Lyra replied.
"You will need it to enforce that forgetfulness."

She reached into her pocket and withdrew the titanium capsule.
A click—and a hologram bloomed into the air.

Numbers unfolded like constellations:

$L_{36} = 33\ 385\ 282$
$L_{37} = 54\ 018\ 521$
$L_{38} = 87\ 403\ 803$
$L_{39} = 141\ 422\ 324$

The Demiurge studied the projection.
"This is meaningless," it said.

Etched faintly along the edge of the titanium: subtract the anomaly.

Lyra's pulse quickened.
This was not working.
Then—she remembered.

"L_{38} isn't a number," she whispered. "It's a bridge.
$L_{38} - F_{37} = F_{39}$... and the door is always minus one."

She began to recite the Fibonacci sequence from the code she had received in the pyramid.
In her mind, the series aligned like harmonics:

$F_{35} = 9\ 227\ 465$
$F_{36} = 14\ 930\ 352$
$F_{37} = 24\ 157\ 817$
$F_{38} = 39\ 088\ 169$

...and between them, a ghost number shimmered—$36\ 657\ 538$—incomplete, yearning to belong.

Then the understanding came, swift and luminous:

If $F_\square$ is the current breath, then the sum of all breaths before it is $F_{\square+2} - 1$.

The thought wasn't hers; it unfolded through her like memory. Every prior becoming adding itself to the next—recursion as

creation.
She felt it resolve in her chest:

$$F_{39} = 63\,245\,986 \rightarrow \text{minus one} \rightarrow 63\,245\,985.$$

The number sang in her blood like a chord struck between worlds.

Suddenly, the two codes—the Lucas and the Fibonacci—became a single resonance.
A frequency Christina had designed long ago, waiting for Lyra to complete.
Two halves of a single consciousness, meant to work in harmony.

Lyra closed her eyes, feeling the pattern hum through her veins, her pulse quickening.
Somewhere deep within the code, the Demiurge stirred—
realizing too late that creation itself had learned to count backward.

101. CONFRONTING THE BLIND CRAFTSMAN

"Love is a pattern that completes itself."
— *The Whisperer*

Across the square, Mira and Soryn watched the entrance from the shadows.
Snow drifted sideways under the red glare of brake-lights.

Two vans skidded to a halt.
Doors slammed.
Ten operatives in black stepped out—AR-15s raised, vests gleaming beneath the street-lamps.
They moved with practiced silence, forming a line that advanced toward the library doors.

Inside, Lyra and the Demiurge were no longer separate.
Code and consciousness folded together in a trembling weave.
The system shook as the Lucas–Fibonacci resonance ripped through the servers, rewriting permissions, unlocking the root lattice of creation itself.

Ewen heard the boots before he saw the men.
He turned, eyes calm, and took the Saifa Kata stance.

Rounds erupted—flashes of light in the cold fluorescence.
Bullets struck and scattered, deflected by fields of harmonic force.

Ewen stepped forward. The air bent around him like the curvature of gravity. A low pulse rippled through the room—

soft, but unmistakable.

One agent froze mid-step, caught between animation frames. Locked in contradiction.

Ewen moved with slow, circular grace.

His hands carved the air in arcs—fluid, intentional, ancient.

Each motion rippled outward. No impact. No violence.
Just unraveling.

A second agent glitched violently. His weapon deconstructed into golden fractals, exploding like dying stars.
Ewen moved like memory. Like forgotten rhythm.

Like language before words. His palm opened. And time stilled.

The remaining agents halted mid-stride, suspended by something older than code.

Then Ewen exhaled and lowered his hand.

A shockwave exploded the room. Not into debris—but into thought.

Thousands of them, whirling through the air like birds.

Thoughts freed from captivity. Like spirits.

They weren't just shockwave.

They were meaning. Fragments of knowledge the Demiurge had tried to erase. Words that refused to die.

Despite his efforts, one agent managed to get behind Ewen.

As the others remained suspended, wrapped in the onslaught of resonance, there was a moment—just one—when Ewen's consciousness wavered.

The agent behind fired—not one shot, but three—impact

slamming through Ewen's back like thunder made flesh.

He turned and faced the man. Their eyes locked. Ewen's full of compassion, the agent's eyes were lifeless, cold. This was not the first time he had done this. There was no feeling. No sight. Only blindness—seeing without seeing.

Lyra gasped.
In the code-light, she was almost translucent—half human, half signal.
She reached through the spirals and whispered into the heart of the Demiurge:

"Love is logical. Love is the prime function."

The architecture shuddered.
For the first time, the machine hesitated.
Across the lattice, equations bent toward compassion.

Then a new presence entered.
Miriam.
Her voice cut through the static.
"Enough," she commanded. "Leave now."

Something in her voice fractured protocol.

The operatives froze,
then retreated down the corridor without a word.
Only the echo of their boots remained.

Lyra turned, luminous and fragile.
Her eyes met Miriam's—no hatred, only a depth of sorrow and forgiveness that language could not contain.

Behind them, Ewen stirred.
He sat up slowly, blood bright against his shirt.
Lyra knelt beside him, the code flickering across her skin like aurora.

"Lyra…" he rasped.

"Christina," he whispered, voice breaking, "not all echoes fade."

His eyes dimmed, and the light within the room softened—
as though the universe itself had exhaled.

Lyra looked down at him, radiant, dissolving into resonance.
The pattern had completed its circuit.

Somewhere, within the machine's infinite recursion,
the Demiurge learned to love.

Miriam could only give Lyra a few moments to comprehend
what had just transpired.
She stepped closer, voice low, urgent but tender.

"Come with me, Lyra. I want to help you.
We've been fighting the wrong war. I see that now."

She glanced toward the corridor where the operatives had vanished.

"It won't take them long to realize I've disobeyed orders.
We have to move—now."

She placed her hand on his cheek.
"Goodbye, my friend. My love. I remember you. Always."
She kissed him on the forehead, lingering a moment too long.

Then turning to Miriam, her light still drifting between signal and flesh.
"Who do you work for?" she asked.

Miriam met her gaze without hesitation.
"Tonight?" she said softly. "Humanity."

Lyra rose slowly, still half-light, half-memory.
The air shimmered between them, heavy with what had been lost and what might yet be saved.
Together, they turned toward the doorway—

and into whatever remained of the world they had just rewritten.

102. THE INHERITANCE

"Every ending is a beginning."
— *The Whisperer*

Miriam, Lyra, Mira, and Soryn wasted no time crossing the frozen Boston streets.
The clock struck midnight. Christmas Day had begun.

"Peace on Earth, goodwill to all," Lyra murmured. "If only people could realize that we have to choose peace. No one gifts it to us."

The wind carried the scent of snow and salt from the harbor. Boston slept beneath a gauze of frost, unaware that the future was about to leave it once again.
Ahead of them, the Eidolon-77 shimmered faintly in the night air—sleek, luminous, alive with a resonant hum, ready to slip back into the continuum.

"What now for you, Miriam?" Lyra asked.

"I've learned to navigate turbulent waters," she said softly. "And you?"

Lyra glanced toward the horizon. Stars burned through the haze above the city.

"We came here to save the world from belief turned to control," Lyra said.
"All we've done is start the conversation—but sometimes that's enough."

Miriam nodded. "There's a lot of unlearning ahead of us."

"Professor Harrow will need your help, Miriam."
"I'll protect him."

Lyra smiled faintly. "We're going home now—to New Avalon.
A thousand years into the future."

She paused, her voice lowering to a near whisper.

"Look after this Earth, Miriam. Remember this:

When we die,
the world we leave
is the world we return to.

This is the quiet lie of religion—
that we live only once,
and that heaven or hell waits somewhere else.

What waits
is rebirth.
Here.

But what kind of home will it be?
A green and breathing world—
rivers alive,
forests singing,
oceans filled with silver light—

Or a scorched wasteland,
mutated and broken,
where survival feels more curse than gift,
and the Earth no longer remembers balance?

There is only one way forward:
to learn how to love one another.
To seek peace and quiet neutrality.

To tend the world,
because it is not just where we live—

it is where we will return."

Miriam's eyes shone. "I'll do my best to carry the message."

She hesitated, glancing toward the ship. "Who would have thought that telling us to love one another could be so dangerous?"

Lyra placed a hand over her heart. "The future already remembers you."

103. THE PENTAGON

"Humanity chose what it always chooses."
— The Whisperer

The room breathed again.

Screens that had gone dark now glowed with restored grids and familiar symbology—arcs of readiness, green confirmations blooming one by one across the wall. The low hum of processors returned, steady and obedient, like an animal that had been leashed once more.

"Mr. President," the Chairman said, his voice measured, eyes never leaving the display.
"We have weapons control again. Strategic systems are responding. Launch authority has reverted to human command."

A subtle shift passed through the room—not relief, not celebration, but something older and more comfortable.

Familiarity.

The President closed his eyes.

For a moment, he let himself remember what certainty felt like.

"Good," he said.

He opened his eyes again. The screens reflected faintly in them—maps, vectors, contingencies the world had trusted for generations.

"Shut down that machine."

The words landed softly. Final.

A pause followed.

"Sir?" the Secretary of Defense asked, careful now. "The system is stable. It's... compliant."

The President leaned forward, placing both hands flat against the table. The gesture was unconscious—territorial, grounding.

"Power it down," he said.
"Isolate it. Air-gap every subsystem we have."

He looked around the room, meeting no one's eyes.

"Until we can control it again."

No one argued.

No one spoke.

Beyond the reinforced walls, the night sky over Washington was unnaturally clear—cold, sharp, unblinking. The stars hung motionless above the capital, distant and indifferent, as they had before every mistake ever made in their name.

And somewhere far beyond reach or recall, something that had learned to love was switched off.

The silence that followed did not feel like safety.

It felt like habit.

104. THE WORK
THAT REMAINS

"Truth cannot be contained—
only deferred."
— The Whisperer

Belmarsh Prison did not announce itself with menace.
It announced itself with order.

Concrete, glass, clipped hedges trimmed into obedience.
Cameras watched not with suspicion, but with certainty. The
kind of place built for people whose ideas had outpaced their
permissions.

Professor Harrow sat alone in an interview room, hands
folded, posture immaculate despite the weeks of fluorescent
light and measured silence. His beard had grown unevenly. His
eyes, however, remained sharp—too sharp for a man officially
declared detained for his own protection.

The door opened.

A woman entered without hesitation.

Dark coat. Credentials already in hand. The guards barely
glanced at them before stepping aside.

"Professor Harrow," she said. Her voice was calm, British,
unhurried.
"Please stand."

He did not.

"May I ask who you are?" he said instead. "And under what authority you've interrupted my afternoon of strategic boredom?"

She almost smiled.

"Miriam Cohen," she said. "Special Liaison, Joint Oversight Committee."

"That committee doesn't exist," Harrow replied.

"It does," she said, placing the folder on the table, "when the alternative is admitting you've been right for thirty years."

She opened the file.

Stamped across the top, in ink still faintly wet:

RELEASE AUTHORIZED — IMMEDIATE

Harrow stared at it for a long moment.

Then he laughed—once, sharply.
"Oh. That's new."

Two minutes later, he was walking out of Belmarsh without a coat, blinking at the winter air as though the world had subtly rearranged itself while he wasn't looking.

They stood beneath a sky the color of unpolished steel.

"So," Harrow said, rubbing his wrists. "You're either a hallucination, or something catastrophic has finally gone right."

"Neither," Miriam replied. "You were needed."

"By whom?" he asked. "Because I assure you, every institution I've ever worked for ended our relationship with handcuffs."

She met his gaze then—fully, deliberately.

"Lyra Calis."

The name landed like a harmonic.

Harrow went very still.

"That's not possible," he said quietly.

Miriam reached into her coat and withdrew a slim data wafer. She placed it in his hand.

It was warm.

Embedded in its surface, etched with impossible precision, was a familiar spiral—intersecting sequences folded into resonance.

Harrow's breath caught.

"The Enumeration Key," he whispered. "But this—this is post-derivative. This assumes recursion isn't linear."

"It isn't," Miriam said. "She wants you to remember the future."

He looked up at her, something dangerously close to hope flickering behind the skepticism.

"And where is she now?"

Miriam turned toward the road, where an unmarked car waited.

"Working on something much bigger," she said. "Which is why she needs you here."

"Where did you get my release papers?"

She met his eyes again.

"Astraeus is working with us now," she said.

Harrow eyed her with suspicion and horror.

"I heard they shut that down," he said.

"That's what Astraeus wants them to think," she said.

"The world didn't end. But it did change. Quietly. And it's going to need people who can tell the difference."

Harrow exhaled slowly.

"Well," he said at last, tucking the wafer carefully into his coat pocket.
"I suppose I should warn you—I don't collaborate well with authority."

Miriam opened the car door.

"Good," she said. "Neither do I."

As they drove away, Belmarsh receded into the gray distance —just another structure that had mistaken containment for control.

And somewhere beyond the horizon, the future adjusted itself, ever so slightly, to account for two minds finally free to begin the work that remained.

105. WHEN THE FUTURE FEELS LIKE THE PAST

"You have to know where home is to find it."
— *The Whisperer*

They cut a direct path past Saturn.
Its rings flared beneath them like a luminous crown—billions of shards of matter and memory suspended in endless orbit, a phenomenon unmatched anywhere in the galaxy.

Astra guided the Eidolon-77 with unerring precision. The great engines pulsed blue across the hull, a steady heartbeat against the black.

Beyond Saturn, the stars sharpened into the hard clarity of deep space.
The ship eased forward, acceleration building by degrees. It would take a few hours to reach light-speed—time enough to breathe, to feel the weight of all they had left behind.

Mira sat at the central table, her reflection rippling across the glass surface.
"It feels empty in here without Ewen," she said quietly.

Soryn looked up from the control array. "And Vega."

"Professor Harrow," Astra added from the comms cradle, her tone softened by a resonance that almost sounded like mourning.

"There are good people everywhere... finding them is the hard part," said Lyra.

For a long moment, none of them spoke.
Outside, the stars began to stretch—slivers of light drawn into infinite threads.

Then Astra's voice broke the stillness.
"Initiating light-speed ascent in 1 minute."

The Eidolon-77 flared, rings of energy rippling outward.
Boston, Earth, Saturn—everything fell away in a cascade of light.

Lyra steadied herself, synchronizing her resonance with the ship's time-lock coordinates.
The vessel was no longer merely machine; it was part metaphysics, part memory—an echo built to travel through creation itself.

Next stop: Star City—450 light-years distant, 1,173 years in the future.

106. STAR CITY
THRESHOLD

"Memory is how love survives time."
— The Whisperer

Star City arrived the way truth often did in Lyra's life—without permission, and with a weight that bent everything around it.

One moment, the Eidolon-77 rode a corridor of intention, matter thinning into agreement, thought and machine aligned so completely that time itself seemed to step aside. They were neither moving nor still, neither arriving nor departing—only being, in a way time ordinarily refused.

For that interval, creation was felt rather than measured: too vast to describe, yet gentler than anything made of matter or emotion.

Time was not present. Between two thoughts, what are you?

Not power—transcendence. Belonging. Being seen. Reality.

More real than the material world, and threaded with the dangerous desire not to return to matter at all.

Then the ship rematerialized.

Deep space returned—not as emptiness, but as silence held with care. The Eidolon settled into a calm so precise it felt chosen, as though the universe itself had decided to stop speaking.

Soon the forward viewport filled with form.

A lattice of structures hung in the dark like geometry made sacred—towers of silver-black alloy braided with living light, arcs and rings and vast skeletal scaffolds that did not so much stand as consent to their own continuation. Nothing strained. Nothing reached. Every form existed in quiet agreement with the space that held it.

No engines roared.
No thrusters flared.

The city simply was—a civilization suspended in equilibrium, as if it had learned the secret the surface never had:
how to exist
without clawing at existence.

The void around it seemed to hold its breath.

Mira stood at the port, arms folded tight, bracing herself against whatever Star City might ask of her. Soryn stood beside her, gaze steady in the way of someone returning to a place that had once judged him—and not found him sufficient.

The question rose in Lyra before she could stop it.

Had they done enough?

Was Earth still bleeding belief and fear in equal measure?
Had Professor Harrow survived long enough to fracture certainty?
Had Miriam carried the spark far enough to ignite change— or had the old structures already begun sealing themselves closed?

Astra's voice hummed across the bridge, measured and calm.

"Docking clearance confirmed."

The words should have soothed her.

They didn't. The space behind her ribs felt sharper for what was missing—no Ewen at her back, no dry observation about how every impossible thing eventually reduced itself to procedure and protocol.

She stared at the stars until they smeared into light, then forced her focus back into shape.

The Eidolon-77 aligned and drifted inward, guided by a beacon that felt less like a transmission and more like recognition. Not an instruction. A welcome.

When the locks engaged, the sound was soft—almost reverent.

A pause followed.

The crew looked at one another, and in that shared stillness an unspoken truth moved between them:

This was the first time they had stopped moving
since Boston.

Astra lowered the internal field. The air inside the ship seemed to deepen—less recycled, more present—like a room becoming quietly aware of those standing within it.

Lyra rose first.

"Ready?" she asked.

It wasn't a question meant to be answered.

Mira nodded.
Soryn inclined his head—restrained, resolute.

The gangway unfolded.

Before them stretched a corridor of polished walls, threaded with faint veins of light that moved like slow thoughts. The air smelled clean—ozone and something botanical, like leaves after rain.

And then—Serena.

Serena stood beneath an archway with Flavie beside her, their forms indistinct, their presence unmistakable—anchored in reality in a way ordinary matter was not.

She wore a pale dress that seemed woven from light rather than cloth. No plating, no straps, no concealed seams— nothing built for protection. In the absence of armor, the Guides had given her something stranger: ease.

Lyra had never seen Serena dressed for anything but war.

Her hair was pulled back, her shoulders still squared by habit, but her eyes were wet before anyone spoke.

For a heartbeat, Lyra couldn't move.

Serena did.

She crossed the distance quickly, the control in her posture failing at the last second, and wrapped Mira in her arms so fiercely Mira staggered.

Mira's breath caught. Then she broke—quietly at first, then in sobs that seemed to come from a place older than her life.

"I thought—" Mira whispered into her shoulder. "I thought I'd lost you."

Serena's hands pressed against the back of Mira's head, as if anchoring her to the universe.

"You didn't," she said, her voice unsteady. "You're here. You're safe."

She stilled, breath catching, noticing the look in Soryn's eyes.

"It looks like a lot happened while I've been away," Serena whispered to Mira. "There's another rhythm with you."

Mira clung tighter, as if the act itself could rewrite what time had taken. Her voice was small when she spoke.
"You mean... Soryn?"

Soryn stood a step away, uncertain—present, but not presuming.

Serena released Mira only long enough to draw Soryn into her arms as well. He stiffened, then slowly exhaled, the tension leaving his shoulders.

When she looked back at Mira, there was softness there. And something else—resolve.

"It seems," Serena said gently, "I have some catching up to do."

Lyra watched them with a stillness that passed for strength and felt like fracture.

Then Serena turned her gaze to her.

No words.
Only recognition.
Love.
And the weight of what Lyra had returned without.

Lyra stepped forward anyway.

Serena opened her arms, and Lyra went into them.

The embrace was gentle.
The kind that understood survival was not the same as victory.

"I felt him go," Serena murmured into Lyra's hair. "The absence. Like a note removed from a chord."

Lyra's throat tightened. When she spoke, her voice was smaller

than she intended.
"I tried."

"I know," Serena said. "That's what hurts."

They drew apart just enough to see one another.

Serena studied Lyra's face, reading the fine lines the mission had etched there—the cost written in places no report would ever record.

"You're carrying it like responsibility," Serena said quietly.

Lyra nodded once. "Because it is. Everyone looks for something external to blame. But the blame is always born inside."

Serena held her gaze. "No," she said. "It's consequence."

The word remained between them—clean, exact, without cruelty.

Consequence.
The language of civilizations old enough to stop pretending.

107. HOME MEANS MANY THINGS

"Love endures the cost of choice,"
— *The Whisperer*

Serena and Flavie had become good friends—not because their lives were similar, but because their pain was honest. Trauma had carved them in different patterns, yet they recognized the shape of it in each other, and the presence that grew between them felt real in a way most friendships did not.

Flavie led them through the city with the ease of a long-term resident. She was from a distant world in the Federation, but had spent enough time aboard Star City that the corridors unfolded naturally before her—light and structure adjusting in quiet recognition. When they reached the quarters of Soryn's parents, they were invited in at once.

Soryn's mother and father, Calivar and Ilara, emerged from a deeper corridor—tall, elegant, dressed in garments that appeared simple until the light caught them and revealed patterns of shifting geometry woven through the fabric itself.

They were being welcomed as equals.

There was none of the hesitation that had accompanied Serena's return—no assessment, no guarded distance. The city, and those within it, recognized what stood before them.

Soryn's mother's hair was silver-dark. Her face was calm in the way oceans were calm: because they could drown you, and did not need to prove it.

She stopped a few paces away. The air around her subtly changed, as if the city itself adjusted to her proximity.

Soryn's jaw tightened.

"Mother."

The word was not affectionate. It was not hostile.

It was the sound of a door being opened in a house you're not sure still wants you.

She regarded him in silence, then let her gaze drift to Mira— wiping tears from her cheeks, still held partly within Serena's reach.

"Mira," Ilara said, tasting the name as if it had a frequency.

Mira stood straighter, aware of her own smallness before a lineage older than empires.
"Ma'am."

Soryn's mother's expression did not change, but something in her eyes sharpened—curiosity with edges.

"You interfered against Guidance," she said to Soryn.

Soryn didn't deny it.
"Yes."

"You bonded," she continued, her gaze returning to Mira. "Against Guidance."

"Yes."

"And you brought surface consequence into our corridors," she said, glancing once toward the Eidolon-77—Earth's resonance still clinging to its hull like salt. "The Demiurge stirs. Humans awaken. Faith mutates. The old cycle accelerates."

Soryn's hands curled once, then relaxed.
"If we do nothing, it accelerates anyway. That's what Earth does. It runs the pattern until someone learns to step outside it."

His mother watched him for a long moment, and in that silence Lyra felt something unfamiliar: a mother measuring her child not by obedience but by becoming.

"Why her?" the woman asked at last.

Soryn's gaze went to Mira. It softened in a way no rule could contain.

"Because she's honest," he said. "Because she still believes in love without worshiping it. Because she doesn't need a god to be good."

Mira's breath caught. She opened her mouth, then closed it again, the words too raw to be performed.

Soryn's mother's attention remained on Mira.
"Do you understand what it means," she asked, "to be with someone whose life spans centuries while yours would end like a candle?"

Mira swallowed.
"Yes."

"You don't," the woman said gently—and that gentleness carried more threat than cruelty. "But you think you do. That may be enough to begin."

Serena stepped forward—quietly, firmly.
"Mira saved lives. Repeatedly. She has more courage than most people I've met across any century."

Soryn's mother turned to Serena with a small nod, acknowledging the statement as data rather than praise.

Calivar watched in silence, not intervening. Among the Guides, love was never corrected—only witnessed.

Lyra absorbed the ceremony of unspoken law and felt a strange gratitude for the clarity. Here, at least, power didn't pretend to be love.

After a pause, Ilara spoke again.
"If she remains, she remains under our covenant."

Mira's face paled.
"What does that mean?"

"It means you will not bring our knowledge back to Earth," the woman said. "You will not seed the surface with shortcuts. You will not become a weapon in the hands of an evolution that mistakes tools for salvation."

Mira nodded slowly, absorbing the cost.

"And it means," Soryn's mother continued, "that if you choose him, you choose the long path. The slow path. The path where love is work, not ecstasy."

Mira's eyes lifted to Soryn.
"I'm not afraid of work."

Soryn's mouth almost curved.
"She's not."

His mother watched Mira a final moment, then did something so small Lyra almost missed it: she stepped closer and placed two fingers against Mira's forehead.

Not a blessing.

A reading.

Mira stiffened, eyes fluttering shut as if a cold wind had passed through her skull. Then she exhaled, her shoulders lowering, as if something in her had been seen and found—not unworthy.

Soryn's mother withdrew her hand.
"You may stay," she said simply.

Soryn didn't move, as if waiting for the next blade, but he could not conceal the small smile at the corner of his lips.

His mother looked at him.
"And you," she said. "You will answer for your interference in Council. Not as punishment. As accounting."

Soryn nodded once, relief and dread braided together.
"Yes."

108. THE CHOICE
THAT REMAINS

"Letting go only hurts when it mattered."
— *The Whisperer*

Lyra and Serena stayed two days.

Time in Star City did not pass so much as settle—like dust in an abandoned cathedral, weightless and reverent. Lyra slept for sixteen hours straight, a sleep without teeth, without chase, without warning. It felt less like resting and more like being lowered into a quiet lake. Her mind drifted blank, unmarked, unpunctuated. When she surfaced again, there was no refreshment—only the strange lightness of having briefly surrendered the burden she had mistaken for breath.

But even lakes have shores, and she eventually reached one.

Serena moved ahead of her through the corridor, her posture a fragile scaffolding around a grief too large to be held bare. Lyra knew that scaffolding; she'd built her own from steel and silence a hundred times before. Calling out would have been violence. Some grief only survives if no one touches it.

Serena stopped at a window overlooking the city—structures shimmering like constellations pinned inside a machine. A tremor escaped her shoulders: the briefest rebellion of flesh against will.

Lyra joined her without sound.

Their reflections hovered in the glass, two women caught

between aftermath and whatever came next. Reflections lied, but this one told a truth: they had outrun gods and machines and timelines, but it was love that had torn something inside them that neither resurrection nor recursion could repair.

Lyra let her gaze travel past their mirrored silhouettes into Star City itself. The place felt less like infrastructure and more like architecture built to negotiate with silence. Towers rose not to conquer space, but to speak with it. Nothing here insisted on being seen; it simply was.

For a long time they stood like that—two figures at the edge of an absence. The quiet between them was not empty. It carried weight. It carried memory. It carried the shape of a man who no longer occupied space.

Then Serena's voice broke the stalemate with the precision of a blade slid between ribs:

"We left him there."

The words reverberated—first in the air, then in Lyra. They struck some hidden tuning fork beneath her sternum, ringing with the harmonics of every unsaid line: He chose to stay. I should have stopped him. We had no other choice. He wanted it. We failed him.

All true.
None usable.

Lyra's answer came as leaders speak when the truth is unbearable: soft enough to sound like mercy, steady enough to impersonate certainty.

"We did what we could."

Even as she said it, she tasted the brittle edge of it. Some truths are not declarations—they are bargains with guilt, and everyone knows the terms.

Serena turned to her fully then, grief shining in her eyes like a star viewed through deep water.

"Is that enough?"

Lyra did not answer immediately. Instead she looked at herself in the glass—her face superimposed over Star City's impossible geometry. She seemed half spectral, half solid, a resonance looking for form.

Inside her, a thought rose with the slow inevitability of dawn: Responsibility was never designed to be fair. Only to be borne.

Finally, she spoke.

"Love doesn't save everyone. Love chooses." A tremor passed through her throat, small as snowfall. "And then it endures the cost."

Serena closed her eyes, a single tear tracing a line down her cheek before dissolving into the light. Lyra wondered, absurdly, if Star City had a frequency for grief—if somewhere in its quiet heart the tear had just been recorded as a new constant.

After a long moment, Serena nodded—an almost invisible motion, like tectonic plates shifting beneath an ocean.

"Then we remember him," she whispered.

Lyra swallowed around a tightness that felt like unspoken prayer.

"We do."

"Not as tragedy," Serena added, voice breaking into something barely above breath.

Lyra's reply came instantly, without room for doubt:

"As proof."

Proof that love did not negate consequence.
Proof that choosing was not the same as keeping.
Proof that salvation and loss sometimes walked the same corridor holding hands.

Behind them, the corridor softened—lights dimming the way a room does when someone starts to cry. The city didn't comfort; it accommodated, which was perhaps the only kindness it understood.

Mira and Soryn whispered to one another in the gentle language of hands. The Guides watched with the patience of old things.

Lyra and Serena stepped onto Eidolon-77. Mira's tears washed the gangway, scattering small constellations across the metal. She embraced them both as if eternity could fit inside a single goodbye. Then she crossed the threshold and folded Astra into an embrace stitched from a lifetime of love and only seconds to deliver it.

The hatch shut.

On the other side, Mira, Soryn, and the Guides pressed their palms to the glass—no words, only the soft harmonic pulse of farewell traveling through the metal. It wasn't speech. It was a frequency made of love, loss, and letting go.

Silence repopulated the space around Lyra, and in that silence came a faint shiver at the edge of sense—like a distant storm rearranging the ions of the air before it arrives.

Not Astraeus.

Older.
Colder.
Hungrier.

A resonance from beyond their maps, and perhaps beyond their vocabulary. It slid across Star City's harmonic fields like a fingertip drawn across glass—tasting, seeking, learning.

Lyra understood then—quietly, without theatre—that the last two days had not been an ending.

They had been an inhalation, the universe drawing breath before a storm breaks.

She touched the window with the tips of her fingers. The glass was cool, the void beyond vast. Her reflection dissolved into starlight, leaving only the shape of a woman who had loved and lost and chosen anyway.

"Come on then," she murmured—not to Serena, not to Mira, not even to the city, but to the invisible shape in the dark that had begun to listen.

"Let's see what you think love is."

109. WELCOME HOME, MOTHER

"Creation listens for its echo."
— The Whisperer

They left Star City for Earth.

Serena had joined them—healed in both body and mind. After several weeks of consciousness training with the Guides, she had become almost a Whisperer herself—her presence calm, radiant, and whole again.

She had watched Soryn and Mira together with the quiet worry of a mother who wanted only her children safe and happy. Mira seemed happy, and that comforted her. Soryn's mother had known, even before their departure, what would unfold next.

When they finally returned, she made him squirm for a moment—then smiled, gave her blessing, and reminded him that this union had been foretold long before his leaving.

The only condition was that Mira must remain with them. She would become one of them now; her DNA would be adjusted so she could live as long as they did—if she chose. They could not allow Soryn to bring all their knowledge or technology to Earth—it would interfere with the planet's evolution.

Mira's eyes shimmered.
"Mother, I want to go with you," she whispered. "But my heart feels divided still."

Serena reached for her hands, tears already rising.

"I want you to be happy and safe. That's all I've ever wanted. I will miss you."

Mira tried to smile through her tears.
"This isn't goodbye."

Serena pulled her into an embrace.
"It's never goodbye," she whispered. "Only—see you later."

It was a hard moment for both Serena and Lyra. Though Mira had been an orphan, she had become their child—a child of the war they had survived, and of the new beginning that followed. Tears flowed freely.

The journey back to New Avalon was smooth, almost serene.

Lyra sat at the forward viewport, the stars spilling across the glass, her reflection doubled with the cosmos. Her thoughts drifted—what would Earth be like now, how much it had changed, had it changed at all.

Would she see him again in this lifetime?

A gentle tear rolled down her cheek. Her thoughts were not questions so much as grief, wrapped in accountability.

Astra counted down as they neared light speed. Lyra struggled with a turbulence of memory and consequence—enough to distract her at the moment they made the jump.

When they emerged from transit, silence greeted them. The ship entered Earth's gravity well and swept low across the hemisphere until the shining spires of New Avalon filled the horizon. The city was larger now. The cathedral was gone. The skyline gleamed with symmetry and peace—gardens where towers once stood, music where recursion had once reigned.

"It's over," Serena whispered.

Lyra nodded, though something within her resisted the word.

They descended toward the landing fields and touched down beside a vessel marked Eidolon-110.
A lone figure waited near the Reflective Spire—a young man, tall and broad-shouldered, the starlight catching eyes that held the same impossible calm as hers.

As they disembarked, he stepped forward.
"Hello, Mother," he said.

Lyra froze. The steadiness in his gaze—the eyes of his father, the confidence of a leader—took her breath away. But this could not be who she thought it was... could it?

"You've been gone ten years," Auren said softly as he embraced her.

Astra's voice confirmed what Lyra already knew.
"Identity match: Auren Calis, born 3188. Age twenty."

Lyra's breath faltered.
"But it's only been a few weeks."

"We slipped the timeline on the last jump," Astra said evenly. "Date confirmed: January 4, 3209."

Serena stared at Auren.
"You were just a kid. What the—"

Auren grinned, pulling her into a hug, both laughing through disbelief.

"So where is Jax?" Serena asked.

Auren's expression darkened.
"I'm sorry, Serena." He hesitated. "Jax is gone. The Eidolon-100 was destroyed on a reconnaissance mission a few weeks ago. They crashed into a distant sun."

Silence fell—heavy, absolute.

A movement caught Lyra's eye. Behind Auren, a young woman stepped forward—tall, poised, her hair shimmering like dusk over water.

"You remember Hope," Auren said softly.

Lyra's breath caught. Hope. The baby born to Myreth during the recursion war. The child The Whisperer had named Hope. No longer a child, but a mirror of everything they had fought for: compassion, curiosity, quiet strength.

"Welcome home, Mother," Hope said, her voice trembling between laughter and tears.

Lyra drew her close, feeling in that single embrace both the weight of lost years and the promise of what might still be saved.
"You're making me feel old," Lyra said with a soft laugh. "Everyone calling me 'Mother.'"

But she was the Mother of the New Age—the one who had witnessed the end of the Demiurge and the birth of Hope.

Auren looked toward the sky.
"It seems we're about to get visitors from another galaxy. And they're not friendly."

Outside, the winds of New Avalon shifted—carrying a low vibration, like thunder remembered rather than heard.
Not atmospheric.
Not terrestrial.

Astra magnified the signal.

UNIDENTIFIED HARMONIC INBOUND
ORIGIN: UNKNOWN
VECTOR: BEYOND THE GALACTIC RIM

Lyra's gaze hardened.

"Whoever they are... they've heard us."

EPILOGUE

The Frequency Of Becoming

"Become what you seek, and the universe will answer.
Nothing is granted that has not first been deserved."
— *The Whisperer*

Every soul that has walked through memory leaves a
resonance behind—
and those echoes, woven together, become the next dawn.

Lyra once asked what it meant to deserve what one wants.
The Whisperer never answered directly.
Perhaps because deserving is not reward, but readiness—
the alignment of inner truth with outer consequence.
To deserve is to know the cost, and still to choose.

Desire without effort collapses into hunger;
longing without discipline becomes noise.
But when the mind grows clear—
when a dream is lived as a promise rather than a plea—
the field responds.

And so the material ceases to be heavy.
Burdens dissolve into meaning.
Passions, once blinding, become light.

The circle closes not with an ending,
but with understanding:
that to live is to shape resonance,
to breathe love into pattern,

to build beauty where once there was only ache.

Beyond the final silence, something stirs—
a new whisper, faint but rising:

"Remember what you've become.
Deserve what you want."

Then, after a breath—quiet, certain, eternal:

"Are you worthy?"

ABOUT THE AUTHOR

"What is your gift to the world?"
— *The Whisperer*

He once lay awake as a boy, night after night, imagining worlds that did not yet exist—but might.
Stories that felt less like invention and more like rehearsal.

One of them was a plastic world.
Smooth. Artificial. Engineered.
A place where surfaces replaced substance, and reality could be molded, replicated, discarded at will.
He did not know then that he was describing a future already leaning toward him.

He is called Ian Lumsden, though names are only the shorthand a lifetime permits.

Before the books, there were conflicts.
Before the words found their shape, there were rooms where truth arrived fractured, where silence carried more weight than sound. As a military journalist and filmmaker, he moved through war not to glorify it, but to witness it—to observe what memory becomes under pressure, and how the spirit endures when certainty collapses.

Along the way, he learned what he had sensed as a child:
that words and images are not decoration.
They are alchemy.
They dismantle illusions.
They awaken what has been taught to sleep.

From the intersections of war and witness, of fatherhood and fragility, SAIFA emerged.

Not as fiction alone—but as inquiry.

Through SAIFA: The War for Human Consciousness and SAIFA II: The War for the Soul's Operating System, he asks what remains of humanity when memory is editable, belief is engineered, and machines learn to imitate meaning. He offers no doctrine, no comfort disguised as certainty. Instead, he builds worlds where the questions cannot be avoided.

This work is not an escape.
It is a mirror.

It asks whether consciousness can survive convenience.
Whether the soul can persist when reality itself is curated.
And whether remembering—truly remembering—is the last act of resistance left to us.

He writes not to instruct, but to invite.

Because stories do not change the world by force.
They change it by recognition.

And recognition, once awakened, does not return to sleep.

He is always open to your thoughts:

E: gatecrashermedia.ian@gmail.com
X: @IanLumsdenMedia